ALPHA'S SUBMISSION

IRRESISTIBLE OMEGAS BOOK TWO

NORA PHOENIX

NORA AFTER DARK

More of what you love...more of what you crave...

Unlock the ultimate experience with **Nora After Dark,** an online platform offering exclusive access to a variety of extras from Nora Phoenix. **Nora After Dark** offers multiple tiers to cater to your unique desires, each with its own array of exciting benefits.

- **Unlock Early eBook Access:** Nora After Dark subscribers enjoy the thrill of accessing eBooks before anyone else.
- **Exclusive Nora Phoenix Swag:** Elevate your reading experience with limited-edition Nora Phoenix merchandise delivered right to your doorstep.
- **Delve into Bonus Stories:** Gain exclusive access to bonus stories and chapters that are reserved just for our subscribers. Immerse yourself in

hidden tales, the perfect companion to your favorite books.

- **Early Works in Progress:** Be a part of the creative process! Nora After Dark grants you VIP access to works in progress, giving you a sneak peek at the magic happening behind the scenes.
- **Collect Signed Paperbacks:** For those who cherish the tangible, our premium tier includes beautifully signed paperback copies of Nora's works.

Visit Nora Phoenix at noraphoenix.com/nora-after-dark to subscribe and indulge in the Nora After Dark experience.

PUBLISHER'S NOTE

1

"I'll follow your lead, alpha."

Lidon gasped as Enar's words echoed through the living room of the ranch. He stood hand in hand with Palani, his face showing both fear and determination. He'd made his decision, had overcome his fears, Lidon realized. They were *doing* this.

He barely had time to let the magnitude of their choice sink in because Vieno had unbuttoned his jeans and pulled them down, whimpering with impatience. His mate needed him, and for now, Vieno's heat would take priority. But how would this work with one omega and three men desperate to fuck him? He couldn't be the only one whose cock ached with need, though the need didn't burn as desperate as the first time he met Vieno.

"Let's move this into the bedroom," Palani said, practical as ever.

Lidon nodded, then picked up Vieno, who slumped against him, his body burning against Lidon's. "Alpha," he moaned, rubbing his cheek against Lidon's chest.

He carried him to the bedroom with ease, Vieno trembling against him, his body flushed and his eyes misty. He was a burning, horny mess, his body drawing Lidon in like a magnet. His cock poked hard as steel against Vieno's body.

"I've got you, sweetheart," he said, his voice raw. God, he wanted him, Vieno's sweet smell invading every cell of his body, luring him in.

He lowered him onto the soft bed where Vieno's soaking wet underwear disappeared within seconds. His little omega had all but undressed Lidon in the living room already, so Lidon took off his own underwear and climbed onto the bed. Before he'd even positioned himself, the omega sprung on top of him, latching onto him in desperation. With clarity, Lidon realized that the solution was as simple as that: they would follow Vieno's cues. Whatever he needed right now would work. Lidon would set aside all jealousy and alpha dominance as long as his mate would get the fulfillment he so desperately sought.

Vieno wanted his cock, so he would get it. With no further preamble, Lidon rolled them over so he topped Vieno, who arched underneath him. "Oh god, finally. Fuck me, please..."

The words tumbled from his lips as if he were drunk, his eyes half-lidded and his cheeks flushed. He took Lidon's breath away, all needy and horny for his cock.

His cock twitched in eagerness, and Lidon could no longer resist. His hands lifted Vieno's hips, angling his body so he could claim him with one thrust, knowing Vieno's hole would be slick in preparation. The omega moaned loudly in his arms, a sound that shot straight to Lidon's balls.

He was so hot inside, so wet for him, shnick-shnick slurping sounds coming from him every time Lidon thrust. His own ass flexed reflexively as his need rose even higher. It was what an omega's heat did to an alpha, and nothing compared to this itch under your skin, this deep need to fuck and fuck and fuck again.

He yanked Vieno down, still buried to the hilt inside that luscious ass, then positioned him with his legs wide and pushed back so he could fuck him in earnest. The first few rounds weren't about creativity. All Vieno needed was a hard fuck. They both did.

He blocked out the somewhat surreal experience of Enar and Palani getting undressed in the same room and focused on his mate, who encouraged him with a stream of whimpers, groans, and noises, his body restless underneath Lidon and his ass clenching around Lidon's dick.

"Harder. Fuck me harder," Vieno begged.

Ah, how he loved to hear him beg, his voice all needy and desperate. Vieno might think it slutty, but Lidon could think of few things sexier than someone who needed him with a want so fierce it blocked out everything else. Vieno had no shame right now, no qualms about communicating what he wanted, and it was such a damn turn-on.

He shoved his legs back as he slammed in again, driven by the need to get that first load out, which would help both him and Vieno. It exploded out of him seconds later, and his vision went white as he came. His cock never even softened, nor had he expected it to. It would stay hard for hours now, fueled by Vieno's need.

"Again," Vieno begged, leaving no room for doubt about what and who he wanted.

"As often as you need," Lidon promised him, his voice raw with want. "Anything you need. God, you're so wet for me, sweetheart, so ready. Look at you burning for me, for us... You're so sexy like this, and I want you so much."

Slick noises filled the room again as Lidon set a steady

rhythm, burying himself with every deep thrust. The bed dipped as Enar and Palani joined them, stretching out beside them to watch.

Lidon checked in with himself. He should be weirded out they observed him fucking, right? Except he wasn't. His alpha merely growled with contentment over the proximity to his mates.

Mates.

Plural.

It sunk in then that he no longer had one mate. If this was to work, if they were together with all four of them, he had three.

Holy fucking hell.

He didn't have time to ponder it, because Vieno thrashed under him, clawing at his arms, needing more than a hard fuck. He refocused on him, bending over to kiss him. "You need my knot, sweetheart? You ready for me?"

"Please, alpha. I need it. I need you."

The begging endeared him and turned him the fuck on at the same time. He sped up until he came again, then folded Vieno almost double and buried himself until he bottomed out, engulfed in Vieno's body.

"Oh..." Vieno groaned as Lidon allowed his knot to swell. It flared at the base of his cock, growing bigger and bigger. "Yes, oh yes... I need you."

He kept babbling until Lidon kissed him, greedily drinking in every sound from his lips. Every little whimper, every groan, every gasp, he wanted them all. He didn't let Vieno's mouth go until his knot was fully formed, immersed in Vieno's slick heat, and closing off his channel. Hot damn, nothing topped that sensation, did it?

One day, he would knot him and impregnate him, creating beautiful babies with his sweet mate. He'd fill him up and watch him grow, his belly all soft and alive. He wasn't ready yet; none of them were. They'd figure out everything else first. But one day...and he couldn't wait. For now, Lidon was grateful Enar could make sure Vieno wouldn't get pregnant.

Vieno whimpered when Lidon's knot had completed, his eyes hazy. Lidon turned on his back with Vieno on top of him so the little omega wouldn't have to bear his weight the whole time. He didn't expect his knot to keep as long as the previous time, but it could still be a while. Vieno let himself be maneuvered, but once he was sprawled on top of Lidon, he moved restlessly, seeking for something.

"What do you need, sweetheart?"

"More..."

Lidon frowned. He was already knotting him. What more did he have to give? Then Vieno turned his head toward Enar and Palani, and Lidon understood. He needed all three of them. He jerked his chin to indicate his approval, and Palani climbed over him to his other side. Seconds later, Vieno sat up on Lidon's knot, his left hand reaching out for Palani, his right for Enar. When they met his hands, he brought Enar's fingers to his mouth and Palani's to his chest.

God, he was beautiful, the way he sat there, softly rocking himself on Lidon's knot, his body displayed for all of them to see, to touch, to worship. Little sighs and moans fell from his lips until Enar pushed two fingers against his mouth, and Vieno eagerly opened up to suck on them. On his other side, Palani came in closer, sitting up to reach Vieno's upper body. He caressed his smooth chest with his hands, then drifted until he reached the omega's nipples.

The sound Vieno made as Palani rolled his nipple between his fingers was pure lust. It shouldn't have surprised Lidon that Palani knew what aroused Vieno, seeing how long they'd been together, but it was mesmer-izing to watch. Palani tugged on those little buds, flicked them, played with them until Vieno's body shook, drool dripping down his chin from sucking on Enar's fingers.

"Look at you...so beautiful," Palani said, his voice filled with love as well as desire. "How do you feel, baby, with that big knot inside you?"

Enar dragged his fingers out, pure wonder on his face.

Vieno moaned. "So full..."

"Details, baby. I wanna hear the details. Tell me everything."

"His cock is so big, so perfect. When he fucks me hard, it hurts so good. But oh god, when his knot forms...it fills me... it presses against this needy place inside me. I want more, Palani. Please, I need more."

His hands searched, fidgeting, clutching onto Palani's arms, then letting go again, as if wanting something else. Lidon didn't know what to do. What did Vieno need? He couldn't read him.

"What does he need?" he asked Palani.

Palani hesitated. "I'm not sure if you—"

"Anything he needs. Anything. We're here for him. This is not about me," Lidon interrupted him.

He hadn't realized how much he meant those words until he'd spoken them, and his alpha signaled his approval. All he wanted was to take care of Vieno. If that meant having Palani function as a cruise director slash pimp, he would suck it up. Besides, Lidon was pretty sure that what-ever the beta would come up with, it would result in an erotic fuck fest they'd all enjoy.

Palani nodded, then turned to Enar, whose eyes were glued to Vieno. Enar's cock creamed precum at the head. No wonder, with the show in front of him.

"Enar, " Palani said, and it took a second before Enar's eyes refocused on the beta. "Are you okay with me telling you what to do?"

Enar's eyes widened, and he nodded. "Yeah. Whatever he needs."

Palani took a deep breath. Lidon wondered what went through his mind right now. He'd taken care of Vieno so long by himself, so what did it mean to him to now share him with two others and alphas at that? Lidon hadn't spotted any annoyance with him, not even a bit of jealousy. He'd thought it before, and he realized it again, how deep Palani's love for Vieno was that he'd always put the omega's needs first.

"Straddle Lidon with your ass toward his face, so you're facing Vieno," Palani told Enar, who sent Lidon a quick look to make sure he was on board with this, and then followed the beta's instructions.

Lidon was treated to the perfect view of Enar's backside, and while his ass wasn't as round and luscious as Vieno's, it was definitely not a hardship to look at. Lidon loved how his golden skin stretched taut around those firm globes. And fuck knew his ass was tight, gripping his cock like a warm, slick fist. It was weird to think about that as he was still knot-deep inside Vieno, who was rocking himself on Lidon's knot, but his mind could picture it perfectly, the way Enar's hole clenched around him, always struggling to take him in.

Lidon couldn't see what happened as Enar's body blocked his view, but Enar leaned in, and then the sucking noises informed him Enar and Vieno were kissing. Vieno wrapped his arms around Enar, his small hands caressing his back. Palani threw a bottle of lube near Lidon's hand, then took position behind Vieno, pushing Lidon's legs wide to make room for himself between them.

As Lidon lay there, his knot still fully swollen inside Vieno, it hit him that he had never felt more right in his life, as if he was doing what he was meant to do, born to do, with the men he was supposed to be with. All three of them were pleasuring their omega, helping him through his heat. It was how it should be.

He threw his head back and let his alpha roar fill the room.

IT WAS LIKE A DREAM, Enar thought, an out-of-body experience. Surely, this could not be happening to him. He could not be the man who found himself in bed with three others, his body on fire and his cock crying with want... Except he was.

Lidon's alpha roar rolled over him, through him, making him want to do things no alpha should. God, he wanted his friend to take him...in front of Palani and Vieno, which was the stupidest thing he could ever allow to happen. Even if Palani knew and Vieno had voiced his acceptance of Enar bottoming, this was not something he should ever engage in with them present. But how he yearned to submit—almost as much as he longed to bury himself deep in Vieno. It killed him, this war inside him.

Vieno attacked his mouth like it was the last thing he'd ever do while his hands roamed Enar's body wherever he could reach him. Small, hot hands stroked his biceps, his pecs, creating a sensual fire everywhere they touched this skin. Enar burned with want, with need, his body demanding more. But what were the rules here?

Palani moved in closer behind Vieno, his hands coming around the omega to play with his nipples again. Apparently, that was a big turn-on for Vieno—something to keep in mind. Every time Palani pinched those little buds, so red and swollen, glistening with the saliva Palani had used on them, Vieno moaned a little into Enar's mouth. It was the sexiest sound ever.

And fuck, the little omega could kiss. He wasn't shy about it either. No coy playing around or pretending to evade Enar. No, he full-on invaded his mouth, gave as good as he got with an aggression that made Enar tremble with want. He needed to be inside him, needed to claim him for himself as well...

Could he? Would Lidon allow anyone else to fuck Vieno? Would his alpha? He'd told Palani it wasn't about him, but Enar wasn't sure if that was realistic. Fuck, he needed the boundaries of whatever they were doing.

Then Vieno's hands trailed from his stomach lower and lower until they found Enar's cock. The omega wrapped his right hand around the head while his left circled the base as best he could from his position. Enar couldn't hold back the grunt of pleasure when Vieno spread the precum around the head of his cock and gently squeezed.

He shifted even closer toward him so Vieno could touch him easier. "Oh god," he groaned, breaking off the kiss to lower his head on Vieno's shoulder.

Vieno rocked his lower body on Lidon's knot, and Palani rutted against Vieno's back—his ass? Enar couldn't see—in the same rhythm. When Enar lifted his head again, Palani's mouth moved in for a deep, wet kiss. They kissed, almost against Vieno's head, both their heads at an angle they couldn't keep up for long, but damn, that kiss stoked the fire inside Enar even higher.

Lidon moved under him. Even over the wet sounds of the sloppy kiss with Palani, the slick noises of his cock being jacked off, and the soft sighs Vieno let out, Enar recognized lube being opened. What was Lidon doing?

Just as he had to break off the kiss with Palani because his neck cramped, wet fingers touched the top of his crack. Holy fuck.

"Ungh..." he moaned as the alpha's finger breached his hole. Lidon didn't ask to be let in; he took. And Enar gave in, like he always did because it was what he wanted...what they both wanted. The thought took hold in his head. Lidon wanted this. Why? Why was Lidon playing with his ass? Just to bring Enar pleasure, or was he prepping him to fuck him? God, it was too much, all these conflicting thoughts and emotions.

Vieno's hands increased their grip on his cock, and Palani rutted faster, letting out a moan that made Enar want to fuck him, too... His balls tightened, and then Lidon shoved another finger deep inside his ass, and Enar lost it. He cried out, pinching his eyes shut as his cock went off in Vieno's hand, cum flying out in staccato bursts with a force that left him panting.

Palani grunted, and Enar felt him spasm. Was he coming too? He opened his eyes, dragging himself out of his postorgasmic stupor, to find Vieno licking off his hand...Enar's cum...with pure bliss on his face. Enar's dick filled instantly again.

Palani kissed Vieno's neck, nibbling on it. "We're gonna make such a mess of you, baby," he said. "Thank you for being such a horny little shit."

Vieno laughed, a sound happier than Enar had ever heard from him, and bent his head sideways for a quick kiss with Palani. "Mmm, cum," the omega said. "I love it, and you know it."

Palani moved away from Vieno, and to Enar's surprise,

the omega moved off Lidon's cock, which had come down from his knot. Enar would've shifted positions as well, except Lidon still had two fingers far up his ass...and now three. What was he doing?

Palani and Vieno shared a soft kiss, and god, it was so sweet to see those two together. The love between them hummed in the air, and it made Enar's heart do something funny and twirly that he didn't recognize.

"I want Enar," Vieno announced, his voice thick with want. He licked his lips as he looked at Enar, whose dick leaked again, fueled by the pheromones that hung heavy in the room.

Enar held his breath, waiting for Lidon to say that was never gonna happen.

"Okay, sweetheart. On your hands and knees," Lidon said, and Enar couldn't move anymore. Was he really going to...? How was this even possible? How was Lidon's alpha okay with this?

Vieno moved into position, his head bent low and his ass sticking up. Lidon pulled his fingers out of Enar's ass. Then he slapped it.

"Go on, fuck him," Lidon said, his voice low.

Enar climbed off him, hesitant to face him out of fear of what he'd see on his face. Maybe he only did this because Vieno wanted it, but he would regret it later?

"Enar, look at me," Lidon said. When Enar didn't obey, he said it again. "Look at me." The alpha compulsion hit him hard, and his head came up, even as he braced himself for what he would see. "You're one of us. You belong here. He's yours, like you are his," Lidon spoke.

Enar shook his head. "I can't..."

Lidon cupped his cheek. "I know it's hardest for you because you so rarely feel like you belong, like you're worthy. But you are. He wants you, and I damn well know you want him. You have not only my permission but also my blessing."

Lidon bent in, and their mouths met, soft lips meeting Enar's trembling ones. Electricity sizzled as his alpha kissed Enar for the first time, and Enar opened up automatically, letting Lidon swipe his mouth with his tongue, moaning at the dominance he craved and loathed at the same time. The kiss was hard, Lidon showing who was in charge, but Enar loved it and let himself be conquered, dominated. Something settled in his stomach, in his lungs, that made it easier to breathe now that Lidon had somehow claimed him. When Lidon pulled back, Enar panted, wanting more.

"Fuck him," Lidon ordered again.

Enar nodded. They wanted him to be a part of them. He *was* a part of them, of this. He still couldn't wrap his head around it, but he'd try. And right now, they made him feel like he belonged.

Vieno sat waiting for him, quivering with need, and Enar wasted no more time. He positioned himself on his knees behind him and thrust in, in one move. The omega's channel was slick with his own natural lubricant and with Lidon's cum, and the thought of adding to that, of mingling his own seed with Lidon's was erotic as fuck. The sloppy wet noises his cock made when it pushed inside Vieno... God, they sounded perfect and dirty, and he wanted so much more. He pulled back out again, dragging a trail of Lidon's fluids out. His body roared with pleasure, the flames of his desire dancing over his skin.

He had thrust four, five times when Lidon moved in behind him, and with blinding clarity, he realized what was about to happen. He fucked Vieno, but Lidon would fuck him. It was his way of showing he was, in fact, the alpha.

Lidon waited behind him, holding still until Enar would signal his permission. Even as alpha, he would never do anything Enar didn't want. Enar's heart filled with peace as his alpha surrendered. He was exactly where he wanted to be, with whom he belonged.

"Yes, alpha."

2

Vieno's head buzzed with the all-too-familiar sensations of a fever combined with having a filter where every signal from the outside had to push through. He acted sluggish and slow, yet he saw everything so much clearer and sharper at the same time. He had this need inside him, this burning, raging want, which demanded to be quenched.

That need was familiar too, but for the first time, he didn't fear it. He wasn't scared of how he would act, of what anyone would think, of being out of his mind with desire, only to have fulfillment be just out of reach for agonizing hours. His heat had always been a source of endless stress, but this time was different.

This time he was safe. Wanted. Cared for. And right now, as Enar fucked him hard and deep, he knew beyond a shadow of a doubt he would be sated when this had passed. Oh, they weren't there by a long shot yet—in fact, they'd only gotten started—but Vieno sensed it, the heaviness of the desire in the air. All three of them would fuck him through it. They not only would allow him to be as slutty and guilty and needy as he wanted to be but also would welcome it, love it, even.

Lidon was fucking Enar, and it was perfect in the most filthy way. Every time he rammed into Enar, the man's cock would jam deep into Vieno. He positioned himself on his hands and knees, his legs spread wide, his ass shamelessly sticking back to receive anything Enar doled out. The slaps of balls against flesh, the low grunts, the slick sounds as Enar fucked Lidon's cum out of Vieno, Enar's moans as Lidon filled him—it made music more beautiful than any song Vieno had ever heard.

He'd closed his eyes to focus on the sensations and jolted when another body pushed against him from the front. He blinked and found Palani positioning himself on his back, shifting downward until he'd placed his cock right under Vieno's mouth. Vieno smiled. Palani knew him so well.

"I love you," Vieno said, his heart so full it felt like it would burst.

"I love you too. Now suck."

Palani...sweet, caring Palani could read Vieno like a book and knew exactly what he needed. Gentle Palani, who could turn into a ruthless beast when Vieno needed him to, when he demanded it of him.

Vieno opened his mouth, drawing in a last deep breath, and then Palani shoved his cock in. Vieno moaned as his mouth filled, the salty taste of Palani's precum teasing his buds. He breathed in through his nose, Palani's sweat making him moan around his cock. He relaxed his jaw and took him in as deep as he could.

It was never deep enough, and Palani's hands found his head to push him down harder, all the way until his mouth and throat were full of cock and his nose was buried in pubes. He gagged once, twice, but it was ignored, as it should be.

"He's gagging," Enar spoke from behind him, worried.

"I know," Palani said calmly. Vieno would have smiled if he could at the pride in his voice. "He loves it."

He pulled back as Vieno got lightheaded. His lungs screamed as he took a desperate breath to replenish his oxygen. Palani gave him a few seconds, then surged right back in.

"I used to spit-roast him like this all the time during his heat. Fuck his ass with this massive dildo, which could form a knot and then make him gag on my cock. He'd come without ever touching himself."

Vieno gagged again, his eyes tearing up with the sheer filthiness of it. His ass and his mouth full with cock...he fucking loved it. Who needed oxygen when you could have this? Right when little black spots danced in his vision, Palani pulled back again. Vieno choked on his greedy breath, his lungs painfully drawing in air. Palani allowed him a little longer recovery time. Vieno never had to tell him where his limits were. Palani knew.

He opened his mouth again and was rewarded with Palani's taste, the beta's whole body tight with control as he fucked Vieno's mouth. Vieno felt Enar speed up, breaking Lidon's rhythm to create one of his own, fueled by the need to come. Palani pulled back and steadied Vieno, his cock still in Vieno's mouth, but not so deep he couldn't breathe.

"Look at you, baby. This is what you dreamed of, isn't it? Three men to satisfy you. You're so beautiful, Vieno, so perfect and gorgeous like this," Palani said.

Enar shouted out and flooded Vieno's insides with his cum. Vieno moaned at the sensation, the perfection of it all. Palani had been right. He had dreamed of this, even if he hadn't known it. One day, he wouldn't have to take birth control. One day, he'd carry his men's babies and become a daddy, his belly all swollen and beautiful. It would be the perfect family.

"Can I knot you?" Enar asked, still panting. He sounded unsure, and Vieno had no trouble understanding why.

"God, yes, please. I need you."

He meant it, felt it deep inside him. He needed all of them. Not only Lidon or Palani. All three of them. And right now, all three of them at the same time.

He whimpered impatiently as Enar's knot wouldn't come.

"Knot him, Enar," Lidon commanded. "He asked you to."

Vieno held his breath as Enar's base swelled. It filled him completely, taking away that harrowing emptiness inside him that had tormented him during his heat. Where Lidon's knot had been dominant and aggressive, Enar's soothed, comforted, as if Enar was sending some of his alpha powers with it. Maybe he was. However he did it, it was perfect.

His knees buckled as his body got tired of kneeling for so long. "I've got you," Enar said, his voice thick with emotion.

He maneuvered them both into a sitting position, his knot still firmly embedded inside him. Vieno sat on him, his back leaning against Enar's chest. Palani looked at them both with a look of pride and love. "You two are so beautiful together," he said.

"They really are," Lidon agreed.

Vieno realized he hadn't heard Lidon come. Had he robbed him of his orgasm? At the same time, the craziness of that thought hit him. They would be fucking for hours, so Lidon would have ample opportunity to come. There was no reason for guilt. He would, however, let the need in that rushed through him again.

He reached out for Lidon's cock with his right hand, and the alpha scooted closer without a second hesitation. His small hand wrapped around it, and he squeezed, letting out a sigh of pleasure at the contact. Palani's right hand found Vieno's nipples again and twisted them with sharp moves that left him gasping.

"Don't think that we are done yet, baby. I'm gonna come down your throat until you choke on my cum," Palani promised him.

Vieno's eyes crossed, and then Enar moved inside him, rocking his knot against a different needy place, and Palani pinched his nipple, and Lidon's cock was silken steel in his hand, and the haze took over until Vieno was a big, gaping hole of need, sucking in whatever he craved. And he got it, every request, every filthy need, every desperate, wanton plea.

Perfection. Absolute, fucking perfection.

PALANI KNEW the moment Vieno's heat had passed. It was as if the frenzy that had kept them all captivated dissipated, like a tornado that ravaged the earth one second and got sucked back into the sky the next, leaving them tired but fulfilled. They'd done it. They had fucked Vieno through his heat, leaving him limp on the bed, his eyes fluttering closed.

"Is he okay?" Lidon asked, sounding worried.

"*He's* fine," Vieno murmured in a tired voice. "But fucking exhausted and sore, so can I please sleep now?"

Palani and Enar smiled at each other. Behind him, Lidon moved as he crawled across the bed to Vieno's other side.

"You can sleep on me, sweetheart. But we need to clean the bed first. And ourselves."

He walked into the bathroom with Vieno in his arms, and Palani slipped past him to turn on the shower. Wordlessly, he and Enar worked together to clean Lidon first, then Vieno, who fell asleep in Lidon's arms, even in the shower. But his skin glowed, showing none of the symptoms he'd had before after a heat. He was sated, fully sated, and healthy. All he needed was sleep and recovery time.

They all did. The pheromones and hormones had kept them going, but Palani's body now protested the fuck-marathon he'd put himself through. His muscles hurt, and he was dead on his feet. Hell, even his dick hurt, oversensitive after so many rounds.

Enar toweled Lidon and Vieno off as Palani stripped the bed of all the stained linens and remade it with fresh ones. Enar helped him as soon as he was done in the bathroom. It wasn't an alpha's job, and again the man showed how much he was willing to give up to be with them. Palani gave him a quick kiss when they were done, catching Lidon's look of gratitude and pride as he stood, still holding Vieno in his strong arms.

"All ready for you," Palani said, pointing toward the bed.

Lidon took position on his back, then lifted Vieno, still asleep, on his stomach on top of him.

"Wanna grab a shower now?" he asked Enar.

"Yeah," Enar said, sighing with pleasure. Palani craved to get clean as well. His skin itched everywhere, and he could smell himself—never a pleasant thing, though Vieno totally got off on it. He loved licking armpits, which Palani never quite got, but whatever. To each his own, and if that turned Vieno on, it was all fine with Palani. The omega could lick every inch of his body as far as he was concerned.

A minute later, he and Enar stood in the shower together. Palani kept his distance at first, not sure what Enar wanted since his face looked closed off until Enar simply pulled him close. He squeezed out some shampoo and reached for Palani's hair, massaging his scalp in firm circles.

"Dude, that's way too much for how little hair I've got," Palani protested with a smile, then moaned at the tension leaving his body as Enar's strong fingers kneaded his head.

"You remember about gift horses, right?" Enar fired back, and Palani smiled.

Palani loved that Lidon's super deluxe shower had two detachable showerheads. Hell, they would even fit in there with all four of them if they wanted to. His mind conjured up an image of Vieno on his knees, pleasuring all of them... or Lidon fucking him, while Enar took Vieno. The options were endless and all arousing as fuck, even though his cock signaled it lacked the energy to get excited right now. No wonder.

Enar took one of the showerheads to rinse Palani's hair, and he closed his eyes and his mouth until the alpha was done. He still thought of Enar as alpha, he realized, even though Enar had demonstrated nothing but beta behavior. He'd wait for his signal, though, for his announcement he wanted to be called something else.

"How was it for you?" he asked when Enar had rinsed out all the soap.

"I don't know if I can describe what I experienced," Enar said, his voice thick with emotion. "I may need more time to process all of it."

"But you're okay with it?" Palani asked.

Enar cupped his cheeks with both hands and pressed a soft, wet kiss on his lips. "Very much so. It was without a doubt the best day of my life."

"Same here," Palani said softly. "It was magical."

He'd fucked Vieno through countless heats, and despite the struggle of not being able to sate him, he'd always felt deeply connected to him at the same time. But this, this was on a completely different level. He'd never felt like this. Not this intimate, this connected, this sense of being a part of something bigger than the sum of its parts, more beautiful than he could describe.

"I know what you mean about not being able to find the words," he said. "Let's sleep, hmm?"

They dried each other off, the lingering intimacy between them almost tangible. When they walked back into the bedroom, Lidon was asleep as well, his stern face so much more vulnerable in his sleep. Vieno was sprawled on top of him, passed out, but his face peaceful. The alpha cradled him with a tenderness that made Palani's heart skip a beat.

"They're beautiful," Enar said with wistfulness.

"So are you."

Enar turned his head, his eyes searching as if to see Palani wasn't joking. His lips curved faintly. "Not as gorgeous as you. Thank you, Palani. I wouldn't be here without you."

Palani put his finger on Enar's lips. "No. No thanks. Remember what Lidon said. You belong. We're together, all of us."

They crawled into bed, Palani's body too tired to do more than find a comfortable position. He held open his arms, and Enar snuggled close, his head on Palani's shoulder. Palani was asleep as soon as his eyes fell shut.

He woke up a few hours later, disoriented as to where he was and what had woken him up. Then he felt Vieno crawling into his arms on his other side, and he smiled, deeply content to hold two men in his arms. He kissed

Vieno's head, but the omega had fallen asleep again already. He met Lidon's eyes over Vieno's head as the alpha turned onto his side and spooned Vieno from the back. His long arm reached over Vieno, searching until it found a spot on Palani's stomach. Palani fell asleep again, connected to all his men, happier than he had ever been in his life.

3

Vieno woke up in a tangle of arms and legs, naked skin brushing up against him everywhere, the scent of sex still in the air, even though the bed linen smelled fresh. He blinked a few times to clear his head.

He was back. His heat had passed. He blushed as memories of the last forty-eight hours rushed back to him. Oh god. It had been perfect. Insane, but so wonderfully right. He couldn't even guess how many times he'd been fucked, how many times he'd been taken, exactly the way he'd wanted to. His throat ached, swollen and raw, he noticed, no doubt from being skull-fucked and... Yeah. No need to rehash the details. They'd thoroughly used him, and it had been pure bliss.

He lay cuddled up against Palani, with Lidon cradling him from behind. Enar's head rested on Palani's other shoulder, looking sexy, even in his sleep. Vieno smiled. They looked exhausted, his men. It had taken three of them to sate him, and he'd fucking worn them out.

He bit back the giggle that threatened to escape from his

lips. It wasn't funny, he told himself, and yet it so was. Here he was, this itty-bitty omega compared to these big men— well, Lidon and Enar anyway—and he'd plain worn them out all by himself. How about that? He held back another snicker, then disentangled himself from Lidon and Palani, crawling out of bed at the foot end. He'd better make them some food because when they woke up, they'd be ravenous.

He threw on a pair of shorts and a shirt, not bothering with underwear since his ass felt sensitive after all the... Yeah, not going there again. Barefoot, he walked into the kitchen, where he gulped down two glasses of water first. All right, he'd better get to work. They'd need protein and carbs, so he'd make a nice pasta, and Lidon could grill some of those big ass steaks he loved so much.

He boiled pasta, meanwhile cutting little tomatoes in half. He'd sprinkle them with olive oil and herbs and grill them in the oven. Combined with the pasta, bacon, some mozzarella, and fresh spinach cut into little strips, it would make for a tasty dish. His thoughts wandered off in every direction as he prepared the food.

A foursome.

They were a *foursome*.

Enar had been right with his theory about Vieno having mated with Palani. Vieno experienced this deep peace in his whole being now that Palani was close again. He'd suffered without him, and he hadn't realized why until Enar had pointed it out. And Palani had experienced the same, being just as forlorn without Vieno. They belonged together.

But Lidon was just as much a part of him, of them. When Lidon's knot had swollen for the first time, the alpha power of his mate had barreled through him. The alpha mark on his shoulder had burned for a second or two, affirming the bond they shared.

Where did that leave Enar? In this reasoning, he consti-
tuted the odd man out because Vieno did not experience
that same closeness with him as he did with Lidon and
Palani. Vieno bit his lip at the realization, guilty for feeling
that way. Enar belonged with them. Vieno knew it with
every fiber of his being, but why did he not sense the
connection with him the way he did with the other two?

He sighed as he cut bacon into small pieces and put
them in a skillet to get crispy. The tomatoes already sat in
the oven, so all he needed to do was prepare the rest and
wait till his men woke up so they could eat. Hmm, he could
fire up the grill already?

As he walked back inside, he almost ran into Enar, who
looked amazingly awake for someone who'd been so out of
it mere minutes ago.

"Hi," Enar said, shoving his hands into the pockets of his
shorts and half avoiding Vieno's eyes.

Vieno smiled. He was insecure, this sexy, strong man.
Vieno might not have all the answers to how he fit with this
man, but this insecurity he could alleviate. He stepped in,
offering his mouth to him. Enar's face lit up with surprise
before he leaned in and kissed Vieno gently.

"Hi to you too," Vieno said, dropping another quick kiss
on the man's lips. He tasted like more. Vieno's omega
reached out, wanting to connect with Enar, and Vieno gave
in. This wasn't about sex. He'd had enough of that for a
while. No, this was about intimacy, about longing to connect
with Enar.

He reached out to pull Enar's head closer, then latched
onto his mouth. Their tongues twirled, dancing around
each other, chasing each other until they met, licking and
sucking and claiming. Enar's taste was still the newest to
Vieno, and he sighed a little into his mouth as he remem-

bered how good the man could kiss. Where Lidon was aggressive and dominant, and Palani kissed with sweetness, Enar was sensual and could reduce you to a whimpering mess with a kiss.

When he pulled back, Enar's cheeks were flushed, his eyes darker than usual. "You taste so good," Vieno whispered.

"You too." Enar's voice croaked, and he cleared his throat. "Thank you."

Vieno stepped back. "I'm making lunch." He looked at the clock. Three in the afternoon. "Or dinner, whatever. Wanna help?"

"I'm a horrible cook," Enar admitted.

Vieno smiled as he sighed overdramatically. "You guys only want me for sex and to cook and clean, huh?" he teased.

"Well," Enar said after a quick look, probably to make sure Vieno was joking, "your ass is heaven, and from what I understand, so is your food, so yeah, guilty as charged."

Vieno pulled the tomatoes out of the oven and put them in a bowl to cool off. "Here," he said. "You can cut mozzarella into little pieces. I'm sure you can't fuck that up too badly, considering you're a doctor and all that."

Enar grinned. "I should be able to handle this, and thank you for the vote of confidence."

Vieno looked at him sideways. "Did you mean it? What you said about me...my ass?"

"God, yes. You're special. I'm sorry. I wish I had better words to describe it. Was it good for you?"

Vieno nodded. "Fuck, yes. Best heat I've ever had. You guys were amazing."

"You look good. Better than I've seen you so far."

Vieno added the bacon to the tomatoes, then the

spinach he'd cut into small slivers. "I feel better than I have in a long time. I think what you said about the alpha hormones and proteins and shit was true. And the knotting felt amazing."

"Mine too?"

Enar's voice was so soft Vieno wasn't sure he'd heard him correctly until he saw his face. Why would he be insecure over that? Unless... It sunk in. "Was that your first time?"

After a slight hesitation, Enar nodded. "I've fucked a few omegas through their heat, but I could never make it further than a half knot. It's not uncommon," he added quickly. "In theory, alphas can knot at will, but the reality is that we often need a connection to achieve a full knot. It's hard when you don't know your partner well, and even harder when you're wearing a condom. So this was the first full knot for me."

"It was perfect. Lidon's first knot took off the edge, quenched the most desperate need, and yours was comforting. Soothing. Fulfilling."

Vieno heard Enar exhale. "Thank you."

Vieno stepped in and pushed against Enar's hands until he put his knife and the mozzarella down to meet his eyes. Vieno wiped Enar's hands off with a paper towel and stepped into his arms, hugging him. It took a few seconds before the man hugged him back, but when he did, he pulled Vieno close, resting his cheek on Vieno's head.

"Don't thank me," Vieno said after a while. "We needed each other. There's no room for thanks there."

Vieno sensed a presence behind him before Enar did, but he made no move to let go. Enar's body froze, and then he pushed Vieno away. "I'm sorry," he said, probably to Lidon, but Vieno didn't turn around. His eyes stayed trained on Enar, who was clearly scared he'd fucked up somehow and that Lidon would be upset with him.

"No," Vieno said, raising his voice. "Don't be sorry."

"You're his omega," Enar explained, his eyes shifting from Lidon back to Vieno.

"I'm also yours. And Palani's."

Enar shook his head. "It doesn't work that way."

Vieno felt Lidon step in behind him, even before the man's hand landed on his shoulder. Palani stood at his side, and Vieno reached out for him, lacing his fingers through his best friend's hand. "It does, Enar," he said softly. "We'll need to talk a lot about this because I don't understand everything either, but I do know this: I was Palani's long before Lidon claimed me, so I belong to them both. And I choose to belong to you as well. You're mine, and I'm yours, and that means we can kiss whenever the hell we want to."

LIDON WATCHED as Enar's face showed all the confusion the man must feel. It seemed the insecurities he'd experienced before had come back in full force now that Vieno's heat had passed. No wonder. It was hard to think when all your body wanted was to fuck. Now that that urge had dissipated, Enar's mind would switch on again.

"Vieno's right," Lidon said. "But let's talk about it over..." He looked at the clock. Quarter past three. Not lunch, but not quite dinner either. "Food. I'm ravenous."

Vieno turned around, sending him a sweet smile. "Grill is ready for you. Steaks are on the counter."

"Thank you, sweetheart. I'm in the mood for meat."

"I figured. I ordered the biggest ones they had for all of you, and the smaller one is for me."

His mate already knew him well. Lidon wasted no time throwing a bunch of juicy, thick ribeyes on the grill.

Vieno was right, Lidon mused. They did need to talk about their relationship. Enar needed it the most. He'd always been a man of rules. As much as he loved breaking them, he thrived on clear expectations, always wanted to know what was expected of him. Maybe it was because he'd always felt like such a disappointment to his father? Lidon had met the man a few times, but his impression hadn't been favorable. He could only hope the man fared better with Enar's younger brothers. At least they wouldn't have to deal with the weight of the alpha expectations.

Enar might need ground rules the most, but they all could benefit from voicing their needs and expectations. As tempting as it was to adopt a laissez-faire approach, it would backfire on them. With four people in a relationship, they would have to be more intentional, even if it would cause some cringy moments and difficult topics. He wasn't the best at communicating shit like this, but Palani and Vieno seemed to be better at it, so maybe they could contribute?

When Lidon brought in the steaks, they all sat down at the table. It looked picture perfect, all set with a table cloth Lidon hadn't even known he possessed and with plates, glasses, and even napkins for everyone. Vieno had been busy the last few days, apparently, ensuring he could serve this.

For the first few minutes, no one spoke. They were all too focused on getting calories into their systems.

"God, that's good," Palani mumbled with his mouth full.

Like Lidon, he'd attacked his steak first. A quick check revealed Enar had done the same. Only Vieno was eating the pasta first.

"Look at you guys devour those steaks," Vieno

commented with a smile. "You'd think you had run a marathon or something."

"Baby, your heats *are* a fucking marathon, even with the three of us," Palani said.

"How can an itty-bitty omega like me wear out three big, strong guys like you?" Vieno teased.

Lidon loved hearing him so carefree. What a difference with how he'd been when he had met him for the first time. If you saw him now, all beaming and glowing, it was hard to imagine the shape he'd been in.

"Two big strong guys," Palani corrected him. "I'm just a puny beta compared to these two."

"Size isn't everything," Vieno said, his eyes sparkling.

"That's not what you said when Lidon had his big cock in your ass," Palani shot back.

Vieno blushed, a lovely heat that crept up from his nose all the way to his ears. Lidon smiled. "Is he teasing you, sweetheart?"

"Yes," Vieno said, demonstrating a cute-as-fuck pout. "Say something, alpha."

It was said in jest, and yet Lidon felt a deep appreciation for the way Vieno turned to him for protection. He still had a lot to figure out about their relationship, but he knew the little omega already had him wrapped around his finger. It was a good thing he didn't realize it and wasn't coy enough to abuse it.

"Do I need to beat him up for you?" he said, laughing.

Vieno pretended to consider it. "Nah," he then said. "He still may come in handy."

The joking continued until they'd all finished their meals. Enar had been quiet, and Lidon shot him a questioning look. "You okay?"

"It's a lot to process."

"You need rules," Lidon said. "I get it. Let's talk."

Enar sighed with frustration. "I got nothing. I don't even know where to start. My head is a mess right now."

"Maybe we start with defining what we are," Palani said. Lidon appreciated the beta's sharp mind more and more. He had the uncanny ability to get right to the heart of the matter.

Lidon nodded. "I like that. So, what do we think we are?"

Vieno responded first. "A foursome. All four of us together."

"As opposed to...?" Enar asked.

"As opposed to Vieno and Lidon being together, me and Vieno being a couple, you and Lidon fucking around, and you and me being whatever the fuck we are," Palani said. "The difference is that we are all together rather than being in individual relationships."

"How does that work?" Enar asked. "I get it in theory, but what does it mean? Does it mean we always do everything with the four of us?"

"Sex, you mean?" Vieno asked.

"Well, for one, but I meant broader. Sleeping, eating, hanging out, and yes, sex...all the things normal couples do together."

"I don't like the word normal," Palani said. "It implies that we're not normal."

"We're not," Enar said. "How many foursomes do you know?"

Palani leaned back in his chair. "There's a difference between not normal and unusual. What we are may be unusual, but that doesn't mean it's not normal. Normal is normative, judgmental."

Enar gestured. "Okay, I'll grant you that. But it doesn't

change my point or rather my question. Do we do everything together?"

Lidon scratched his chin. "That seems impractical to me, considering our conflicting work schedules."

"So you would have no problem with me hanging out with Palani or Vieno," Enar said.

Lidon's eyes narrowed. "You say hanging out, but you're talking about sex."

Enar threw up his hands. "I'm trying to figure out how you can be okay with this. Are you telling me you'd honestly be good with me fucking Vieno behind your back?"

Lidon leaned forward. "It wouldn't be behind my back, now would it? And yes, I would be okay with that as long as Vieno wants it, but you'd never do anything against anyone's will."

"I don't understand this. I get why you'd be okay with Palani, since it's clear he and Vieno are mates as well. But me, that's different. I'm not your mate, Lidon. Sure, we fucked occasionally, or rather, you fucked me, but we didn't mate. And I'm sure as hell not mated to Vieno or Palani. So what am I doing here? Why are you all so okay with me being a part of your threesome?"

His words hung in the air, his pain almost tangible. Lidon hadn't realized how deep his friend's insecurity ran until that moment.

Vieno reached across the table to grab Enar's hand. "Because we're not a threesome. We never were. It was me and Palani and then me and Lidon, and when we figured out that we were more, you were a part of that."

"But I'm not your mate," Enar said again, his voice filled with desperation.

"Don't you get it? You're something much more powerful. I didn't choose to mate with Palani. It just happened, maybe because I've always loved him or because we've been so close the last few years. I don't know. And I didn't choose to have this fated mates connection with Lidon. The goal was to marry him and hopefully grow to love him, but I didn't choose all this. I'm grateful that it's there, but it wasn't by choice."

Everyone's eyes were focused on Vieno as he spoke with such passion. Lidon felt the words originate in Vieno's very soul, knew them to be true in the depths of his own being.

"But you, Enar, you I choose. I choose you to be my third mate. You're the only one I chose myself. Don't you see how special that makes you?"

Hours later, Lidon, Palani, and Vieno were asleep again, still tired after Vieno's heat, but Enar couldn't sleep. In the light of the moon that fell through the cracks of the curtains, he watched his men sleep. Vieno lay cuddled up against Lidon, using his shoulder as a pillow. He was a snuggler, the little omega, always seeking someone to nestle himself against.

Palani lay closest to Enar, his face turned toward him. Enar gave in to the temptation to brush his forehead. He was so strong and yet so kind and soft, knowing when to be bossy and when to embrace, when to push and when to let go. It was a rare quality.

He checked the clock. He'd been awake for over an hour now, and his body wasn't showing any sign of wanting to go back to sleep. Careful not to disturb the others, he crawled out of bed and found a quiet spot outside on the porch. It held a swinging porch bench that Lidon's grandpa had built, a sturdy wooden thing that made no sound as Enar gently swung back and forth on it, his legs pulled up. It was quiet outside, crickets chirping in the background, interrupted by the howl of a coyote every now and then. Enar wished his head was as tranquil.

He was still trying to come to terms with what they had discussed. Vieno's words rang true, yet still he struggled with accepting it. They didn't understand who he was inside, of how fucked up his mind was...or his body, wherever it had gone wrong inside him. All he knew was that he wasn't a real alpha, and he never would be. No matter how hard he'd try, he'd never be able to conform to the norms, the expectations society had of him as an alpha.

Sure, they all suspected, Palani probably on a deeper level than Lidon and Vieno, but Enar had never put it into words to them. How could he? He still had trouble defining it himself, let alone accepting it. Acknowledging his true status meant losing everything he'd built. Maybe not with them but definitely in society. And it shouldn't matter, but it did.

Even thinking about the hurtful words his father had hurled at him over the years made his heart contract painfully. As a child, he'd already felt different. The alpha behavior that should have been so natural to him instead felt forced. He'd always been more content to follow than to lead, and that was about the worst thing for an alpha.

Sure, he could be a full alpha if it suited his purposes. His alpha powers were weak and seemed focused on empathy and comfort—something that came in handy with his job—but they were present. And he could be dominant and bossy if he wanted to. It was more that he didn't want to, most of the time. It felt completely unnatural to him, so forced it sucked him empty.

He had to, in his job and in society, to fulfill the role that was expected of him. That's why he'd built up to a "code yellow" every few months, when the pretending got too much. Having Lidon boss him around, allowing him to be a beta, had kept him sane. Those few stolen hours, every two, three months, had been enough to last him till the next time he could lower his defenses and be himself—more or less.

He'd never been more himself than with Palani, though. He wasn't sure how the beta had seen through his pretense so easily, but he had. That stupid joke he'd wrongly reacted to had been a catalyst, but Palani had been so damn understanding and accepting. Lidon had been as well but in a different way. They'd never talked about it, not even after the first time Lidon had taken him, which had only happened after Enar had all but begged him.

No, Palani understood him on a level no one else did, and it was what made this whole foursome-thing so damn scary. What if he fucked it up and lost not just his best friend but also the man who truly got him?

And Vieno, sweet Vieno, didn't have clue beyond that Enar liked to be fucked every now and then. He thought Enar was the alpha he portrayed. What would happen if he found out? He'd reacted well to Palani's rather blunt statement about Lidon having fucked Enar, but this was on a whole other level. He might be certain he chose Enar as a mate, but would he change his mind if he discovered the truth? Enar counted on it.

He heard the door opening behind him and sensed who it was without looking.

"Couldn't sleep?" Palani asked.

"No. My head's too busy."

Palani studied him for a second, then lowered himself onto the swing next to Enar, lifting up Enar's legs and placing them on his lap when he'd found a spot. "Wanna talk about it?"

Did he? Every time he talked to Palani, he ended up sharing more than he had planned to. The man possessed an uncanny ability to make you say things you didn't want to, simply by listening and asking the right questions.

"Turn around," Palani said, pushing against Enar's legs.

Enar was confused for a second what he meant, but the beta grabbed his arms and turned him so he ended up with his head against Palani's shoulder, his body resting against him and his legs stretching out in the other direction. "Why'd you do that?" he asked.

"Because you seem to be able to talk better when you're being held."

Enar almost sat up when that truth connected with him. Fuck, Palani really had his number, didn't he? How had he figured that out so easily? "You're good at reading people," he said.

"True, but I'm especially good at reading you."

Enar chuckled. "And so modest."

"Modesty gets you nowhere, not in my world."

"No, I would imagine not. You've accomplished quite a bit for a beta." He cringed at his own words. "That came out wrong. I meant—"

"I know what you meant. Don't worry, Doc, I have thick skin. I can't be offended that easily."

Enar pondered that. "You can't afford to in the kind of work you do."

"Exactly. But let's get back to the part where you were complimenting me."

A slow smile broke out on Enar's lips. "I respect the hell out of you for the work you do. Being surrounded by alphas, and then doing as well as you're doing is nothing short of amazing. You should've been born an alpha."

Palani's hand found Enar's neck, and he scratched it with the habitual affection of a longtime married couple. Enar's skin jumped up in goose bumps before it settled down again, but his increased heart rate still told him how much he liked being held and petted like this.

"Now that Vieno is taken care of, I'm happy with who I am."

"Are you? Don't you wish you'd been an alpha? Don't you feel like one at times? You're quite bossy and pushy for a beta."

Palani laughed, a melodious sound that danced over Enar's skin. "Aren't you full of compliments tonight?"

Then he kissed Enar's head, another one of those little gestures, which made Enar experience things inside he'd never felt before. "Back when Vieno was so sick, that's when I raged at being a beta. I wanted to help him, wanted to be enough for him, you know? But it was always because of him, never because I felt like an alpha deep down...unlike you."

Enar's breath caught. The air grew thin, as if he wasn't breathing in enough oxygen. He'd admitted parts of the truth before when they had talked, but was he ready to open his heart? Handing his heart to Palani meant risking having it broken, but hadn't the beta showed already he knew how to handle with care?

"Yes," he admitted softly. "Unlike me."

He rubbed his head against Palani's shoulder, which earned him another neck scratch.

"I don't feel like an alpha at all, but I don't feel like a beta either," he admitted, forcing the words out.

"You don't?" Palani asked, surprise audible in his voice.

"No. I *am* one, deep inside. I can act like an alpha, but deep down, I'm a beta...always have been. It's what comes naturally to me, what I know to be true at the core of my being. I'm so tired of pretending to be someone and something I'm not."

"So stop pretending," Palani said, but it wasn't flippant.

"How? It's not gonna be accepted."

"Not in the outside world, no. Not at first anyway. But here with us, you can be yourself or experiment with your identity and behavior to find out what works for you."

Enar's eyes welled up. "You'd accept it, just like that..."

"Hell, I already have. You may not realize it, but you're acting more like a beta with me already, Doc, and I love it. I love that you feel safe enough to show me who you really are."

"I do feel safe with you," Enar admitted. "Even more than with Lidon, and he's known me forever."

"Lidon's not a talker, like me. I process through words, and I think that helps you do the same. But he's accepted you as much as I have, and so has Vieno."

"Vieno doesn't know about me," Enar said, frowning.

"Oh, you can be so stunningly naïve at times, Doc. Of course, he knows. Not in the right terms, but he can see you're different from other alphas. And he's fine with that. He chose you as mate anyway."

The realization that his different-ness was so obvious both scared and comforted Enar. He'd always thought he kept it well hidden, but maybe it had come out more than he'd been aware of with his men. And Palani was right. They had accepted him anyway.

"I'm not ready to tell them yet," he said.

"That's okay, Doc. Whenever you're ready. And in the meantime, if you want to talk about it or experiment with me, you're more than welcome to. I want you to be able to be yourself with me because I like you the way you are."

"You do?" he asked, his eyes welling up again.

This time, Palani grabbed his neck and pulled his head sideways for a soft kiss on his lips. "You have no idea how much I like you... One day, when you're ready, I'll tell you."

4

———————

Lidon was working through a load of mail, sighing at the intimidating stack of bills. Every month, he dreaded this, having to go through all the bills and receipts, make sure his finances were all in order. He really needed to hire an accountant to do this for him, but the trust issue had kept him from even looking for someone.

At least it was less lonely with Vieno vacuuming the living room. They'd shared a lazy breakfast after Palani and Enar had left, then an equally lazy round of making out in the bathtub. It was unlike any day off Lidon usually had, but he could get used to this. He'd worried Vieno's sexual appetite would diminish after his heat, but that was a week ago, and he'd been interested, not to say enthusiastic, every single day.

Over the sound of the vacuum, Lidon heard his phone signaling someone was at the front gate. He swiped to get the camera view and recognized the car. He waved at Vieno to shut off the vacuum and opened the gate with the app on his phone.

"Jawon is here," Lidon announced. "My cousin. He'll get

started on the renovations outside," he added when Vieno looked confused.

"Ah, him. Sorry. I can't wait. I'm so excited."

Lidon kissed the top of his head. "So am I."

They walked outside where a big pickup truck was pulling up in front of the house. Lidon hadn't seen his cousin in a while, and they greeted each other with a hug and a few slaps on the back. For a beta, Jawon was bulky, his body muscled and hardened by manual labor and spending most of his days outside.

"Jawon, this is my mate Vieno," Lidon said.

As was custom with a mated omega, Jawon didn't shake his hand but bowed his head in a quick gesture of tribute. "It's so nice to meet you, Vieno." He turned toward Lidon. "Mom was ecstatic about your marriage."

Lidon winced. "And probably pissed as hell we didn't invite her, right?"

Jawon grinned. "Like I'm gonna get between my mom and you. Good luck with that."

Lidon's Aunt Sophie was a wonderful woman, a true force of nature, but family was everything to her. She'd been a second mother to Lidon since his parents had passed away, so he could only imagine her disappointment when she learned about him getting married.

"There were extenuating circumstances," he said weakly.

"I'm sure there were. Still not touching it with a ten-foot pole. Now, let's talk about what you want me to do."

Lidon gestured to Vieno. "I'll let him take you on a tour and explain everything."

Vieno pulled his little notebook from his pocket, and Jawon grinned. "You're organized. I like you already."

"I have a lot of ideas," Vieno said apologetically.

"Good," Jawon said with a warm smile, affirming to Lidon he was the right man for the job. "This place could use it. Let's get started."

Lidon followed them as they walked outside of the gates. It was a beautiful day, the warmth of the sun already strong, even though it wasn't even midmorning. Birds darted through the sky, chasing each other, making Lidon envious with how carefree they were. The land stretched out before him, acres and acres of potential. Of home, his home. It hadn't felt like that in a while, though the pull of the ranch had always been there, but somehow, the heart had been missing. That was being restored, and he couldn't be more excited as Vieno described what he wanted. Jawon asked questions every now and then but mostly listened.

"The vegetable garden is a priority for me," Vieno said.

Jawon pointed to the half-collapsed barn the plot of land sat up against. "We'll need to renovate that first so you have a spot to put all your tools and equipment in. What scale are you thinking?"

"Scale?" Vieno asked.

"Do you want to keep it at a scale where you can do everything manually? Or should we plan so you could scale it up if you wanted to and bring in farming equipment, like tractors?"

"Is that even an option here?" Lidon asked, surprised.

Jawon nodded. "It sure is. I looked at some old maps and asked my dad about what this place was like in the past to get an idea of what the possibilities were. Dad said Grandpa used this as an operational farm with livestock, dairy, and agricultural crops."

He pointed to the plot of land in front of them. "This would be most suitable for smaller crops that have a shorter life and can be replaced quickly, like lettuce, radishes, and fresh herbs, or in the winter, spinach and cabbage."

He gestured to another area. "You have a plot there that's perfect for veggies that need more space, like zucchini, melons, and pumpkin. But on the other side of the little creek, you have a piece of land to grow crops like potatoes, corn, even grain if you wanted to. We could fence off a large plot for livestock...and horses, if you wanted."

Lidon swallowed, a sadness invading him. Why had he let the place go so much? It had all been too much after the death of his parents, dealing with the grief, trying to find his way in the police academy and then on the force, losing Matteo...then the whole mess with Rodrick, and he'd stopped caring, stopped living.

"I didn't realize your dad had memories of this place," he said in a soft tone.

Jawon's face showed nothing but kindness. "Lidon, he grew up here, just like your dad. Only your dad was the alpha heir, so he inherited, but Dad told me he still lived here, even after your parents got married. After Grandpa passed away, they all moved out, Dad and his siblings."

Lidon sighed. "I never got the time to talk about this with my dad. Tell your father I'd love to learn about his memories of this place and any advice he has on how to rebuild it. I'm sure he's been frustrated for years with how I let it go..."

Jawon put a strong hand on his shoulder. "He under-stands. It was a lot you had to deal with. I won't deny he was over the moon when I told him you called me in to start working on it, though."

Lidon nodded, turning to Vieno. "What do you think?"

Vieno looked pensive. "I don't think we want to start on

that scale right away, but it would be foolish not to plan for it. What would it entail now?" he asked Jawon.

"It would mean we'd renovate the barn and make it the right size so it could hold tractors and bigger farming equipment when needed. Everything else can wait and can be done gradually."

Vieno nodded. "Okay, I like the sound of that. The barn first, then, and the vegetable plot. I also want to restore the chicken coop."

"Yeah, that makes sense. Fresh eggs are wonderful, plus they'll be able to eat a lot of your food waste. I would also create a compost corner," Jawon suggested. "You'll have to fence it off well to keep out wildlife, but it's a great way to create natural compost for your veggies."

They discussed more details while Lidon's thoughts wandered off. He'd known Uncle Leland had grown up here, but somehow, he hadn't registered how much he had lost too. His father, when Lidon was born. His home, when he moved out. And then his brother and brother-in-law, when Lidon's parents had died.

And still, he'd never been anything but kind to Lidon, even though it must have broken his heart to see the ranch grow neglected. He'd never brought it up, had never even tried to fight the will that had left everything to Lidon's father, and then to Lidon, unfair as it might have been. The alpha heir—the oldest alpha son—inherited everything. That's what Lidon's dad had told him. It wasn't fair by any standard, but it was common practice.

Maybe he should invite his uncle and aunt over for dinner. Word about the foursome relationship he was in would leak out soon enough anyway with Jawon and his men working here, so he might as well stay a step ahead of it and introduce his men on his own terms. The weird thing was that Lidon didn't even fear their reaction. Somehow, he knew they'd be okay with it, considering how much his uncle valued the old ways, as he called it. The shifter ways.

And not only could he introduce his men and show his uncle the improvements he'd planned but also could ask about what it had been like on the ranch before he'd been born. Uncle Leland might have insights and ideas he could use and maybe some stories he'd love to hear. He hadn't been ready yet to hear them, but things had changed now. Hell, everything had changed, and it felt like the right time.

Vieno and Jawon were wrapping things up now that Jawon had his marching orders.

"I can't wait to get started on this," Jawon said.

"Do you have the manpower?" Lidon asked. "When can you start?"

Jawon shuffled his feet, looking embarrassed. "I can start today if you want. Business has not been good lately," he said. "With the economy in a slump, small businesses like mine are suffering. People are doing renovations themselves, or they're postponing them, and I don't have the skills, manpower, or tools for the bigger construction jobs. So in all honesty, Lidon, working on this project would be a godsend. It would keep me afloat for a while."

Lidon clamped his hand on his cousin's shoulder, and Jawon looked up to meet his eyes. "I'm happy it's working out this way. We're family, so we need to take care of each other. What timeline are we talking about until you're done with this phase?" Lidon asked.

"That depends on how many outsiders you want me to bring in."

"As few as possible. It's outside the gated area of the house, but it's pretty close."

"I know, no outsiders inside the gates." Jawon grinned.

Lidon was glad to see him relaxing again. "I was raised the same way. Look, I can bring in Ori and Servas. I hire them whenever I need extra manpower, and I assume you'd be okay with them, right? They could use the job."

Lidon nodded. Ori and Servas were two other cousins, both sons of his father's younger sisters. "That's fine. I also asked Urien to stop by to service the pool. I had the impression he's looking for extra work, so he could pitch in as well?"

"That's good thinking. I know he's struggling financially after that stunt his ex pulled."

Lidon raised his eyebrows. "I didn't know about that. What happened?"

"A gambling problem he didn't know about. She lost all their savings, then ran up a massive debt in both their names. He filed for divorce and was awarded full custody of their daughter, but he still had to cough up half of his ex's debts. It was nasty all around."

"Fucking hell, that sucks," Lidon said. "Poor guy. Let's see if we can employ him first, make sure he can provide for his daughter."

Jawon nodded. "Will do. I'll draw up a preliminary budget for you to sign off on before I start the work."

Lidon waved him away. "I don't need one. You're family. You're not gonna screw me over."

"That's what Urien thought as well, and look how that turned out."

"That's different. You're my blood. You wouldn't fuck me over. Besides, we have big plans with this place. You're gonna be busy here for a while. I want family for this job, and you know I'll pay you well. In return, I ask for your loyalty and your discretion. If I hear you talk about me or my family behind my back, you're out."

Jawon's face was dead serious as he stuck out his hand to Lidon. "You have my word, alpha."

5

Ten days after Vieno's heat, things had settled a bit with the four of them in their complicated relationship, much to Palani's relief. Not that they'd figured it all out, and he sure as fuck objected to how much Enar worked and the ridiculously long days he made, but they'd found a rhythm together. Sort of.

Palani decided to work on Project X today, his investigation into Ryland, the cop Lidon suspected of being dirty. For Lidon to mention him by name to Palani, he'd have to be damn sure something fishy was going on, considering his strong loyalty to his brothers in blue. Ryland and Excellon were connected, even if he hadn't figured out why and how, so Palani figured that investigating the drug would also lead him to dirt on Ryland.

His previous investigation into dirty cops had hinted at involvement in the White-Collar Division where Ryland was the second-in-command, but Palani hadn't dug deeper at that time. His boss had been reluctant to even publish what Palani had found out about lower-level cops, so the beta had figured it wasn't the time to aim for higher-ranking officers. Lidon's request changed that.

He'd already deduced from his conversation with Lucan something suspicious was going on. It made zero sense to let a suspect like Lucan go unless they were either protecting a bigger case they were investigating...or a bigger name. Call him jaded, but Palani's money was on the second. Ryland's boss, an alpha by the name of Lester Cournoyer, didn't seem to do much actual leading. Technically, he headed the White-Collar Division, but Palani found out the man was months before his retirement...and Ryland was set to take over from him.

Lucan had sent him a screenshot of the statement he'd supposedly signed, and the signing officer had been one Alec Kimble, who reported directly to...Karl Ryland. It was too much of a coincidence, and Palani didn't believe in coincidence in the first place. So he'd start at the outskirts and work his way inward until he struck gold.

Lucan had provided him with some names of doctors who illegally prescribed Excellon, so he went down the list and called them, one by one, promising them off-the-record quotes and deep background only to get them to talk.

"It's a crime against omegas," one doctor argued passionately. "Excellon is far more effective in preventing pregnancy, and yet doctors won't prescribe it."

"Why? What's keeping them from giving their patients access to this drug?" Palani asked.

The doctor hesitated.

"We're off the record," Palani assured him again. "This will not lead back to you in any way."

The doctor sighed. "There are rumors that doctors are being bribed or pressured to prescribe one of the other three drugs rather than Excellon. I don't know for sure, since no one ever contacted me, but I'm known as an omega advocate. I'd start with doctors who are in it for the money rather than for a personal passion."

"Have you ever reported your suspicions?" Palani asked.

"I haven't, but a friend of mine has. He didn't get anywhere with the cops."

Palani asked for his name, then called this Dr. Vandermeer next.

"I did report it, first to a telephone hotline the cops have for reporting fraud. That was months ago, but I never heard back. So a few weeks ago, I stopped by police headquarters and filed a report with the department that handles fraud."

"The White-Collar Division?" Palani checked.

"Right, that sounds familiar."

"Do you remember who you spoke to?"

"One sec." Papers rustled in the background. "Erm, Alec Kimble, it says here. I requested a copy of the report I filed."

Palani sat up straight. If they had changed one report, what were the odds of them doing it again? "Any chance I could have a copy of that?"

"Sure, I'll scan it real quick and email it to you."

Palani gave his email address and, after a few more questions, hung up. He leaned back in his chair. A picture was emerging. Even though he still possessed no hard evidence for the bribes against Excellon, he gathered enough to confirm his gut feeling that it was true. And while Ryland hadn't been implicated so far, his division sure as hell wasn't jumping in to investigate this. Palani needed more.

First, it would help to have a copy of the report in the internal system of the police for what Vandermeer had filed. If it didn't match what the doctor had sent him, he'd have evidence of tampering. He couldn't simply call the force and ask for a copy. Sure, they'd give it to him under the Freedom of Information Act, but he'd also alert them he was investigating them. No, he needed inside access, and he'd do what he could to keep Lidon out of this. The man had taken enough of a risk to even talk to Palani about this. He had a couple of sources within the police force who had helped him before, so he started there.

"Palani, I respect the hell out of what you're doing, but take my advice. Don't go up against Ryland," Susan, one of his best informants on the force, told him. The urgent tone of her voice left little doubt how much she meant it. "He's not like your previous targets, the lower-level cops you exposed. Ryland will fight back, and it won't be pretty."

Palani frowned. "What do you mean?"

Her voice dropped to a whisper. "He's gotten at least ten people fired, and he replaced them all with his own men. I swear some of them act like they never even graduated from the academy, but they blindly follow his every order."

"You're kidding me," Palani said. "That's fucked up."

"I'm sorry, Palani, but I can't get you that report. I'm too scared of what Ryland will do if he finds out."

After what she'd told him, Palani couldn't blame her. Susan was a secretary in HR, so she'd know, wouldn't she? "I understand. I don't want you to get into trouble," he assured her.

Susan sighed. "Trouble I can handle, but this is on another level. IA has been trying to make a case against him for months, but every time they think they have him, evidence disappears, or witnesses do. It's disturbing."

Disturbing was too tame a word, Palani thought. Susan was as level-headed as they came, so for her to be this worried, the threat was real. "It's okay. I'll manage another way. You be careful, okay?"

After ending the call, he sat there for a few minutes. This was far more complex than he'd counted on. Cops being fired and replaced by what sounded like unqualified friends of Ryland? That was some serious shit. All the more reason to keep Lidon out of this if Ryland's reach was that long. He'd better focus on Excellon for now.

He needed proof of the actual bribes. The question was how to obtain this. Money trails were easy to follow once you knew where to start. Since he didn't have a solid lead where the money was coming from, this would be a challenge. No, he'd either have to show up with an omega and try to get a doctor to prescribe Excellon, or...

Enar. He could use Enar. Not in their city, since he was probably too well known, but another big city in the state? That had to work, right? Enar was a fellow doctor. He might get other doctors to talk, brag about how much they were making off this? It wasn't ideal to involve Enar, and neither was taking this outside the city.

The omega wasn't a bad idea either, but there was no way he was involving Vieno. Aside from his persistent agoraphobia—he hadn't left the ranch since he'd moved in —Palani didn't want him anywhere near this. He'd have to find someone else who could do it, but that was a long shot for now. He'd have to focus on different avenues of getting more intel on this bribery. What if he kept it simple at first and called doctors to see if he could get a prescription for a fictitious omega husband? It wouldn't prove anything, but it might show him how big the issue was.

Two hours later, he had called fifty-three doctors with the same story about his omega husband about to start his first heat, and they'd hired a caretaker and could they please prescribe Excellon, since he'd heard it was effective against male pregnancy. Only six of them had been willing to prescribe. A vast majority had denied it was more effective, others had cited severe side effects, and a few had claimed it was off the market due to an investigation of fatal allergic reactions to one of the components.

This quick exercise had shown Lucan had been right. Doctors *were* reluctant to prescribe Excellon, and since the medical trials showed it was effective, money seemed to be a logical motive. Still, he had to make sure the bit about the side effects and allergic reactions wasn't true. How to check that?

The easiest way was to call Lukos, the company who made it, but Palani hesitated to do so. The fact that Lukos had produced three effective drugs in a short period was already an anomaly, but Palani had realized something else. Lukos had to know by now something was stopping doctors from prescribing their far more effective birth control. So why weren't they protesting this?

Palani had seen nothing in the news about it—and he'd done a thorough online search after that thought—and as far as he knew, it wasn't being investigated either. The latter could be explained if Ryland, the de-facto head of the division who would research this had there been a complaint, was indeed dirty, but wouldn't Lukos had gone over his head? If you had concrete evidence other companies were obstructing your sales, wouldn't you bring it to the highest officers you could think of? Even government?

Yet Lukos hadn't, and that made Palani suspicious. It reeked of something else going on there, something he had no idea of yet what it was, but he would find out. But first, he could check the claim about the side effects with Enar.

"Am I interrupting?" he asked when Enar picked up.

"No, I'm in the car, on my way to a patient. What's up?"

"Do doctors get information about newly discovered side effects of drugs? Or if a drug is pulled because of fatal allergic reactions?"

"Yes to both, provided they use the electronic patient file system, the EPF. That shows warnings every day with new interactions. They also pop up when we prescribe a drug. So if I were to prescribe you a cough suppressant through the EPF, for instance, the side effects pop up. The system also shows known interactions with other meds you take, provided your file is updated."

"Do most doctors use the EPF? It's mandatory, right?"

"It is. Some doctors feel it's an invasion of patient privacy, so they won't always list every procedure they perform on a patient. Or they omit certain medications they prescribe, since a patient's legal guardian or alpha may have access to that file. Hypothetically speaking, of course."

Palani grinned. Enar was being a total smartass here. But the man was prudent to speak in generals and not discuss anything specific. "Have you heard of any new side effects of Excellon? Or allergic reactions?"

"No," Enar said. "Nothing."

"Okay, thanks. That's all I needed to know."

"Palani, be careful, okay?"

He smiled at Enar's care. "Right back atcha, Doc."

Not bad for a few hours' work, Palani thought. Now he needed to report to Franken and get his boss to agree to put more hours into this. Nailing Ryland was one thing, but Palani's ultimate goal was to discover what was going on with Excellon. Because aside from Ryland being dirty, he now had credible evidence of the bribery, but he needed more proof of who was behind it. The drug companies, maybe, or insurance companies, as Lucan, the pharmacy technician Lidon had arrested, had suggested, but speculating had no place in a newspaper, as Franken always told Palani. He needed facts, cold hard facts, so he'd need to do more digging.

6

Enar rubbed his neck with his right hand while he kept his left hand on the steering wheel and his eyes on the road. Damn, he was tired. It had been a long day, drawn out by the complications in the delivery of a baby. Everything had been fine until it hadn't been, and when the baby's heart rate bottomed out, Enar performed an emergency C-section to save the mom and the baby. It was touch and go, but it looked like both would be okay.

He called Vieno to let him know he wouldn't be home till after midnight, and Vieno was all sweet and understanding. He promised Enar there was a meal waiting for him in the fridge if he wanted it. Enar wasn't even sure if he was hungry or not. Right now, he was too exhausted to care about food. Even the thought of having to microwave a meal was intimidating. He just wanted to crash.

He considered going back to his townhouse, which would've saved him a twenty-minute ride, but decided to drive over to Lidon's after all. It was strange because they wouldn't be awake anymore. They'd be in bed, the three of them, together. And that thought made him happy and sad at the same time.

He belonged with them, so they had assured him. Vieno had said it crystal clear that he'd chosen Enar as his mate. Enar had still been super careful not to cross any boundaries or lines he wasn't aware of, but no one had called him out on anything in the three weeks they were together. Not even Lidon.

It was him Enar struggled with most. With Palani, he knew where he stood. Even though they'd only known each other for a short time, their connection was easy. Palani got him, and that was mutual. With Vieno, it was simple as well. He had a naturally sunny disposition and such an innate sweetness. Plus, he was so free with his affection that Enar couldn't help but get pulled in by him. And he couldn't deny Vieno's attraction to him, at least physically. They'd shared some sweet moments together...and a few seriously hot ones.

But Lidon, that was different. They'd known each other forever, since kindergarten, but their dynamic had changed over the years. They'd started out as equals, two alphas trying to find their way in the world, but after Enar had submitted to him, things had changed. Enar wasn't sure if Lidon treated him differently since he'd started fucking him or if Enar's perception had changed, but something had. They were no longer equals, Lidon always the stronger, more powerful and dominant. Enar hadn't fought it, not until Lidon had asked him to join their foursome.

God, he'd wanted to...desperately. But that last step, that final acknowledgment of Lidon's dominance over him, had been so damn hard. Like the final step in accepting that he wasn't a real alpha, which he'd always known deep down, but still. Stating that to Palani was different from voicing it toward Lidon, and Enar couldn't explain why. Maybe because Lidon was the ultimate alpha? Acknowledging Lidon's alpha power over him had been like admitting defeat, hadn't it? Then why had it felt so right?

A headache brewed behind his eyes, thrumming in his forehead, and he rubbed his face again, trying to get rid of the tension. It bothered him that he couldn't figure out his relationship with Lidon. Sure, the alpha had fucked him during Vieno's heat three weeks ago, and that had been perfect, but he hadn't touched him since. Well, that wasn't true. He hadn't fucked him, but he always kissed him when they came home, but it had felt obligatory to Enar. Like Lidon accepted Enar because of his connection with Vieno and Palani, but not because he himself wanted him. Or did he?

They'd never talked about their relationship in the past other than Enar calling or texting him with a code yellow and Lidon giving him what he needed. They'd never put what they did into words. If it was a friends-with-benefits thing or Lidon merely being nice or what. Why had he done it? Enar had never asked. Maybe because he'd never dared to, but now it mattered, and he didn't know what to do with that, how to bring it up, or if he even should.

By the time he reached the gates, he had come no closer to an answer, and his headache had worsened. The lights were still on in the kitchen, and he smiled. That must've been Vieno, wanting to make sure he would feel welcome.

"Hey," Lidon's voice sounded, and Enar all but jumped.

"You scared the bejesus out of me," he gasped, his hand flying to his heart as Lidon walked in from the living room. "I wasn't expecting you."

"I've barely seen you the last few days, and since I have a

late shift tomorrow, I figured I'd stay up." Lidon's voice was
friendly, yet it had an undertone that put Enar on edge.

"Oh."

He set his bag down and kicked off his shoes, then
reminded himself to place them in the shoe rack in the
hallway and to put his bag in the cubbies Vieno had set up
there.

"You look like crap," Lidon said as he walked back in.

"Jeez, thanks for staying up to tell me that," Enar said,
keeping his voice light.

"Have you eaten?" Lidon asked.

"I'm not really hungry."

Lidon's eyes narrowed. "That wasn't the question, but I'll
take that as a no. Sit down. I'll warm up the dinner Vieno
left you."

"You don't have to..." Enar started but shut up when
Lidon shot him a look that left little to the imagination. He
sat his ass down at the table and waited while Lidon put his
plate in the microwave, then grabbed him a seltzer from the
fridge.

He closed his eyes and tried again to rub the tension out
of his neck. He'd performed the emergency C-section in the
woman's living room, knowing he didn't have time to get to
the hospital. The light had been bad, and he'd craned his
neck to make sure he didn't fuck up. That, in combination
with the other procedures he'd done today, had caused his
muscles to cramp. That had to be why he had a headache,
though he had them more lately.

"Here," Lidon said, and Enar's eyes flew open. "Dinner is
ready."

"Thank you," he said meekly. The smell of the barbecue
ribs with mashed potatoes hit him, and his stomach
rumbled.

"Not hungry, huh?" Lidon said. "Don't bother answering. Just eat."

Enar obeyed, keeping in a moan as the rich barbecue sauce hit his tongue. Damn, that was good. "You're gonna watch me eat?" he asked with his mouth full. "At least talk to me. How's work?"

Lidon raised his eyebrows but obliged by sharing an investigation he was involved in right now. Enar knew he could talk to no one else about this. Palani was too risky, considering his job, and Vieno...no one wanted to burden Vieno with anything heavy. It was how they rolled. So Lidon talked while Enar ate and listened, asking the occasional question.

When he'd cleared it, he pushed his plate back with a satisfied sigh, licking the last bits of sauce of his fingers. "Thank you," he told Lidon.

"You're welcome."

The silence hung between them, thickening.

"I don't know how to do this with you," Enar blurted out. "Everything has changed between us, and I don't know how to navigate this."

Was that relief he saw on Lidon's face? If so, it mirrored his own feelings because he was glad he'd said it, awkward and uncomfortable as it was.

"Me neither," Lidon said. "I've never been good at the whole 'let's talk about our feelings' thing, and with you, it's even harder."

"You two are adorable and frustrating as fuck at the same time," Palani spoke, startling Enar and Lidon both.

He walked into the kitchen, dressed in the bright red boxers he always slept in, his eyes remarkably sharp, considering he must have been asleep already. He walked over to Lidon first and gave him a kiss. The alpha's hand drifted to

Palani's butt, and the beta let out a little moan when that big hand squeezed it. Then Lidon slapped it, sending Palani over to Enar.

Palani kissed him, a soft, sweet kiss that made the tight muscles in Enar's face relax a little. "You have a headache," Palani said, and Enar nodded.

Palani pulled Enar's head against his chest, cradling him and holding him while his fingers found sore points in his neck. "Long surgery?" he asked.

"Yeah. Wrong position too."

"Hmm," Palani said, his fingers still kneading Enar's neck. Enar moaned when the beta hit a sore spot, causing his arms to tingle and his skin to rise in goose bumps.

"Why don't you two take a bath?" Palani said. "It will help you relax your muscles."

"Together?" Enar asked, then wanted to clamp his mouth at the surprise that was so clearly audible in his voice.

"Yes," Palani said, his tone patient. "Together. Let Lidon rub out the tension in your neck and back while you two talk. Use one of the guest rooms so you don't wake Vieno up. He's cleaned most of them by now."

He stepped back, letting go of Enar.

"Would you like that?" Lidon asked, his voice uncharacteristically insecure.

"Yes," Enar said. "If it's okay with you."

Palani rolled his eyes. "God, you two crack me up. Of course, he wants to take a bath with you, Doc. He wants you to lean on him, so lean. Stop dancing around each other and give in to what you both want and need already. I'm going back to bed. Take care of each other."

With one last kiss for both of them, he left them alone.

"So," Lidon said. "Bath?"

They filled a bathtub in one of the guest bedrooms, one that also had a master bathroom attached to it. The thing had a massive bath that would easily fit them both. As Palani had said, it was sparkling clean, and there was even bath salt on a shelf. Enar threw some in and let the bath fill. He looked at Lidon as they both got undressed. Why was he feeling so damn insecure, even though they'd had sex and had seen each other naked many times? What was it about Lidon that threw him off-balance?

"Was Palani right?" Lidon asked, his voice soft. "Do you want to lean on me?"

That was an easy one to answer. "Yes."

"I'm always so scared of getting it wrong with you, of inadvertently hurting you," Lidon admitted.

Enar met his eyes and saw the concern in them. "I know."

Lidon reached out his hand, and Enar took it, allowing himself to be pulled close. "Why are you reluctant to lean on me when I see you have no trouble doing it with Palani?"

He wasn't ready yet, not when he had to face him. Not when the chance of rejection felt so big.

"Can we... Could you hold me when we're in the tub? Like, not opposite each other, but—"

"I'd love to," Lidon interrupted him.

He let go of Enar and got into the tub first, opening his legs so Enar could find a spot between them, leaning back against his chest. The angry voices inside his head screamed when he did so, shouting at him he was a betrayal to his kind. He ignored them, but it wasn't easy. Then Lidon folded his strong arms around him and pulled his head back so it leaned against him, and the voices quieted.

"Like this?" Lidon asked.

"Yeah, exactly like this," Enar whispered.

They were quiet for a long time, but the silence felt peaceful this time.

"I'm scared to lean on you because deep down, I fear you'll judge me for it," Enar finally said. He felt Lidon tense underneath him and reached for his hand, holding it to his chest. "My mind knows you won't, but my heart, the voices inside my head, they're telling me you'll laugh at me, judge me, condemn me for being weak."

"I won't," Lidon said. "I... See, this is where I hesitate. Because I'm not good with words, and I don't want to hurt you."

"Tell me...be honest with me."

"I *want* you to lean on me. Hell, I want to force you to stop being so damn stubborn and let me and Palani and Vieno take care of you, but I'm holding it back because I don't want to overstep. You came home, and it was so easy to see you were bone-tired and struggling, and I wanted to tell you to eat, relax, and take some painkillers... And to stop working so damn hard, because you're not taking good care of yourself, and I miss you."

"You *miss* me?" Enar focused on the last part because the first part was too overwhelming to even let it sink in.

"When you're not here? Hell yes, I do. I haven't figured it all out either, how you and I fit, but I want you here."

The words hit him like a hammer. They'd all said the same, that they wanted him here. Then why couldn't he feel it? Why was his heart telling him that sooner or later, they'd discover they were better off without him? That they fit together, the three of them, a real alpha, a real true beta, and a real omega, without him fucking things up?

He leaned against Lidon, his body surrendering, but his head pounding with the screaming voices all over again.

≈

VIENO WOKE UP DISORIENTED. The room was much lighter than usual when he woke up. Warm arms held him, cuddling him from the back, so he wasn't alone. He didn't need to turn around to know who held him. He'd recognize his smell anywhere.

"Good morning, baby," Palani said softly. "Did you sleep well?"

Vieno blinked a few times, then looked at the clock. Nine? Why the hell had they let him sleep so long?

"I need to make breakfast," he said.

He tried to move, but Palani tightened his arms to hold him back.

"It's all good. No worries. Lidon and Enar went for a workout, and they can take care of themselves, you know? We stayed up late two nights in a row, so we all agreed you should sleep in a little. Come cuddle with me a little longer."

Vieno breathed with relief. "Oh."

He pushed against Palani's arms so he could turn around. His best friend's brown eyes were full of love as their eyes met. "It's been a while since it was just us," Palani said.

Vieno smiled. "Missed me?" he teased, then offered his lips so Palani could kiss him.

It was the perfect of kisses, as only Palani kissed him, all soft and dreamy and slow.

"Mmmm." Vieno sighed into his mouth. "I love waking up like this."

Palani rolled over, taking Vieno with him so he ended stretched out on top of him, his head on Palani's chest. Vieno was still naked after Lidon had fucked him last night, a quick fuck because he'd been hard and Vieno's hole had ached with emptiness, and it had worked out well for both of them. Palani and Enar had sixty-nined, something they loved to do, and Vieno loved to watch 'cause hello, super-fucking hot, Enar especially. The man rimmed like he got graded on it.

It was amazing how his appetite for sex seemed to have adjusted to him having three mates. He'd never denied any of his men when they wanted him. On the contrary, as soon as they touched him, he got all slick and ready for them. Lidon took him almost every day, sometimes more than once. The alpha had unrivaled stamina because some days he fucked all three of them...and he would get hard again in an instant. Maybe the mating thing had triggered something in him as well?

"How are you, baby?" Palani asked. "So much has changed. Are you happy?"

"God, yes. I never thought I had the capacity to be this happy." He realized something as he spoke. "I haven't been depressed since we got together..."

"You haven't?" Palani asked with wonder in his voice. He rolled them over and leaned over Vieno on his elbow, watching him. "I'd noticed you seemed content but hadn't realized that. That's amazing."

"It is. I'm so happy with you all," Vieno said. He bit his lip. Would Palani be hurt that he hadn't been enough? They'd never really talked about it after it had all happened.

Palani rubbed a wrinkle between his eyes. "That's your worry-frown. What are you worrying about?" he asked, his tone kind as always.

"Are...are you content?" Vieno asked. "Happy?"

Palani sent him a soft smile. "God, yes. At first, I was

happy because you were. It's all I ever wanted, for you to be safe and loved and taken care of."

Vieno's heart filled with love. "You're incredible, and I love you so much."

Palani's face broke open in a sweet smile. "I love you too, and seeing you happy is everything to me. But I'm happy for myself as well."

There was something in his eyes, on his face, that touched Vieno deep. "You're in love with Enar," he whispered.

"I am. I don't know how and when it happened, but I love him. I haven't told him yet, because he's not ready to hear it."

"He loves you," Vieno said, knowing with absolute certainty he was right.

Palani's eyes glowed. "I think he does, but I'll give him time. It's hardest for him, you know, navigating the four of us?"

Vieno nodded. "I know. And Lidon?" he asked.

"I love seeing how sweet and tender he is with you. I have to admit he surprised me with that. He's such an alpha, but when he's with you, he dares to show this softer side."

Vieno smiled, and Palani traced Vieno's lips with his finger. "You're in love with him," Palani said, his voice filled with wonder. "No, don't let that smile disappear. It's a good thing, baby, a wonderful thing."

"Is it?" Vieno asked. "You're not jealous or disappointed?"

"Are you jealous that I'm in love with Enar as well?"

Vieno considered it. How did he feel about that? Jealousy would in a way be normal, he guessed, since he and Palani had been together for so long. Sure, they'd never dared to develop their relationship beyond the fuck fest they had every three months with his heat, but that had been pure self-preservation. The love had always been there between them, for as long as Vieno could remember. There had never been a time when he hadn't loved Palani, and yet the idea of Palani loving someone else as well didn't scare him or make him sad.

"No. It's like it makes my love for you bigger, if that makes sense? Like you and me are still together, but a part of something much bigger." He tried to put it into words. "It's hard to explain, but you and I didn't truly work until we'd become four. We need all four of us to make it work."

Palani nodded. "I get what you mean. The three of you all provide something else I need...and allow me to give a different part of me as well."

"Exactly. Like, Lidon gives me something you couldn't..." He stopped when he realized how hurtful his words could be interpreted, but Palani cupped his cheek.

"I understand, baby. Don't hold back. Nothing but truth between us, please. I could never satisfy you sexually. Is that what you mean?"

Vieno breathed out in relief. "Yes, but it's more. Because he's such an alpha, I can be more of an omega. I'm weaker with him, needier, even more dependent, and it's freeing, stupid as that may sound."

Palani smiled. "Lidon loves it when you go all needy on him."

"Oh god, he totally does. But I don't do it for him. He brings that out in me, and I love it. I don't have to be tough or strong with him."

"So, what does Enar bring you or what can you give him?" Palani asked.

Vieno let out a sweet sigh. "He's... God, he needs us. He's so lonely and hurting, and I just wanna hug him all day long and make the pain stop. I guess he brings out the opposite of Lidon, in a way, like me caring for him."

Palani kissed his nose. "He does need us. He still hasn't fully accepted he's part of us. You can see the doubt every day, like when he's kissing you and Lidon walks in. He always expects to be cast off, and it breaks my heart."

They were quiet for a bit. Then Vieno asked, "But you didn't answer my question about you and Lidon. How do you feel about him?"

Palani let out a soft sigh. "I really like him. I love how he treats you, and I love the sex with him...damn, he's so fucking big. It always takes my breath away at first when he fills me, you know?"

Vieno grinned. "Your poor beta hole a little too tight for his cock?" he teased.

"Not too tight but close enough, yeah. Unlike your greedy little ass, huh?" Palani teased right back.

Vieno's ass twitched at even the mention, and he laughed. "Greedy is the right word. I can't get enough of you guys." Then he sobered. "Do you think that's weird?"

"What? That you love having sex?"

Vieno bit his lip. "That I have sex with three guys...that I have sex multiple times a day. I mean, you jokingly called my ass greedy, but it often feels so empty." He swallowed, then lowered his eyes. "I really like it when you guys fuck me," he whispered. "Isn't that, like, slutty, even for an omega?"

"Oh, baby, who cares? You're ours, so the only opinions that matter are Lidon's, Enar's, and mine. And obviously your own. We don't think you're slutty. Hell, we love your greedy ass. You keep us all satisfied. One itty-bitty omega and three of us, and we can't get enough of you. You're gorgeous and sexy, and we'll fill your emptiness as often as you want to."

Vieno didn't know whether to laugh or cry from the giddiness inside him at that perfect answer. So he did the only thing he could think of. He'd felt Palani gradually harden against him during their conversation, and of course his own hole was slick and ready. So he rolled on top of him and positioned Palani's cock at his entrance, then lowered himself with a happy long moan.

"Oh fuck, baby, that's so good," Palani grunted. "I love it when you take me in like that."

Vieno sat upright, his eyes closed, Palani's cock completely swallowed up in his hole. He loved how perfectly it fit, how sweet and comfortable it felt, like...

He opened his eyes. "You know what you offer me?" he said, his voice soft. "Home. You're my home, Palani. You always have been. It may not sound sexy or—"

Palani moved his hips, thrusting even deeper. "It sounds perfect. It's everything I could hope for, baby. Now, let me fuck you. What are you in the mood for? You want sweet and soft, or hard and quick?"

This was classic Palani, always focused on what Vieno needed. Vieno checked with himself. What was he in the mood for? "Sweet and soft sounds perfect," he said.

Palani's smile made the butterflies in his stomach dance. "Sweet and soft it is, baby."

———

7

Palani sighed as he sat himself down behind his desk at the newspaper. There was so much happening in his life at the same time that he struggled with keeping track of it all. Adjusting to life with the four of them and to living on the ranch rather than in his apartment, the whole Excellon thing, the Melloni gene... It was like this massive juggling game where he feared he'd drop a ball any time now.

His brothers had been a tad upset when he'd finally met up with them yesterday evening for drinks. Not because they hadn't seen each other in a while, but because Palani hadn't told them sooner about his men. Despite the initial shock he was with three men instead of just one, they took it well, and they were happy for him—though they'd warned him he'd better find a good way to tell his parents. Thank fuck they were taking the long cruise they'd talked about for ages to celebrate their twenty-fifth wedding anniversary, so he still had a little time there.

Franken hadn't said anything yet, but Palani felt his work had suffered. He'd done his job, but it had been a B minus for effort, rather than the A plus he usually put in. He hadn't made any progress on project X either since his last effort to dig deeper. It was all just a lot.

He vowed to do better, and if anything should help him achieve that, it would be today's interview with George York, the leader of the Conservative Wolf Party. If he wanted to ask the man even remotely intelligent questions, Palani had better get some fucking focus and research the shit out of this political party that had his boss so worried. He followed the news, obviously, so he understood what the CWP was about, but he needed more than the current headlines and talking points. Franken's concern was that this party had come out of nowhere yet seemed to be doing well in the polls. Palani figured he'd start with how the party was founded and what their platform was.

In the four hours he spent researching, he found a ton of information about York, his party, and their platform. It was...illuminating. Borderline crazy at times, though Palani couldn't deny some of their proposals would improve life for omegas. They proposed a universal health care system for omegas, for instance—an idea so revolutionary it had dominated the news for days. Palani could see the appeal of their ideas for omegas and even for betas, but why would alphas ever support them? Something he intended to ask York.

George York turned about to be a classic, imposing alpha with gray hairs sprinkled in his dark hair and a beard with equally mixed colors. He was handsome in that way older men could be, though his stance still showed his alpha dominance and virility. Palani betted he affected most non-alphas, present company included.

"Palani Hightower," he introduced himself. He didn't extend his hand, leaving it to the alpha to initiate physical contact. He did with a strong handshake that left Palani impressed.

"I'm a huge fan of your investigative reporting," York said, surprising Palani. "Your pieces on the corruption within the police force were exceptional. I'm sure you must have caught serious flak for those."

Palani settled in the chair York indicated opposite him at a small conference table. He got his legal pad and pen from his messenger bag and put it on the table, right next to his little recording device he always used. It prevented people from claiming he'd misquoted them. "Thank you. Few alphas appreciate it...or at least, dare to voice their approval."

York smiled. "No small talk, huh? I like that. You'll find that in many ways, I'm not a typical alpha."

Palani raised his eyebrows. "Can you give me some examples?"

"The standard MO of most alphas is to cover for each other, correct? That's not how I operate. I'll support other alphas when I agree with their viewpoints or condone of their behavior. If not, I won't hesitate to speak out."

"That's a surprising strategy for a politician," Palani commented.

"Maybe, but I've discovered many people appreciate my honesty. I'm a straight talker, so they know exactly who I am and what they're going to get with me."

"Which is what?"

York leaned forward in his chair, his eyes intense as he looked at Palani. "A return to a better society. A fairer society. A society where we get rid of all the restrictive rules and restore alphas, betas, and omegas to their rightful, natural order."

"I've read your political manifesto and your party's platform. For a conservative party, it's quite radical."

"Maybe, but it's not new. It's how it was, many years ago, and how it should be again. If we want to flourish again as a society, as a species, we have to return to the order and dynamics that helped us thrive in the past."

"This natural order you refer to that's at the core of your party's ideology, it's based on how you think our shifter ancestors lived, correct?"

York's eyes flashed before he got himself under control. He'd touched a nerve there, hadn't he?

"I wouldn't use the word *think*. We have done extensive research on this."

"Who's we?"

"Myself, but also some members of our think tank who are specialized in wolf history. They've developed a clear view of how society functioned back then."

"Let's assume their findings and interpretations are correct—"

"They are," York interrupted him. "We're not talking about amateurs. These are highly qualified historians who know their facts."

"Are they all alphas?" Palani asked.

York smiled. "No, because you and I are both aware that alphas tend to see history through the lens of their own alpha bias. That's why we created a multidisciplinary team consisting of alphas, betas, and even omegas—men and women."

Palani couldn't help it. He was impressed when he heard that. "I'll admit that sounds better than I had expected," he said. "But back to my question. You say their findings are correct, so let's go along with that for a sec. How can you apply these to a culture that has completely changed? Can you use the dynamics that worked in a society a hundred years ago, before so many modern inventions, and apply them to our current day society?"

"You don't seem to object to the dynamics themselves," York noted, deftly evading the question.

"I have my reservations," Palani assured him, "but my bigger concern is how you can claim that what worked a century ago would still work."

"You'll need to share those reservations with me, as I'd be most interested to see where you have doubts. You're most certainly a proponent of more independence for omegas, judging by some of your articles."

"I am, but that doesn't mean I agree with your view on how that independence should be achieved. You state all omegas should marry, for instance, and by doing so achieve more legal autonomy. What if they don't want to?"

"All omegas want to be in a relationship," York said. "It's in their very nature. It's how they're wired. To deny themselves that would be unnatural."

"I don't agree with you, but even so, how would that work when so many alphas refuse to enter into a serious, committed relationship? I'm neither an alpha nor an omega, but I've learned from stories how hard it is for omegas to find alphas willing to settle down."

York scratched his beard, sighing. "I agree that's an issue we need to address. Many alphas need to grow up and leave their antics behind them to start a family."

"And you think you can achieve that with a marriage bonus?" Palani said, referring to one of their political key promises.

"Not with that bonus alone but with a broad spectrum of measures and incentives, yes."

"Getting an alpha to marry an omega is still not a guarantee for a family," Palani pointed out. "Male infertility is a big issue, and so are pregnancy complications and the high mortality rate during delivery for male omegas."

"Yes. That's why we propose a massive increase in funding for research into the causes of these health issues and for treatment. Health care options for omegas are way too limited, especially for those who are single or from lower-income families. That has to change. We applaud the efforts of doctors who have been on the front line of male omega health care for years, fighting a lonely battle, and we would support them with grants for research, training, better facilities to treat omegas, and more."

Palani had to fight to keep his face neutral. The man was referring to Enar, no doubt about it, but how did he know? It was not something Palani was going to discuss, not with someone he was interviewing, not with the leader of a political party, and most definitely not while his recorder was on.

"Those measures can only be described as revolutionary," he said. "How will you get other alphas to support this, considering they don't seem concerned about this issue right now?"

"We have some educating to do," York said. "Alphas don't realize that these problems do affect them. The number of children born from male omegas is still declining, though slowly, and this is a worrisome trend. If we don't change something, fertile male omegas capable of delivering a healthy baby and surviving to actually parent the child will become a rarity. That is not a reality that any alpha should want. The problem is that many don't start caring until it's their omega who can't get pregnant. We need funding for more research. We need to stop the government from being influenced by lobbyists who are blocking reform on this issue. There are drugs that have proven to be more effective in preventing pregnancy in male omegas for instance, but lobbyists from certain drug companies are blocking their approval."

This time, Palani could not keep himself from reacting. What drugs was York referring to? Was he referring to Excellon? How the hell had he found out about it? "Are you sure that's an accusation you want me to print, Mr. York? That's a bold statement coming from a political candidate."

York leaned back in his chair again. "It is, but it's the cold hard truth... There is evidence of coordinated efforts by companies to block access to successful drugs for omegas. You know that as well as I do, Mr. Hightower."

Palani wasn't sure what surprised him more, the reference to him already knowing about this issue—by now it was crystal clear he was alluding to Excellon—or York addressing him as Mr. Hightower when the colloquial "Palani" for a beta would have been far more customary. It was the second time York had mentioned knowing more about Palani, and it creeped him out a bit. Enough to not acknowledge he knew what York was referring to, that was for sure.

"The elections are in three months. Polls show you have a chance of winning as many as forty of the hundred-and-fifty seats in parliament. With the other seats divvied up between six other parties, you're looking at becoming the biggest party. That would be the political upset of the century...and would make you prime minister. Do you think these polls are realistic?"

"No, I don't. Right now, our support comes mainly from omegas and betas who are tired of omegas being suppressed. We don't have enough alphas supporting us yet, which is why we'll focus on explaining why improving the positions of omegas is beneficial to alphas as well."

Palani couldn't help it. "Good luck with that," he said.

Back in his car after the interview, he pondered the many things York had said. The man seemed to have a genuine passion to grant omegas more rights, and yet Palani shuddered at the vibe he picked up from him. Sometimes the man sounded passionate and honest, but other times he was one step away from being a ranting lunatic.

Take his insistence that returning to the societal structure from a century ago not only would improve the lives of alphas, betas, and omegas but also would strengthen their shifters' abilities. Moreover, he wanted to fund research into restoring the ability to shift. The Conservative Wolf Party didn't merely want the dynamics from the shifter-society. They wanted a full-blown return of shifting itself. If that didn't sound like pure science fiction, Palani didn't know what would.

And what was up with York digging into Palani's personal life? The reference to Enar had been worrisome, but the one to Excellon had been scary. That was not a topic anyone should be aware he was working on, not even his boss, so how had this man found out? Palani had some more digging to do, it seemed.

BETWEEN his longer commute to Lidon's house and his crazy hours, Enar had little time to think about the mysterious Melloni gene. But today was Sunday and Palani was off, so Enar had forced himself to free his schedule as well. They'd found a quiet spot in the study to see if they could come up with any answers. Hell, Enar would be happy if they could develop a solid theory at this point. He'd called Melloni again a few days ago, but the doctor hadn't made any breakthrough developments on the origin of the gene.

"Let's write all the facts on separate Post-its," Palani suggested. He found a block of bright pink Post-its in a drawer and handed Enar a black marker. "That always helps me to see things in a different light."

"Okay, I like that," Enar said. "But you'd better write 'cause my handwriting is illegible."

Palani grinned. "You just wanna look at my ass as I bend over to write," he teased.

"True. But you really won't be able to read my scribbles."

"All right, I believe you. Let's start with what we know to be true."

A few minutes later, they'd stuck various Post-its on the cream-colored wall in front of them. Enar studied them, his mind trying to figure out connections. "All male," he said. "Symptoms are high fertility, low birth mortality, high sex drive, excessive behavior during heats."

"Depression," Palani added, writing another note and sticking it on the wall. "Multiple cases in the same family, which suggests it's hereditary."

Enar hesitated. "The first, yes. The second we can't support with data yet. There can be other reasons why it affects siblings."

"Such as?"

"Environmental causes, for instance. Siblings grow up under the same environmental conditions. If it's something in, say, the water, it will affect them all."

"Good point. I'll just add a note with the McCain family, then, without speculation for the cause." He wrote the note. "What else?"

"Irresistible smell to the point where it triggers even mated alphas."

Palani nodded and added it to the wall. "I wonder if Vieno's smell will change now that he's mated," he said.

"He smelled damn good to me last time," Enar pointed out.

"Yeah, but he'd only been mated for a short time, and I'm not sure if he was technically mated to you yet, and if he was, it was probably not long enough for it to affect his smell."

"Good point. We'll see at his next heat, then."

Palani added the question to a Post-it and stuck it a little to the side of the others. Enar studied what they had accumulated so far. "I'm not sure if depression is a symptom or a result," he said. "It could be caused by the gene, but it could also be a result of the consequences of the gene. Many of the omegas we've seen with the gene have been assaulted or raped, which is a known cause for depression."

"Vieno showed the first symptoms of being depressed before his first heat."

"Melloni speculated this was not a natural cause, remember?" Enar said.

"Because of how fast it popped up," Palani said. "I remember. He said that if it had been a natural cause, even an environmental one, it would've developed more slowly over time."

"Exactly. It suggests a human intervention of some kind. But what common characteristics do these omegas share to link them to a possible human origin? Vieno didn't know the McCains either, did he?"

"No," Palani said. "And he hadn't heard of the beta Lidon almost arrested either or his omega husband, 'cause I checked with him. They're all from roughly the same neighborhood, but that's still a big area, and they didn't have any personal contact. Aside from the McCains who obviously knew each other, I haven't found any links between the carriers of the gene."

Enar studied the wall again. There had to be a connection, something that linked all the omegas who had this gene, but what?

"Let's hypothesize for a second," Palani suggested. "Let's say it was human intervention. How would you gain access to a child to administer something to change his genes?"

"You can't," Enar said. "You'd have to..." He stopped, checking his own reasoning.

"You'd have to...what?" Palani asked.

"Genes are formed in the womb. To change someone's genetic makeup, you'd need to do it during pregnancy."

"But what woman would give permission for that?" Palani wondered. "Take Vieno's mother. She's not exactly mother of the year, but I can't see her give permission for some strange genetic experiment on her baby."

"So they didn't know. They were given something during their pregnancy, and they weren't aware of it," Enar said.

"But who would have access to them?"

The answer was so obvious, Enar couldn't believe he'd missed it so far. "Me. Their ob-gyn."

Palani's eyes grew big. "Shit, you're right."

"You have no idea how easy it would be for me. I give pregnant patients shots all the time, like vitamins or antibodies or meds to prevent morning sickness. They would never know if I switched the syringe and shot them up with something else instead."

"We need to know if they all used the same ob-gyn. It would make sense, since they're all geographically close. No pregnant woman wants to go across town for checkups."

Enar froze. "They all had female omegas as mothers," he

said. "They have that in common too. None of them was birthed by a male omega, right?"

"Right. Not as far as we know. All the McCains had mothers," Palani said, his voice excited. "I can ask Vieno who his mom's ob-gyn is. Maybe he remembers."

"I'll ask him, and you could call a few of the McCains instead, since they know you?"

Vieno was outside with Lidon and his cousins. They were putting topsoil on his vegetable plot, and the omega was almost dancing with excitement, so it took a while before Enar could get him to focus on something else. Once he had his answer, he headed back inside. When he walked back into the study, Palani was wrapping up a conversation.

"Thank you, Mrs. McCain. I'll be sure to keep you informed, I promise." He hung up, then turned to face Enar. "They didn't share the same ob-gyn, the McCain mothers. Two of them did, but the third had another doctor."

"Vieno said his mother switched doctors all the time, so he had no idea who it could have been."

Palani sighed. "Yeah. Apparently, it took her a long time to get pregnant with Vieno. His parents were already married ten years when he was finally born. It was one of the things they held against him, that he was such a disappointment after all the trouble they'd gone through to get pregnant and the money they'd spent on..." He suddenly stopped talking, his eyes widening.

Enar wanted to ask what was wrong, but Palani held up his finger. "Wait. Let me think 'cause I'm having a déjà vu."

Enar stood, patiently waiting. He wouldn't dream of interrupting Palani, not with the concentrated frown the beta was sporting.

"Robert McCain," Palani said, his face lighting up. "His mother couldn't get pregnant. That's what his boss said, that she'd told him that at the funeral. He was an only child because his mother struggled with infertility."

"Yeah, so?" Enar asked. Why was Palani so enthusiastic about this? Then it hit him. "They have that in common, Vieno's mother and Robert's mother."

Palani nodded. "What if they had the same fertility treatments?"

"God, yes. What better way to administer something aimed at changing the genetic makeup than during conception? Holy crap, we need to find out of this was true for the others as well."

Palani whipped out his phone. "On it."

"Mrs. McCain, I'm so sorry to bother you again," he said seconds later. "I have a rather personal question, if that's okay."

Enar waited while Palani talked to the mother, his eyes fixed on Palani's face for any signal. Palani's eyes popped.

"Are you sure?" he said, reaching out for Enar's arm. He held on to it with such force that Enar was certain bruises would show the next day. "I promise you we'll come talk to you as soon as we confirm this."

When he hung up, his eyes were still wide open in shock. "They all used the same fertility drugs. The McCains. I didn't realize it, but they're three sisters who married two brothers and a cousin, and they all struggled with infertility. A genetic thing, she said. Her oldest sister got pregnant after using them, and they all followed her example."

"What's the name of the drug?"

"It was a clinical trial. It never went to market, she said. The drug was labeled X23 in the trial."

Enar's head buzzed with the implications. "I've never even heard of it, but that's not surprising as this trial had to be done, what, twenty years ago?"

Palani's grip on his hand intensified. "Wait. Something doesn't add up. Robert McCain was twenty-two when he died, which means his mother would've been in that trial twenty-three years ago, give or take. So was Colton McCain. But Vieno is twenty-three...that's a whole year older. And the other McCains who passed away were younger...Adam was twenty and Lance twenty-one. We're talking about a three-year period between the youngest and the oldest... What clinical drug trial would take that long?"

He was right. That was a way-too-long period for a drug to be in a clinical trial. What the hell had happened? He tried to make a timeline in his head and realized something else. "There's another complication with this theory. The first cases of the gene were over a decade ago. Melloni mapped the gene ten years ago and gave it its name. That would put this trial at a running period of fifteen years. That's impossible."

"You're right... But the fertility drugs are too obvious a connecting element to ignore. We should inform Melloni of our theory, see if he has any theories."

Enar shook his head. "No, that's too soon. We'll need to dig what we can find out about those drugs the McCains took first and see where that leads us."

"If we operate off the assumption that fertility drugs were the common factor, that gives us also tools to discover more potential carriers of the gene," Palani added.

Enar's blood froze in his veins. "It also means I have to contact my brother, Sven. Remember what I said, that my mom had trouble getting pregnant again after me? How much do you wanna bet she used fertility drugs, considering she did end up having two more kids pretty close to each other. What if she took the same drugs? Sven is twenty and could have his first heat any moment."

8

Every time he drove through the gates, a strange calm washed over Lidon's heart. It had always been home to him, his ranch, but for a while, he'd lost that feeling. It had felt empty to him, but now things had changed. As soon as the gates closed behind him, he felt different. Safe. Calm. As if he was exactly where he was supposed to be.

It could be because of the renovations that had started, he mused. In the last weeks, Jawon had cleared the plot where Vieno wanted his vegetable garden and covered it with topsoil or whatever it was that made plants grow, preparing it for Vieno to start sowing and planting.

He'd also knocked down the old chicken coop, clearing the land for a new one. Vieno had become well versed in growing vegetables by doing extensive research online, and he knew more about chicken breeds than Lidon ever had thought possible. It proved how well Vieno matched with this place, which filled Lidon with a deep contentment and pride. He'd chosen his mate well, or rather, fate had chosen well for him.

After some debate, he and Jawon had decided to tear down the old barn, though they would reuse as much of the old wood as possible. Jawon had put up a big tent to temporarily store the equipment that had been in the barn. He'd promised Lidon they'd have the new barn up in a few days as soon as the ordered wood had been delivered. In the meantime, he would finish building the new chicken coop, using the wood from the old barn, and would focus on fixing the rainwater irrigation system, much to Vieno's delight. He looked forward to using it once his veggies had started growing.

Vieno was over-the-top excited with how things were going, which endeared Lidon. He loved the pride Vieno took in making the ranch shine again, even if it was in little steps. He'd cleaned his way through the rooms they already used and had suggested opening up a few more rooms. Lidon had shoved a credit card into his hands and told him to buy whatever he wanted or needed.

Lidon was pleased to see the changes and renovations, even though they were just getting started. He'd walked over to his cousins a few times when they were working. It was good to see them and even better to know that he was helping them financially. They still lived with their parents except for Urien, but Lidon was sure they were dying to move out. It wasn't easy in this economic climate, and it made him realize once again how fortunate he was with his wealth. At least he could help his family out by giving them work. Fuck knew there was enough to keep them busy on the ranch for months to come.

He trusted them around his ranch and around Vieno. Jawon and Urien were betas, which posed a medium risk with an omega around, but Ori was an alpha. That in itself was remarkable, that an alpha would work for a beta and a cousin at that, but Ori seemed happy in that role. Lidon had watched him like a hawk the first time he met Vieno, but Ori had shown nothing but friendliness and had kept a respectful distance.

Servas was an omega, which was even more remarkable, because they rarely had jobs like this. Jawon had assured Lidon Servas was a hard worker who pulled his weight on his crew and that he would stay home around his heat to not entice anyone. Lidon was fine with it, as he figured Servas would know better than anyone else what would work. The guy was twenty-two, so he'd already had his first heat. Thank fuck he didn't have the gene at least, Lidon had thought when he'd heard his cousin had experienced his first heat at eighteen, the normal age.

All these changes made the ranch feel more like a home, but it was more than that. Palani hadn't spent a night at his own place since Vieno's heat almost a month ago, and Enar had been back to his townhouse once or twice when he'd been too tired to drive to the ranch. That, Lidon thought, was also something he needed to figure out a solution for. He did not like Enar driving by himself in the middle of the night in the first place, let alone when he was dead on his feet like ten days ago. The man had slowed down a little, but he was still working more hours than Lidon thought was healthy.

Maybe he should bring it up with him. After all, Enar hadn't protested when Lidon had said he wanted to order him to do shit, right? Still, he hesitated. In bed, he had no trouble dominating the hell out of all three of his men, though somehow, Vieno was always at the center. But during Vieno's heat, Lidon hadn't asked if he could fuck Enar. He'd assumed he could, though he had waited for him to consent. But outside of the bedroom, it was hard to navigate because he didn't want to humiliate Enar. Ugh, why was this so damn complicated?

He parked his car in the garage and headed inside. As soon as he stepped into the hallway, a mouthwatering smell informed him Vieno was cooking. Something Indian, judging by the faint aroma of coconut and spices. Korma, maybe?

He heard his mate's giggle before he reached the kitchen, and his heart warmed. Then the giggle transformed into a moan, and his cock stirred. Who was Vieno playing around with?

He walked in to find Vieno pinned against the wall, with Enar kissing him as if his life depended on it. Enar unzipped his shorts, taking out his hard cock. Mmm, talk about a nice dinner show.

Enar broke off the kiss when Lidon walked over to the fridge to grab a water. There was always a flash of hesitation and insecurity in his friend's features in moments like this, as if he still doubted Lidon would allow him to play around with Vieno. Lidon gulped down some water before sauntering over to the two.

"Hi, sweetheart," he said to Vieno, bending over to kiss him.

He always kissed him first and not just a quick peck either. Somehow, his alpha demanded he lay claim to his omega, to his mate. Then he turned to Enar and, without a second's doubt, bent in to kiss him as well. When Enar opened up eagerly, he deepened the kiss, not stopping until he'd conquered his mouth and tasted him on his tongue.

"Don't stop on my account," he teased him, then slapped his butt when he walked away to take a spot at the kitchen table. "I'm in the mood for a little dinner show."

Vieno giggled again, that happy sound that made

Lidon's heart jump up in his chest. "You heard our alpha... He wants a show."

Enar smiled. "And the alpha always gets what he wants..."

Enar took Vieno's mouth again, his hands making quick work of both their shorts. He hoisted Vieno up and settled him onto his cock. Lidon tilted his head to get the perfect view of Enar's big shaft sinking into Vieno's round ass. Man, what a gorgeous sight.

Vieno moaned as Enar bottomed out. "Ungh, so good..."

Enar folded the omega's legs around his waist, then pinned him against the wall as he fucked him with slow, deep thrusts. His grunts mingled with Vieno's groans into a mix that made Lidon's cock weep with excitement.

"Hi guys," Palani called out as he walked in, then laughed as he spotted Enar and Vieno. "I see we're all in the right mood for the weekend."

His eyes searched around the kitchen until he found Lidon sitting there. He walked over, his eyes scanning Lidon's face for permission before leaning in for a kiss.

"Hi," Palani said, breathless after Lidon had kissed him thoroughly. What a lucky man he was, to have three men to kiss. Three men to claim.

"Wanna keep me company and watch the show?" Lidon said with a soft smile, delighted when Palani nodded. He pulled Palani on his lap, slipping his hand under his shirt.

"Hey, you said *watching*," Palani teased.

"I'm *watching*, using my hands," Lidon said, his smile widening.

They sat like that for a while, Lidon's hands roaming Palani's tight body while they observed Enar fucking Vieno into the wall. Palani wasn't as vocal as Vieno, but by now,

Lidon could read his body language better. The beta liked being manhandled a little, though he did his fair share of bossing around as well. God, watching him and Enar together was entertaining as fuck. Palani could be both brutally bossy and super sweet with him, and Lidon loved that his friend got to be himself with the beta. Palani *got* Enar, somehow.

Palani shifted restlessly on his lap, his ass rubbing against Lidon's cock in the best way, even with layers of fabric in between. It made Lidon's cock grow to steel, and he didn't doubt Palani had noticed. It seemed he was in the mood to play, which suited Lidon just fine. Watching Enar and Vieno made him horny as fuck, and he'd love to take that out on Palani's ass.

"You sure *watching* was all you wanted?" Palani asked.

"What are you suggesting?"

Palani grinned, then whipped off his shirt and pulled on Lidon's. "I say we give those two a show of our own."

Seconds later, their clothes lay discarded on the floor. Palani grabbed a big bottle of lube from the kitchen counter. Bottles of that stuff stood everywhere in the house now, including several places in the kitchen. Highly convenient. At some point, he'd have to thank Vieno, who made sure to constantly restock throughout the house.

Lidon prepped Palani with rough moves, smiling when the beta fucked himself on Lidon's long fingers. "I've got something better for you," he promised, pulling his fingers out.

Palani lifted himself up, then lowered himself onto Lidon's cock. Lidon spread his legs to ground himself on the chair, content to watch Palani's ass take him in.

"Dammit, you're so fucking big," Palani grunted.

"You say it as if it's news to you."

"I keep underestimating your size, fuck you very much..."

Lidon grinned as he put his hands on Palani's hips to help him steady his balance. "Wait till I knot you."

"Not gonna happen. I can damn well guarantee you that... Oh!" he moaned as Lidon finally bottomed out.

Lidon pulled Palani with his back against his chest, holding him close. "Fuck, you feel so good. You're so snug around my big cock, your body struggling to take me in. It's such a damn turn-on."

Palani relaxed against him, wrapping his hands backward around Lidon's neck. "Mmm, this is good." He turned his head for a quick kiss.

"Look at Enar, ravishing our boy's ass," Lidon commented. "He's so focused when he fucks."

Enar had Vieno whimpering now, begging him to speed up and make him come as well. Judging by the streams of cum that dripped from Vieno's ass every time Enar thrust in, he'd dumped a good load there, but Vieno hadn't come yet. The little omega clung to him with all his might, but he was losing the strength in his muscles.

"Quit tormenting the poor man and make him come," Lidon called out to Enar.

"Don't you have your own man to fuck?" Enar called back over his shoulder. "Why don't you focus on making *him* come and let me handle this one?"

Palani chuckled. "He's got a point."

Suddenly Lidon realized with blinding clarity why the ranch felt different, why it felt like coming home every single day. It wasn't the building or the renovations. It was them, these men, their foursome. They had turned the house into a real home.

"I want you guys to move in here," he said with a fierce

passion that came straight from his heart. They were *his*, and they belonged here with him. "Permanently."

VIENO WAS seconds away from a mind-blowing orgasm, his balls already painfully tight against his body when Enar froze halfway inside him. What the hell was he doing? Vieno vaguely remembered Lidon saying something, but he'd been too preoccupied with the agonizing torture of Enar's way-too-slow fucking after he'd shot his load inside him to focus.

"You want what?" Enar said over his shoulder.

"I want you to move in here. Sell your house and come live here for real."

Vieno let out a frustrated growl. "Can he finish this first, please? We were just getting to the good part."

Lidon's laugh boomed through the kitchen, and then Palani joined in as well. Vieno groaned with frustration, knowing it was only a matter of seconds, till... Yes, there it was. Enar's body was shaking with laughter.

"I hate you all right now," Vieno muttered. "Seriously. Two, three more seconds, and I would've... Ugh."

Enar pulled out and gently put him down. "Sorry, little one. I'll admit Lidon's timing wasn't ideal."

"It fucking sucks," Vieno said, still frowning.

He had to hold on to Enar until the blood flow to his legs had been restored. When he could walk again, he stepped past Enar to find Palani on Lidon's lap, the alpha's cock buried deep inside him. What, Palani did get to come while Vieno was denied?

"We need to have a discussion about your priorities," he told Lidon. "Or rather, your lack thereof."

He saw the others smiling, thinking he was joking around, but he meant it. A strange irritation had a hold of him. As much as he loved the idea of Palani and Enar moving in, why couldn't Lidon have waited until after he'd come? His body was aching now, his hole protesting the emptiness and lack of fulfillment. He felt denied. Ignored. Frustrated. And he sure as hell resented it.

"Vieno," Palani said, his voice loaded with meaning.

It would've been Palani to first pick up on Vieno's mood, tuned in as he was to him after all these years. Tears formed in Vieno's eyes.

"I'm sorry," he said. "I'm being unreasonable."

The three men looked at him, each with a different expression. Enar was studying him, probably determining what the issue was and how he could fix it. Palani's eyes showed worry because he'd seen Vieno's volatile emotions before, and he knew these were not a joke. And Lidon's face turned from flabbergasted to determination in a blink.

"Palani," he said.

"I know," Palani said, lifting himself off the alpha's cock, aided by the man's strong hands on his hips. He stumbled as he got to his feet, but Lidon held him until he'd found his footing.

"Come here, sweetheart," Lidon said, and Vieno came almost running.

He didn't even do it on purpose, but as soon as Lidon lifted him on his lap with their faces toward each other, he sought his cock, needing to feel it inside him. He couldn't even capture the emptiness inside him in words. All he knew was that he needed what Lidon was offering, even if it meant Palani was slighted.

He took him in, in one surge, more tears forming as

Lidon was fully seated. The alpha looked at him quizzically. "What's wrong?" he asked, his voice kind and soft.

"I don't know. Honestly, I don't. I felt empty and ignored and so fucking frustrated, and I needed you." He bowed his head, looking up at Lidon between tear-stained lashes. "I'm sorry for being selfish."

"You're not selfish, sweetheart. I'm trying to understand what happened."

Vieno bit his lip. "I needed that orgasm. I wanted it, and I was so damn close, and then you..."

"I distracted Enar, and the moment was gone." Lidon understood.

"Yes. It doesn't make sense, but..."

Lidon lifted his chin up with a single finger. "Emotions don't always make sense. Brutal honesty, remember? You don't have to understand, but please tell me what you need. Your needs come first."

Vieno frowned. "What do you mean? There's four of us."

Lidon's face showed surprise, he noted, as if his own words had shocked him.

Lidon looked at Palani and Enar, then back at Vieno, and his face softened. "I'm not sure where that came from, but it's the truth. You're...you're the center of us. You're what binds us. And you're both our strength and our vulnerability."

Vieno reeled with the implications of those words, his mouth unable to form words.

Palani stepped in behind him and put a soft hand on Vieno's shoulder. "He's right. You come first."

Enar's hand touched his other shoulder, more hesitant. "I'm sorry. I fucked up."

"You didn't know," Palani said immediately.

Vieno's heart warmed. Palani always jumped in first to

affirm Enar. He was more vulnerable than he let on, the sexy doctor, and Palani was adamant to ensure he didn't get hurt.

"What do you need, sweetheart?" Lidon asked.

Vieno repositioned himself on Lidon, his heart millions of pounds lighter than it had been before. "I need you," he said, letting his omega dictate his words. "I need you all. I need to be at the center. Make me feel seen. Wanted."

Lidon smiled softly. "We can do that."

Vieno closed his eyes as strong hands lifted him off Lidon's cock and put him on the kitchen table.

"Here, put this underneath him," Enar said.

The same hands raised him again and lowered him on a fluffy towel. They grabbed his ankles and yanked him down till his ass perched on the edge of the table.

"God, look at him," Palani said. "He's so fucking gorgeous."

Vieno jumped when something covered his eyes. "Sshh," Enar said. "Close your eyes. We've got you."

The smell of the detergent in the kitchen towel Enar tied around his eyes tickled his nose. Before he could say anything, his mouth was taken in a deep kiss. Enar. He'd recognize his men's different tastes anytime. He kissed him back, his body relaxing, even as hands roamed his body. Palani, playing with his nipples, which he loved so very much. Lidon, holding his hips and positioning him, before filling him up with his cock again. A warm hand wrapped around his cock. Lidon too? Vieno didn't know, and seconds later, he didn't care.

Enar's mouth caught every sigh and moan he let out as hands roamed Vieno's body, and oh, Lidon fucked him so perfectly deep. His orgasm snuck up on him, his balls emptying with fervor before he even realized it, spraying cum all over his chest. Enar chuckled, and his mouth traveled from Vieno's mouth to his chest to lick up his cum.

Vieno protested the loss of his mouth on his lips with a mewl and was rewarded with another mouth that claimed his. Palani. He teased Vieno's mouth with his tongue, tracing his lips and licking inside his mouth until Vieno growled with want. Only then did Palani kiss him, one of those deep kisses where Vieno barely remembered to come up for air.

His men claimed every inch of his body as they pinched his nipples, tugged and twisted, licked and scratched, making the pleasure inside him rise to unbearable levels. The hand around his cock alternated between tight and loose, fast and slow, bringing him to the brink, only to let him teeter on the edge without falling over.

And oh, his hole, no longer empty but perfectly filled with that fat alpha cock taking him, claiming him, filling every bit of him until he felt so full he could burst. His body seemed to detach from his mind, a separate entity that rose higher than he'd thought possible. He surrendered to the myriad of sensations barreling through him that set every nerve in his cells on fire as his three men pleasured him until he came again with such a force it left him limp. Only then did Lidon explode inside him.

And it wasn't selfish, Vieno realized. It was right. He was their omega, and he was exactly where he was supposed to be: at the center of them.

9

Enar wished he shared Palani's enthusiasm about moving in with Lidon. The beta's "yes, please" at Lidon's question had been absolute and instant—well, after Lidon had asked again once Vieno had been pleasured to his heart's desire—and he'd ended his lease the same day. Enar understood why. Palani's home was wherever Vieno was. The suffering their separation had imposed on both of them had made that abundantly clear. Plus, Palani seemed to have an instinctive trust and optimism about their foursome relationship.

For Enar, it was different. He didn't share that optimism, that sense of belonging. He felt it at times, after his bathtub-moment with Lidon, for instance, or after talking to Palani, but then a day later, doubt would creep back in. The doubt that nagged him that he wasn't a part of them, that he would never be. The thoughts that pestered him that they'd be so much happier without him. The ever-present voices in his head that whispered or even shouted he was a poser, a fake, and that he would never belong anywhere.

Still, he'd said yes. Truth be told, his reasons were more

practical than anything else. He'd considered putting his townhouse up for sale before and find something cheaper. He was never home anyway, so an apartment would be fine and much more affordable. That's what he told himself as he signed the sales contract for his house, smiling at the young couple who bought it hours after he'd put it online. They were excited to start a family in the desirable neighborhood Enar was in.

He couldn't blame them. It was a perfect place to raise children, which is why he had bought it, years ago when he'd still harbored hope he'd find an omega who accepted him and even grow to love him. It hadn't happened, and it was time to face that. If things with the four of them didn't work out—as he expected—he'd find an apartment. Fuck knew he needed the money from the sale to finance new surgery equipment. That shit was expensive as fuck, and his income didn't allow to take on an extra loan.

"You ready to load, Doc?" Palani called out from outside.

They'd rented a moving truck to transport his things to Lidon's ranch. He'd wanted to sell most of his furniture, considering Lidon had a decorated living room and everything, but Lidon had suggested he'd put it in the empty rooms that had been closed off till now. That made sense, and if he wanted to move out, at least he could take everything with him again.

"Yeah. Everything's packed and ready to go," he told Palani, who walked in to find him when Enar hadn't answered.

"Okay, I'll tell Lidon's cousins."

Enar nodded, then looked around his empty house one last time. He felt strange leaving it, as if he was abandoning a dream he once had. Maybe he was leaving it for something better? If the four of them did work out by a miracle, they could start a family someday.

The thought of Vieno with child stirred a deep longing inside Enar. The omega would make such a sweet, caring daddy. He seemed to have a double dose of the nurturing instinct most omegas had, wanting nothing more than to please others and take care of them. The difference he'd made in Lidon's ranch was remarkable. He'd turned every room sparkling clean, everything dirty was gone, and the whole house smelled fresh and homey.

Vieno was born to be a daddy. And Lidon would make an amazing father. Strict but loving and just. He certainly had the genes for it. It was a shame that betas couldn't produce offspring with male omegas anymore, because Palani would have made an amazing father. God, he was so kind and attentive, always tuned in to the needs of others.

Enar wasn't so sure if he wanted kids anymore. Well, not biological kids anyway. He was so busy with his work that he'd barely have time to see his kids. Besides, his DNA wasn't the most suitable to pass on. His fucked-up identity, what if that was hereditary? What if his kid would never figure out where he belonged, like Enar himself? And even if he'd have a child with a clear sense of identity, what role model would Enar be? He couldn't show how to be an alpha, but not how to be a beta either. He was always something in between.

He *had* a perfect alpha role model for his kid, though, didn't he? Lidon could show him how to be a real alpha. And Palani was a classic beta who could lead the way there. And in Vieno, his son would have an example of a real omega. In that sense, his son wouldn't need Enar to be perfect. Hell, he could have a girl, and the whole problem would be solved. The thought was exhilarating and frightening at the same time. What an idiot he was, daydreaming of creating babies with Vieno when five minutes earlier he was certain he didn't even belong. God, his head wore him out more sometimes than the long work hours ever did.

"You okay?" Lidon asked, startling him.

He spun around. "Yeah. Just lost in thoughts for a minute."

"Not having second thoughts?"

Lidon's eyes studied him as they so often did, his gaze analyzing yet kind.

"No. Some doubts, I guess?" Enar confessed, not wanting to keep all his emotions a secret. He could share a little to see how Lidon would respond.

"Come here," Lidon said, but it was more a gentle request than a command, even as his hand reached out to pull Enar toward him.

Enar went, allowing himself to be pulled, to be held by those strong arms. At first, Lidon merely held him, and even that calmed Enar. Lidon's presence always did.

"I know you still struggle," Lidon spoke after a while, his voice soft and kind. "I see the battle in your eyes, in your body language when we're together. Not just with the four of us but with me most of all."

"It's so hard to figure out how I should behave," Enar whispered, coming as close to the truth as he dared to.

"I won't say I understand, because I can't even begin to imagine what this must be like for you. I know you're trying to come to terms with far more than our relationship and something far deeper than what we're building with the four of us. And you don't have to talk about it with me, 'cause I think you're not ready, and I know damn well I'm not good at talking. But I think you've found that person in

Palani, and that makes me happy. And when you *are* ready to talk, I promise I will listen and I will accept."

Lidon had seen and understood more than he'd given him credit for, Enar realized. He'd simply respected Enar's need to work through it himself first. "Thank you. I will talk about it...soon."

"Okay. We'll be ready."

"Lidon?" he asked, his heart beating fast. "I have a request."

Lidon pushed his head back until they faced each other, his brown eyes serious. "Tell me."

He wanted to beg him not to laugh at his request, but then realized he didn't have to. Lidon would never laugh at him. He'd sense the need the request originated from and would honor it. He let go of his nerves.

"Could you please kiss me? Not because it's required or expected, but because I want you to...because you want to?"

Lidon smiled. "With pleasure."

The alpha's strong hands cupped his cheeks, his brown eyes caressing Enar's face. "You're so much braver than you think," he whispered. "I wish you could see yourself the way I do, the way I know Vieno and Palani do. Someday you will, I hope."

Before Enar could answer him, Lidon kissed him. It was a soft kiss at first, warm lips pressing against his, then a tongue slipping into his mouth. It was so easy to surrender, so he did, letting Lidon in, allowing him to swipe his mouth, taste every corner, claim every little bit. He pressed him against the wall, his hard, strong body pushed against Enar's in a way that made Enar's head spin. His cock grew hard, his heart rate jumped, and his breaths quickened.

"Are you guys ready?" he heard Palani call out.

Lidon ripped his mouth off and, with his eyes trained on

Enar, called back, "You guys go ahead. We'll follow in my truck!"

Palani laughed, and Enar watched Lidon as they both waited till the house grew quiet, the definite click of the front door indicating everyone else had left.

"Lidon, you don't—"

"I wish I could fuck you right now, but I don't have any lube, and I refuse to hurt you. So we'll improvise."

Enar's eyes widened. He'd not been expecting this. Sure, Lidon was hard, but he'd never fucked him without Enar asking for it or outside of Vieno's heat. Enar hadn't even been sure Lidon wanted him like that.

"I-improvise?" he asked.

"Take your clothes off," Lidon ordered, and Enar obeyed, even though Lidon hadn't used alpha compulsion.

As soon as he was naked, Lidon's hand wrapped around his cock, which already stood at attention but grew even stiffer in that tight embrace. "You know what I think? I think I've been too focused on trying to give you space, trying not to force you to do anything you don't want," Lidon said conversationally.

Enar swallowed. Where was this going?

"I've approached it all wrong. Before, I never asked you what you wanted. I took because I knew that's what you needed. You need to stop thinking, to not have to make a choice, and that's what I provided. So we're going to try that. I'm gonna take, and you're gonna give me what I want... aren't you?"

He nodded automatically, but his heart raced at how right it felt.

The hand around his dick tightened, and his breath caught. "What do you say when your alpha asks you a question?"

Could it really be this simple? Maybe he'd overcompli-
cated things. Maybe they both had. "Yes, alpha."

Lidon unbuttoned his jeans, then whipped his shirt over
his head. He was a god the way he stood there, all muscles
and glorious skin, rippling with power.

Lidon held out his hand to Enar's mouth. "Spit in my
hand," he told Enar.

Enar obeyed without questioning.

"More."

When he was satisfied, Lidon used the spit to slick both
their cocks, then grabbed them in his strong hand. "I'm
gonna jack us off together, and you're not gonna come until I
do, are you?"

"Yes, alpha. I mean, no alpha."

He moaned as Lidon rubbed them together, so slick with
his spit, so perfect and filthy, those two big alpha cocks
together. He rutted against his hands, his hips moving of
their own accord. Lidon sought his mouth again, pushing
him against the wall, even as he jacked them off, completely
invading Enar's mouth, his will, his soul.

Enar surrendered, letting himself be swept away until
Lidon came with a satisfied growl. Enar fought back his own
release, even as Lidon's cock pulsed against his, his cum
landing on Enar's stomach.

Lidon took a step back, his hand still tight around them,
his eyes seeking Enar's. And Enar submitted all over again
as he waited for his alpha's permission.

"Come for me."

10

P alani was decidedly discontent with the lack of progress on his Project X. He'd made little headway in the last weeks. He'd been able to confirm that Internal Affairs was indeed looking into Ryland, but his source had refused to provide more information than that, displaying the same distress and panic Susan had shown weeks before. What the hell was it with this Ryland guy that people feared him this much?

He'd wanted to do more digging, but in his defense, he'd struggled to find the time. He'd focused on writing a series of articles on George York and the Conservative Wolf Party first, a series well received by both Franken and readers of the newspapers. Palani had managed to dig up some interesting tidbits from the CWP's program that had sparked debate about the position of omegas and how to improve certain systematic problems. Many people agreed that while the problems were real, the CWP's solutions seemed farfetched. That, of course, made Palani wonder all over again where the support for the CWP came from.

Franken had asked him to keep focusing on York and the CWP and follow up with new insights, and so Palani had. He'd interviewed staunch supporters of the party as well as opponents and concluded the latter were a hell of a lot better informed than the first. Some supporters possessed no clear concept of what the party advocated beyond "more omega rights," as one man he'd interviewed worded it.

The opponents, on the contrary, seemed well informed on the CWP's revolutionary ideas and spared no effort in trying to convince Palani of the sheer stupidity of said plans. Some belonged to existing political parties, but a few confessed to supporting another new group called the Anti Wolf Coalition. That name didn't deserve points for originality, but it made the main objective crystal clear, Palani had to admit. And like their counterpart the CWP, the AWC was getting traction.

It made for captivating articles, and Franken was happy with him again. That was a big relief, so maybe he should be grateful for that instead of berating himself for not following up on Excellon. Today, he'd finished work early, which left him with a few hours to spare, so he decided to pick his investigation back up and see if he could make some headway.

He read through his notes on Excellon and Ryland. What should he focus on next? He'd tried three different sources to get access to the police version of the report that Dr. Vandermeer filed but with no success. It left him no choice but to ask Lidon, so he called him on his private cell.

"Hey you," he said when Lidon answered.

He still struggled with what to call him, how to approach the alpha. He was so damn sexy, but so was Enar, except Lidon was also fucking intimidating. There was something about him, an aura of power and strength that reached deep inside Palani and made him want to serve the man, somehow. Well, he did serve him regularly...that morning, in fact, as he and Vieno had worked together to give the man a blow job he wouldn't soon forget. He'd been rewarded by being fucked thoroughly, and his ass still throbbed with the aftereffects.

"As much as I like to listen to you breathe, I assume you called me for a reason?" Lidon said, his voice dripping with amusement.

Palani felt his cheeks heat. "Yes, sorry. I got distracted by...yes, anyway."

Lidon chuckled. "Memories of this morning?"

"Yes, sir. Very happy memories, in fact. But that's not why I called." He quickly made his request. "I tried my usual sources, but they won't touch this."

"Why?" Lidon asked, his voice serious now.

"Can you talk?" Palani checked.

"Yeah. I'm outside, getting a decent coffee instead of the absolute dredge they serve at headquarters, before a meeting with city officials. Talk to me, what's going on?"

"I get the feeling Ryland is bad news. My contacts are terrified of him. One source mentioned he'd gotten people fired, then replaced them with his own men. IA has been trying to nail him, but their witnesses and evidence keep disappearing."

"What?"

Palani heard the horror in Lidon's voice, and he cringed. It had to be hard for the man who boasted such high morals to hear this about a fellow officer.

"I'm sorry," he said, swallowing back the "baby" that teetered on the tip of his tongue. Somehow, that term of endearment seemed inadequate for Lidon, and he doubted the alpha would appreciate being called that.

"Let me see what I can do," Lidon said, his voice tight.

"Be careful," Palani said, echoing the sentiment Susan had communicated to him.

"Yes. I will be. And, Palani?" Lidon's voice had softened.

"Yeah?"

"You can call me *baby*..."

Lidon's laugh drifted into Palani's ears before the cop hung up. He'd caught on to that, huh? Not surprising, as the man was sharp as a tack. He didn't miss much, though he preferred dealing with information rather than with emotions. The way he and Enar danced around each other was as frustrating as endearing. These two strong men, who felt so much for each other but seemed unable to express it. They'd made another step on moving day, Palani had noticed, but progress still continued at a snail's pace.

But he'd leave the issues between Lidon and Enar for another day. He had a task to get back to. While waiting to see if Lidon could get him that report, he'd do a little digging into Lukos. His fingers flew over his keyboard as he searched.

Lukos was founded seven years ago but didn't have registered employees until five years ago. Huh, interesting. How had they survived the first two years without employees?

It took him a while to wade through the legal structure behind Lukos for which complicated proved too tame a word. It was owned by a shell corporation, which was owned by another corporation, which was owned by...the list was endless. He'd dug six layers deep now, but he was no closer to finding out who owned the damn company. Sure, there was an official website, which showed a CEO and a board of directors, but it mentioned nothing about the owner. Hmm, weird.

Their website showed their main products, including Excellon. It also listed Optimon, a birth control method for male omegas, categorized as "pending final approval by the Drugs Agency." The third drug was named Mollison, but the "X34" behind brackets made clear it was the heat suppressant Enar had told him about. They had three products, all aimed at male omegas, Palani noticed.

Palani's suspicion about the three award patents in such a short time was still fresh in his mind. How had they pulled that off?

He made a quick phone call and requested all three patent files from the patent office. They responded much faster than he'd dared hope, and an hour later, the three files popped up on his screen. The medical jargon meant shit to him—he'd have to ask Enar if he could spot anything strange there—but one thing stood out: all three patents listed the same name as the doctor claiming the patent on behalf of Lukos: Dr. Jerald Eastwood.

He googled him but found no information other than an official bio that listed all his degrees and shit, but nothing personal. Granted, his list of degrees was impressive, but how had this man managed to get three patents awarded this fast? Palani leaned back in his chair to ponder it. Five years was a ridiculously short time for research, especially medical research. Eastwood had to possess experience in this specific field, or he'd brought knowledge in from a previous employer? Or patents?

Palani did a reverse search on the patent website to see if the man had any other patents registered to his name, and what did you know, a few results popped up. He clicked them, curious what the good doctor had worked on before his career with a brand-new start-up. Antidepressants, fertility drugs, and three different pregnancy vitamins—all for male omegas. What was the man's fascination with omegas? These were all registered by him while working for a company called Ulfur. Why would a renowned doctor like Eastwood have switched to a start-up like Lukos?

Palani did a little more Internet-sleuthing and discovered the answer within a few minutes. Ulfur had gone under six years ago, so Eastwood would've gladly jumped ship to ensure employment. And by the looks of it, Ulfur had allowed him to take his research with him to Lukos, which explained the fast patents in the five years Eastwood had worked there.

Okay, so now he knew how a start-up had registered successful patents this quickly, but who was trying to block them from more success? Their competitors formed the most likely suspects, but Palani had a hard time envisioning three companies that size working together. Plus, Lukos was peanuts compared to them, and birth control wasn't *that* crucial to the market share and income of the other companies. Insurance companies made more sense, but again, how would they all work together, and why would they target one specific drug?

Palani sat up straight in his chair. Unless it wasn't just Excellon. What if Lukos's other products were targeted as well? Optimon still hadn't been approved, and X34/Mollison was held up in clinical trial. That was far beyond the scope of insurance companies or rivaling drug companies. That reeked of bribery on the highest government levels. He didn't even know where to start if that was the case. It would explain why Lukos hadn't complained about the bribes against Excellon. If this was a concerted government effort, complaining to said government wouldn't get them far.

His email dinged with an incoming message. Lidon had sent him a copy of the report on file for Dr. Vandermeer. The accompanying email was brutally short but had Palani grinning nonetheless. "FYI," Lidon had simply written, but he'd signed off with "XXX, your baby." The man had a sense of humor that Palani could appreciate. He shot back a quick "Thanks, babe," the smile never leaving his lips.

As expected, the report Lidon had sent differed from the version Vandermeer had provided. The whole report read word for word the same...except for the name of the drug Vandermeer had reported. Instead of Excellon, it said Trigadon, which research revealed to be a stomach acid reducer, produced by a different company than Lukos.

Fraud. Palani now possessed crystal clear evidence of fraud within the White-Collar Division, and the only logical explanation to change a report like that was if someone was being bribed. Or multiple someones. In this case, Ryland and Kimble formed the most likely suspects. But why the hell was Ryland protecting whoever was blocking Excellon or even Lukos in general? What was in it for him? If Palani could find out that, he'd have something solid. So far, his gut said something was horribly wrong, but he still had little factual evidence to back that claim up. More digging it was.

LIDON DIDN'T USE his desk at the precinct all that often, since a lot of his work took place in the field. That's why it surprised him to see a white envelope with his name on it propped up against his computer monitor. It didn't list a sender, and it also didn't have the stamp to signal it had been delivered by the police department's internal mail system. What the hell was this?

When he opened it, a sheet of paper fell out, and he folded it open. His breath caught in his lungs when the printed words registered.

Tell them to back off.

Oh god. He recognized the other beta in the picture instantly. Shit, shit, shit. The guy had been right. They *were* watching him.

He folded the sheet back before his partner, Sean, spotted it. He was a good kid but way too curious.

"Sean, I'm gonna need an hour to do some personal stuff," he said.

Sean looked up, his eyes narrowing. "Everything okay? Trouble at home?"

The news about Lidon's marriage had made the rounds, even more so after he'd taken off for Vieno's heat. His coworkers had no idea about Palani and Enar, of course, merely that Lidon had married an omega. He could use that to his advantage. "Vieno's not feeling well," he said.

Sean waggled his eyebrows. "Is he...?"

"If he is, you'll be the last person I would tell," Lidon shot him down. He knew damn well the likelihood of Vieno being pregnant was small, since Enar had made sure he'd been on birth control.

He tried to stay calm as he walked outside. He didn't know who had put the letter there, but it had been an inside job. It had to be Ryland, right? But how had he found out about Lucan—the pharmacy technician—and Palani? Lidon's heart grew cold. They'd both been in the picture, so the message was clear. Whoever had sent it, knew about Lucan talking to Palani and about Palani researching this. Palani hadn't published anything yet, and he hadn't spoken to Lucan since they'd met in the coffee shop. So what had triggered this warning now?

He stopped in the middle of the hallway when it hit him. He'd requested the file about that doctor's report, Vandermeer. He hadn't been as stupid as to go straight into the system and request it but instead opted for asking Sean to look into an old case he'd been able to tie it to—with a little creative thinking. So Sean had requested it, but still they'd traced it back to Lidon. Ryland must have placed a trigger on certain files that alerted them whenever someone looked at them or downloaded them. Dammit, he'd been stupid. After Palani's warnings, he should've known, should have anticipated this. Even Charlene had warned him, weeks ago. He had placed both Lucan and Palani in danger.

Chances were they were watching him to see what he would do. Thank fuck he was in plain clothes. His first stop was a store where he bought a few burner phones. Once he had one set up, he got into his car. He already held the phone in his hand to call when something hit him. If they were serious about watching him, his car would be a prime target. He'd better have it checked for bugs before he made any more calls. He never had his phone hooked up to his car in the first place, since that made him way too vulnerable to hacking, but if they'd planted a mic somewhere, they would be able to hear his end of the conversation.

He drove to a car shop he had good experiences with. The owner was a woman whose husband technically owned the shop, even though she did all the work. She also happened to be known for her electronic skills. Aside from being a first-class mechanic, the woman could hack into almost any car software system known to man...and knew how to check for wiretaps and bugs. Lidon had used her services a few times when he did undercover work.

He parked his car in the lot, then walked inside. He spotted her crawled under a classic Mustang.

"Laura," he called out.

She slid from under the car, smiling when she spotted him. "Detective Hayes. Always a pleasure." Wiping her hands on a rag, she got up. "What can I do for you today?"

"I need a checkup," he said, handing her the keys. "I think you may want to run a check on the electronics as well."

She nodded. "No problem."

"Do you have a place where I can make a phone call without *interruption*?" he asked.

"Yes, sir. The office is quiet."

He whipped his phone out before she'd closed the door behind him. At least he was certain this place wasn't bugged. And thank fuck he'd memorized this particular number. It only rung once before it was answered.

"Palani, it's me," Lidon said.

"Why are you calling from an unknown—"

"We have a problem. Lucan was right. He *was* being watched."

"Fuck, what happened?"

"I got a letter today, a threat. It was a printed picture of you and Lucan, taken in that coffee shop where you met him a few weeks back. It said, 'Tell them to back off.' This is not good, Palani. I'm worried about you but about Lucan as well."

"Dammit. How did you receive it? Any way to trace it?"

Lidon smiled despite the gravity of the situation. "You realize you're talking to a cop, right? Plain white envelope, printed standard paper, my name written on the front, hand delivered to my desk."

Palani sighed. "So they know you're involved. What do we do now?"

"I think me requesting that Vandermeer report may have triggered it, even though I didn't request it myself but had my rookie do it. I suppose asking you to stop investigating Excellon and Ryland would be useless?"

"Yes. This thing is big, Lidon. I can't give up now."

Lidon leaned his forehead against the wall in Laura's office. What was it that Charlene had said? Ryland would come after him, and Enar had warned him about his weak spots. He had to protect them: Vieno, Palani, and Enar. They were his weak spots.

"Do you have a way of contacting Lucan?"

"Yeah. We have special email addresses that aren't linked to anything else."

"Email him. Tell him to pack his essentials. He's moving into the ranch. I don't want it on my conscience if they're coming after him."

"He lives with his dad, the author?"

Lidon vaguely remembered Palani mentioning that. "Then he moves in as well. And I'm arranging security for the ranch. Vieno is too vulnerable out there by himself, even with Jawon and his men around."

"Are you sure that's necessary?" Palani asked.

"I'm not taking any chances after what you said. If half the stories are true, Ryland's got a lot to lose if it comes out. He'll go to extremes to protect himself and those around him, so I will have to do the same."

"Okay, I trust your judgment in this. Lucan mentioned his brother had a security firm. Maybe you could involve him?"

That wasn't a bad idea. Surely, he'd be interested,

considering his brother was at risk. And it wasn't like Lidon had a long list of people he trusted right now.

"Ask him for a name, and I'll contact him. You can text me at this number."

Half an hour later, his car was serviced, swept for bugs—Laura hadn't found any, she said—and Palani had texted him a name and number for one Bray Whitefield, owner of Whitefield Security. Lidon called Sean from the car to inform him he was taking the rest of the day off, then called Bray Whitefield and arranged to meet him at the ranch. Whitefield had sounded surprised, but he'd been willing to meet on short notice, which Lidon considered a good sign.

He met him at the gate, where Whitefield parked his car. He was a tall alpha, built like a wall, with a stern but sharp look. And he was a hell of a lot younger than Lidon had expected for someone who ran a security firm, since he guessed him twenty-five at most.

"Can I see your ID, please?" Lidon asked.

He checked the driver's license handed to him. It was legit. And he'd been spot on; the guy was twenty-five. That was young to run his own company. "Okay, come on through," he said and opened the gate for him. "You can drive up to the house."

When Lidon had walked up, Whitefield stood waiting for him next to his car. Lidon extended this hand. "Lidon Hayes."

"Bray Whitefield."

"Your brother is in trouble, Whitefield, and I'm responsible for it. We may need your help to keep him safe," Lidon said, his eyes trained on the man to see how he would react.

Whitefield merely blinked. "Call me Bray. Is Lucan safe right now? Do I need to get him?"

"He's being brought here as we speak, with your father."

Lidon quickly explained the situation, omitting Ryland's name and the name of the drug Palani was investigating. The fewer people who knew about that, the better.

"Damn," Bray said when Lidon was done. "All because he tried to do the right thing."

"The right thing?" Lidon asked, wanting to make sure he understood correctly.

"You can't tell me you agree with this idiotic restrictive policy for these birth control pills?" Bray said. "It's one more step in a long series of measures aimed at boxing omegas in."

Lidon smiled. "Glad to hear you feel that way. Before I ask you inside, would you mind waiting here for just a minute? I need to check on something real quick."

"Sure thing."

Lidon hurried inside. It was the first time he'd brought a strange alpha to the house, to Vieno. He needed to make sure Vieno was okay with it—and that Bray wouldn't react to Vieno. The chances were low, since he'd already had his heat, but it was important to be certain.

"Vieno?" he called out as he stepped inside.

The music told him where he could find his omega. He was singing along to a tune Lidon recognized but didn't know the name of, while mopping the kitchen floor.

"Hey, sweetheart," he said, raising his voice to be heard over the music.

Vieno spun around. "Hi. What are you doing home already?"

Lidon signaled for him to turn the music down, and when he did, he said, "There have been some developments. Can you step outside with me to meet someone?"

Vieno put the mop down and wiped his hands on his shorts. "Sure, but who is it?"

"His name is Bray Whitefield." He then realized they hadn't told Vieno about Lucan, since they'd wanted to shield him from that whole mess. Well, he'd have to explain that later. That was too long a story for now. "I have a lot to tell you, but Bray may be around to arrange extra security for the ranch. I wanted you to meet him and make sure you're okay with him being around."

"He's an alpha," Vieno said.

"Yes."

"Why do we need security?"

Lidon sighed. "That's part of a long story I need to tell you, but not now."

Vieno's face tightened. "You want to make sure he can't smell me."

"Yes. Just a safety precaution."

Vieno nodded after a slight hesitation. "Okay."

Lidon felt the tension in the omega's body as he held Lidon's hand while they walked outside, where Bray stood waiting for them.

"Bray, I want you to meet my mate, Vieno."

Bray did a courtesy dip of his head to Vieno. "It's nice to meet you, Vieno."

"You too," Vieno said, hiding half behind Lidon.

Lidon held on to his hand as he pulled him forward. "Bray, I'm gonna ask you a weird question, but please trust me when I say this is necessary. Can you tell me what you smell on Vieno?"

Bray's eyes widened almost imperceptibly, but he stepped forward and sniffed. "You, mostly," he said, then sniffed again, cocking his head. "And some other smells? A mix."

It made sense he would smell Enar and Palani on him as well, but he hadn't reacted in any way. Vieno's hand relaxed in his, and Lidon bent toward him for a quick kiss. "Go back inside, sweetheart. Thank you."

Bray waited with speaking until Vieno was inside. "Wanna tell me what that was about? Why the hell does your mate have the scent of two other men besides you, and what does that have to do with me?"

11

P alani had instructed Lucan to pack essentials for him and his dad and take a cab to the airport. It was the best place he could think of where he could pick them up. If someone was tailing them, they'd have a hard time staying close enough to keep an eye on him amidst the hectic kiss and ride.

When he pulled up to the spot he'd told Lucan to wait, the guy almost immediately walked up to the car. Another man, an alpha, stood waiting on the curb. He looked enough like Lucan that even without prior knowledge, Palani would have been able to identify him. His dark hair sported some silver streaks in it, but he was a lot younger than Palani had expected. When Lucan had said he lived with his dad, Palani had pictured an elderly man, but this guy was early forties if he had to take a guess. If that was Lucan's dad, he must have been young when he fathered his older brother.

"I'm so sorry," Palani told Lucan. "It's a shitty situation you're in."

Lucan's face was tight. "It sucks. For my dad, too, since he had to come with me."

Palani slapped a hand on his back. "We'll get you squared away, okay? Let me introduce myself to your father."

He extended his hand. "Palani Hightower."

The alpha's handshake was strong. "Grayson Whitefield. It's a pleasure, Palani. I'm a fan of yours."

The man's voice rung deep and commanding, and Palani, who wasn't easily impressed, found himself a tad flustered. "Thank you, sir. Likewise. I love your books."

The alpha smiled. "Then it's even more of a pleasure. Call me Grayson, please."

"Dad doesn't like formalities," Lucan said with a little eye roll that made Palani grin. This, apparently, frustrated Lucan. It fitted Palani, who'd never been big on all that überpolite and formal shit anyway, to a T. He hated the ass-kissing so many alphas insisted on from betas and omegas. Ugh. They were people too, not gods.

"With pleasure, Grayson," he said and watched with satisfaction as the alpha grinned while Lucan did another eye roll thing. He was such a cute nerd.

Minutes later, they'd loaded everything into his car, and Palani drove off. Lucan took the back seat, as expected, while Grayson rode shotgun.

"Where are you taking us?" Lucan asked.

"To Lidon's place. He has a huge ranch, and there's more than enough room for both of you."

"I didn't realize you two knew each other that well," Lucan said, the unasked question clear.

How the fuck did he explain this? Palani didn't want to lie, but they hadn't discussed what to tell others about the four of them. Lidon being a cop complicated things even more. Then again, Lucan and Grayson would find out anyway if they stayed at the ranch.

"Lidon is my partner," Palani said. "One of them."

"Oh, you guys are in a threesome with an omega?"

In for a penny, in for the whole damn thing, right? "A foursome. With another alpha."

When Lucan stayed quiet, Palani shot a quick look in the rearview mirror. The other beta's mouth had dropped open.

"Sorry," Lucan finally said. "I did not see that coming."

"It's unusual now, but it wasn't before," Grayson spoke. God, his voice was rich, the kind of voice you wanted to listen to for hours as he told captivating stories of times past.

"Before what, Dad?" Lucan asked.

"Before we stopped shifting. Back then, threesomes, foursomes, and even more sharing one omega were normal."

"Really?" Lucan asked.

Palani thought back of what Melloni had explained, about the fated mates and how there would be all kinds of combinations. He hadn't realized it at the time, but the man had mentioned only combinations with one omega. Apparently, the common factor was to share one omega. Their combination with Vieno wasn't so abnormal, then. Huh. That offered an interesting perspective.

"Someone else explained to me that poly relationships occurred far more back then," he said to Grayson.

"It was how packs functioned," Grayson said. "One alpha who led the whole pack and who formed a poly relationship with three or more others, but always with one omega. The pack itself consisted of any alpha-beta-omega combination but usually not more than three."

It fit what Melloni had said.

"So your foursome isn't something to be ashamed of," Grayson said with a finality that left little room for discussion. The little smile that played on his lips showed his approval even more.

"Thank you," Palani said, amused. He was gonna love having this man around. He would certainly shake things up.

"And I'm not surprised to see Lidon Hayes in a relationship like that."

"You've heard of him, Dad?" Lucan asked, the surprise in his voice clear.

"I've never met him, but I know his name and family. I did some research into his bloodline. His grandfather was a good man, well respected in the community and with strong ties to his family. It seems his grandson takes after him."

Palani frowned. What Grayson said confirmed what Enar had told him, though the omission of Lidon's father caught his attention, but there was an undertone he couldn't place, something that sounded a lot like reverence. "Why does it not surprise you of Lidon specifically?" Palani asked.

"He's the strongest alpha I've come across, and his family history is legendary."

"Dad," Lucan said with a mix of embarrassment and begging.

Grayson huffed. "You and Bray, always telling me to pull my head out of the clouds. I love you both, but you are so focused on science and facts that you forget there are things that can't be measured, that can't be known with any scientific method. One day you'll find out what you've missed all these years."

Palani couldn't pinpoint how and why, but something in what Grayson said connected with him. "I'd be very interested in learning more about Lidon's history, and I think he'd be as well."

Grayson nodded. "Good. We'll talk."

Palani opened the gate with the app Lidon had installed on his phone. A strange car stood in front of the house, but Lucan sighed as soon as he spotted it.

"He's already here," he said miserably.

Palani parked right behind the vehicle. "Who is?"

Lidon came walking out, a tall, bulky alpha next to him.

"This should be entertaining," Grayson commented. "Come on, Lucan, let's see if we can calm your brother down."

Ah, Lidon had worked fast, then, if this was Bray Whitefield. Fuck, that alpha was badass. He was taller than Grayson and a lot more muscular. For an alpha, Grayson's build was a bit on the lean side. Not that it looked bad on him, but he wasn't as imposing as Lidon or Enar or this guy.

Bray hugged Grayson first, a manly but loving hug. "Dad, always good to see you."

"You too, son. Cut your brother some slack, will you? He did the right thing."

To his credit, Bray hugged Lucan as well. "Glad you got here safely," he said. He let go of him, then put both hands on his shoulders and shook him a little. "What the hell were you thinking?"

Palani stepped in. "Hi," he said, extending his hand. "Palani."

It was ballsy as fuck, of course, to interrupt an alpha like that, but he didn't care. This was his turf, and his own alpha was standing right there, an amused smirk on his lips that told Palani Lidon knew exactly what he was up to.

Bray released Lucan and grabbed Palani's hand for a strong handshake. "Bray Whitefield, which you knew already, of course. Nice try interrupting me lecturing my brother for being careless with his safety."

"You have no idea what's going on, so maybe you should try listening to him first," Palani said, crossing his arms.

"Lidon filled me in already, and besides, I don't take orders from a beta."

Palani looked past Bray to Lidon, who nodded to him with a twinkle in his eye, knowing without words what Palani was asking. A rush of adrenaline flowed through Palani. "You will have to if you're gonna lead security here. This is my home too."

Bray's initial amusement died when he spotted Palani's face. Lidon walked over and, in front of everyone, claimed Palani's mouth for a bruising kiss. Palani surrendered to his demanding mouth, led by a deep desire to show everyone he belonged to Lidon.

Lidon broke off the kiss, leaving Palani almost out of breath. He dropped his arm around Palani's shoulder and pulled him close. "He's right," he said casually. "You can consider anything he tells you an order from me."

Palani fought hard not to gloat. He didn't want to make enemies with Bray, not if the man would be around. But he was giddy with how Lidon had set him straight. Palani didn't have the time or the patience to deal with that alpha posturing anymore, especially not in his own home.

"My apologies," Bray said. "I wasn't aware of these dynamics."

Palani caught Lucan holding a hand in front of his mouth to keep from laughing, though his eyes showed his mirth. No wonder, he'd just witnessed his older alpha brother being dressed down. That had to feel good. Grayson's eyes sparkled as well, though he succeeded in keeping somewhat of a poker face.

Grayson stepped forward. "Lidon Hayes, it's an honor to meet you. Grayson Whitefield."

Lidon let go of Palani to shake the man's hand. "Mr. Whitefield, the honor is all mine. I apologize for the circumstances."

"Call me Grayson, alpha."

Palani watched Lidon freeze, and like Bray and Lucan, he stared at Grayson. Why had the older alpha used that title for Lidon? Custom said Lidon should call him alpha because of his seniority, not the other way around.

"I... Why are you referring to me like that?" Lidon asked, as confused as everyone else.

Grayson's look was steady and his voice calm as he spoke. "Because you are the alpha of this pack."

IT TOOK a little getting used to, having strangers in the house, but after a few hours, Vieno was comfortable having Lucan and Grayson around. Lucan's dad didn't protest when Lidon asked him to smell Vieno and report anything strange. Like his son Bray, the alpha only detected Vieno's men on him with a faint trace of his own scent, but nothing other than that.

It reassured him, but it also triggered Vieno's curiosity. Would he still be irresistible during his heat? They'd have to find out, but Palani and Enar seemed to suspect it would be much less because of the interaction with Lidon's and Enar's alpha hormones. Or maybe the alpha claiming, Enar had explained. It seemed that resulted in effects the famous Dr. Melloni had studied before becoming an expert on the gene that carried his name.

They finished dinner, and the others retreated to the living room while Vieno loaded the dishwasher, his mind wondering why Bray was here. Lidon had only mentioned he wanted extra security, but why? He'd given Bray a thorough tour of the house and the land, and after that, Bray had stated he wanted to call in some extra men. Lidon had agreed instantly, sharing a look with Palani that worried Vieno. Bray had waited for his men to arrive, and then they had set up a circle around the house, making sure no one got in.

What the hell was going on? His heart rate sped up, and his heart clenched painfully. It had to have something to do with Lucan and Grayson, but Vieno couldn't figure out how or what. He wasn't even sure where Palani had met them and why Lidon seemed to know Lucan as well. Were they in danger, somehow? From whom?

"Let me help," Palani said, startling Vieno from his worries.

"I can do it."

Palani kissed him quickly. "I know, baby, but you don't have to. You already had your hands full taking care of us three, and now there's two more. That means we need to pitch in."

Vieno put the plates he'd been holding on the counter and turned toward Palani for a hug. He always felt better when he was being held by one of his men. Palani's arms came around him, and Vieno rested his head against the beta's shoulder, melting against him.

"I'm worried," he said.

"We'll explain everything, baby."

"Do I have reason to be worried?"

"A little. You know I never lie to you. But you have a lot of men around you whose single focus is to protect you, okay?"

He felt Lidon's presence before the alpha's strong arms

came around them both. "He's right, sweetheart. We won't let anything happen to you."

"Enar," Palani said, letting go of Vieno to pull their fourth man into the embrace. Enar apparently had wandered into the kitchen as well.

"We'll protect you above all, little one," Enar said.

Vieno's eyes welled up. He had three men surrounding him, holding him, all focused on making sure he was okay. How had he gotten so lucky to have them in his life? It was nothing short of a miracle. His fears floated away as his body responded to the strength his men exuded.

They settled in the living room after the kitchen had been tidied, with mugs of coffee and tea and a big plate of the pecan cookies Vieno had baked earlier that day. Vieno sat tucked away against Lidon on the couch, as he often did when they were sitting here. The alpha's physical proximity always had a calming effect on him.

"It's a wonderful home you have, Lidon," Grayson commented.

"Thank you. I'm glad to see it being restored to its former glory. It's been in my generation for a long time."

Grayson nodded. "The PTP ranch, I'm familiar with it."

"Grayson told me in the car he researched your bloodline," Palani said to Lidon.

"Really? Why mine, specifically?"

"Dad does a lot of research for his books," Lucan said. "Shifter legends, that kind of thing."

There was a not-too-subtle stress on the word legends that Vieno picked up on. "But your books, alpha, they're fiction, yes? These are legends, not reality."

Grayson's sharp blue eyes looked at Vieno with kindness. "So my son would like to stress, as you noticed. He feels that what he calls legends belong firmly in the fiction category. I disagree. And call me Grayson, please."

"You don't think they're legends?" Enar asked, leaning forward.

"No. Well, some of them, sure. But I think many have a kernel of truth in them. If you dig deep enough, you discover what that truth is."

"There are legends about Lidon's family?" Vieno asked, intrigued.

"God, yes. Too many to count. Lidon may remember some himself, though most likely as stories he was told as a kid."

"Can you tell us one?" Vieno asked.

Grayson's eyes shifted from him to Lidon. "Only with the alpha's permission."

"Why do you keep calling him that? You said it outside when you called him the alpha of this pack. What are you referring to?" Palani asked.

"Do I have your permission to explain?" Grayson asked Lidon.

Lidon's arms tightened around Vieno for a second before he answered. "Yes, please."

"Let me start with a question. What happened half an hour ago? Vieno was in the kitchen, and we were all here. First Palani got up and went to the kitchen, then Lidon, and then you, Enar. Why?"

Vieno frowned. What did that have to do with anything?

"I sensed Vieno needed me," Palani said. "I was sitting here chatting with you, and suddenly I had this urge to check on him."

"Same here," Lidon said.

Vieno looked up at him, and the alpha's face was filled with wonder.

"My rational mind says it's not possible, but that's what I felt. I wasn't even in the living room but in the bedroom getting changed," Enar said, his face displaying the same look as Lidon's. "What are you saying, Grayson?"

Grayson leaned forward and met their eyes one by one. "What I'm saying is that you're a mated foursome, tuned in to each other but above all into your omega. He's at the core of who you are, and over time, you'll be able to sense his emotions even stronger. My guess is that Palani feels them the most, as he responded first, so maybe he mated first with you, Vieno?"

Vieno couldn't do anything else but nod. How was this even possible?

"I came second and Enar third," Lidon said, his voice filled with the wonder Vieno was experiencing himself.

Grayson nodded. "That's what I suspected. You're new together, so it's only getting started, but ultimately, all of you will be able to sense when one of you is in danger, and you'll be able to feel Vieno's emotions above all."

Vieno's head dazzled with the implications of what Grayson was saying. Was that even possible, that they had sensed his stress, even when they weren't in the same room? It sounded impossible yet strangely true at the same time.

Palani and Enar looked at each other. "Would Melloni know more about this?" Palani asked.

"Doctor Melloni?" Grayson asked. When Palani nodded, Grayson said, "He should. He's doing groundbreaking research into this, even wrote a whole book about the effects of alpha claiming that was based on research he did on fated mates."

Enar nodded. "It's out of print, and he doesn't own the copyright, so he can't make it available as an e-book. For some reason, his publisher doesn't want to republish it."

Grayson's face tightened. "That, I believe. There's a powerful lobby against anything having to do with the old ways. I have the book, so you're more than welcome to borrow it and read it."

"The old ways?" Palani asked. "You mean the shifter ways?"

Grayson nodded.

"But how do you explain the rise of the Conservative Wolf Party?" Palani asked. "I interviewed George York, and their ideas are revolutionary. They're making no secret they want to reinstate many of the old ways, as you call it. If there's such a lobby against this, how are they gaining so much ground?"

"I've read your series about George York." Grayson's voice was sharp, and it startled Vieno. "You'll want to be careful with him. He's charming, but underneath, he's ruthless. I don't trust him."

Palani grinned. "I'm naturally inclined to distrust anyone."

Grayson relaxed. "Yeah, I'm sorry. I should've known, since this isn't your first rodeo, so to speak. I didn't mean to go all alpha patronizing on you. It's just...he worries me. That whole development baffles me because as you pointed out, I can't understand what their appeal is and how they gained so much popularity. That they're interesting to betas and omegas I can believe, but alphas? I can't see that happening."

"I'd love to talk more with you about this 'cause I still haven't figured out how they're doing so well in the polls," Palani said. "But right now, I'm more interested in why you keep calling Lidon alpha."

Grayson smiled first. Then they all did, and Palani held up his hands. "I know, I'm a little pitbull with things like this, but my mind won't let it go. So, please, Grayson, enlighten us?"

"Let me show you with a little experiment, with your permission?" Grayson looked at Lidon, who nodded. "Palani, can I use you for this?"

"Sure."

Grayson stood up, then looked at Palani. "Kneel!" he suddenly spoke, his voice booming through the room.

Everyone froze for a second, and then Lucan dropped to his knees, a startled look on his face. "What the hell?" Palani said, looking from Grayson to Lucan.

"Sorry, son," Grayson said. "I couldn't warn you, or the experiment would have failed."

"You fucking alpha compelled me," Lucan muttered as he got up.

"I don't understand," Palani said. "I should have... Why didn't it affect me? And Vieno? We should've at least felt it, so why didn't we?"

"Because you're Lidon's, and his alpha outranks mine. Your beta and Vieno's omega know who they belong to. Lucan is my son, so he'll always respond to my alpha. But allow me to do one more experiment to show you?"

Vieno had shot up into a sitting position when Grayson had given his command, and so had Lidon. Now, Lidon's face showed his curiosity with what was happening.

"Lidon, give us a command and use your full alpha powers. We'll all try to resist."

Something tingled in the air, a ripple that made the hairs on Vieno's skin stand on end. What was happening here?

Lidon rose to his feet and closed his eyes for a second. Vieno felt the power before he heard the word, and he was already on his feet before Lidon had finished speaking. "Bow!"

As one, they bowed to him, everyone, including Grayson, and they did not move until he released them.

"Holy crap." Palani was the first to speak. "What the fuck just happened?"

They looked at each other in stunned disbelief, Lidon as confused as the rest of them. The only one who seemed unaffected was Grayson. His voice was calm and deep when he spoke.

"Pack, meet your alpha. Alpha, meet your pack."

Vieno took a deep breath. He had this. The roast was in the oven, the potatoes for the mashed potatoes were almost done, the salad was ready to be served. What else did he need? Beans. He wanted to serve green beans as well.

He put another pan on the stove to boil water, then took out the sour cream for the mashed potatoes as well as the bacon bits he'd made before. A little fresh chives, a splash of milk, and of course salt and pepper, and they'd be all set. He'd put some grated cheddar on the table as well, in case someone liked their mashed potatoes loaded.

He wanted to make a good impression on Lidon's uncle and aunt, the first family members they were officially introducing themselves to as a foursome. Jawon and Lidon's cousins knew, of course, but they'd agreed not to say anything yet. It was one more example of Lidon's alpha powers because he'd easily convinced them to keep that news to themselves.

Palani's brothers were aware but hadn't come down the ranch yet, and he'd only told his parents the day before when he'd visited them after they'd returned from their cruise. They'd been shocked at the news and asked for a little time to get used to it before meeting his men. It was the best reaction they could've expected from Palani's parents.

He himself hadn't been able to tell Tiva, who hadn't contacted him since the wedding. Vieno suspected his parents had found out she'd been the one to warn him. He worried about her, but there was little he could do. Thank fuck his parents had never been physically abusive. He'd have to find out when her wedding was. Maybe Palani could sneak in and make sure she was okay. For now, he'd focus on welcoming Lidon's uncle and aunt in the best way possible.

He was grateful that Grayson and Lucan had offered to stay in their rooms, to not make things even more complicated. It was hard to explain their presence without explaining all kinds of things about the gene and Excellon and whatnot. Vieno's head had whirled when Palani had detailed what had been going on and what had necessitated the security for all of them.

Grayson and Lucan were no bother at all. On the contrary. After being alone during the days for years, Vieno discovered he liked having people around. Grayson usually worked during the mornings. He was an early riser, as Vieno often heard his keyboard clack when he got up to make breakfast for his men. But after lunch, the man was done, he'd explained to Vieno. The rest of the day he would do research, read, hang out with Vieno and Lucan, and help out outside as well.

Lucan struggled, Vieno had noticed. No wonder. He'd held a full-time job till recently, and now he'd been confined to staying on the ranch with little to do. He'd tried to help Vieno with household stuff, but he lacked the aptitude. Finally, Grayson had taken pity on him and had given him a long list of stuff to do for him, like creating a character bible for his novels, doing specific research, and more. It seemed to keep his son busy for now, but Vieno wondered how long it would last.

And jeez, Grayson's casual revelation of Lidon's alpha powers had been a shock. Lidon himself had had no idea of his abilities, he'd confessed to them afterward, when they were in bed. It had stunned him as much as everyone else to see them bow for him. Only Grayson had known, and it made Vieno wonder. What else did that alpha know? He excelled at keeping his mouth shut, considering he made money telling stories. Lidon had asked a dozen questions, but Grayson had told him it wasn't time yet. Whatever that meant.

"Everything under control here?" Palani checked in.

Vieno nodded. "I think so. Did you set the table?"

"Yes, baby. Like you asked me to an hour ago."

Vieno looked sheepish. "Sorry, I'm nervous. I wanna make sure it's perfect..."

Palani hugged him from behind, nuzzling his neck. "You could burn the potatoes and serve dry meat, and they'd still love you," he whispered. "No one could not love you, baby."

Vieno smiled and leaned back in his embrace for a few seconds. "Thank you."

When the bell rang minutes later, he pushed down his nerves. He had this, dammit. All the food was prepared, ready to be finished and served in a few minutes. He took off his apron, smoothed his hair.

"You look gorgeous," Enar said, laying his hand on Vieno's shoulder.

"You're so sweet." Vieno sighed, and he couldn't resist leaning into the man's strong body for a little. He turned his head and rose to his toes to kiss him and was rewarded with a sweet, soft kiss that made his belly flutter.

"What the hell?" a deep male voice sounded, and Vieno jumped away. Lidon's uncle, Leland, was smaller than him, but the resemblance was unmistakable. Vieno cringed a little under his stern look. Oh fuck, he'd messed up right out of the gate. Now what?

"Enar Magnusson, what the hell do you think you're doing, kissing your best friend's mate?" Lidon's aunt, Sophie, was petite, but her fierce blue eyes were blazing as she all but stormed at Enar, who raised his hands.

"Aunt Sophie," he said, and Vieno realized he must've met them plenty of times, having grown up with Lidon. "I can explain."

Then Palani stepped into the kitchen, and Lidon took position right next to them, his long arms around them as he said calmly, "No, that's my job, and since we're all here, let me introduce you. Uncle Leland and Aunt Sophie, these are my mates Vieno, Palani, and you've met Enar, of course."

The kitchen grew quiet, the bubbling of the boiling water for the beans the only sound audible.

"You have three mates?" Aunt Sophie said, her voice rising high.

"Yes," Lidon said. "I've alpha mated and married Vieno, but Palani and Enar are my mates as well."

Vieno held his breath, his hand clutching Enar's so tightly the man would end up with bruises for sure. Lidon's uncle and aunt would explode, he was certain of it. There was no way they would approve of this, no matter how much Lidon assured him they'd be accepting. No one in his right mind would accept his nephew being in a foursome, right?

Then Lidon's uncle stepped forward, extending his hand to Enar. "Welcome to the family, alpha."

Vieno's breath left his lungs with a swoosh. Lidon had been right. How the fuck was this even possible?

Lidon's uncle shook Enar's hand, following protocol by going by status. They'd have more explaining to do at some point, but since Enar had never come right out and said anything himself, this seemed fine for now.

"Thank you, Uncle Leland," Enar said.

Palani was next. "I recognize your name and face, son. That's some mighty fine reporting you're doing. Welcome to the family."

"Thank you, sir."

"That's Uncle Leland, son. You're family now."

The man's face showed nothing but kindness as he gave Vieno a nod, keeping with protocol and not touching a mated omega. "It's such a pleasure to meet you, Vieno."

"Thank you, Uncle Leland," Vieno said, earning a broad smile from the man.

Aunt Sophie enveloped Enar in a tight hug. "I couldn't be happier with you," she said, emotions thick in her voice. "I've always liked you, you know that."

Enar smiled, a carefree smile that showed Vieno how much he loved this woman.

"He was such a sweet kid, even as a young boy. Always finding wounded animals here on the ranch and nursing them back to health," she told Vieno and Palani. "He was a healer, even then."

Vieno looked at Enar, trying to picture him as a little boy. To his surprise, it wasn't hard at all, and his heart warmed. Like him and Palani, Lidon and Enar had such a history together, so many memories. They'd have to share them sometime.

Meanwhile, Aunt Sophie hugged Palani, who seemed amused by her affection. She patted his cheek in a gesture that was so maternal it made Vieno tear up. God, how he wished for a mother like that. He tried to wipe the wetness away before she would see it, but he wasn't fast enough.

"What's wrong, sweetheart?" she asked, and that familiar word from her lips sent even more tears to his eyes.

"I'm sorry," he said. "It's just..." God, how did he explain this without looking like a total loser? Could he be any more awkward and emotional? Talk about making a horrible first impression.

Palani came to his rescue, as Vieno could've known he would. "He's a little overwhelmed with how sweet and welcoming you are," he said. "Vieno's parents are not very supportive, and I think seeing you made him feel that."

Aunt Sophie's eyes welled up, and then she opened her arms and pulled Vieno close. "Oh, honey, I'm so sorry, but it's their loss. You are beautiful and sweet, and you take such good care of your men, now don't you? I saw it walking in, how perfect the house looked and how clean it smelled. And that roast in the oven smells delicious. And don't you worry about a thing, sweetheart. You'll do just fine, you hear me? And if you ever need anything, I'm here to help."

Vieno laughed at her wonderful barrage of words, smiling through his tears as he hugged her back. "Thank you, Aunt Sophie. I already love you."

"Me too, sweet boy. Me too." She let go of him, wiping his eyes with a gesture that made him fall in love with her on the spot, then dabbed her own. "Now, let's eat, and you must tell me everything."

～

LIDON COULDN'T EXPLAIN how he'd known his uncle and aunt would be okay with his men, but they'd reacted much like he'd expected. Aunt Sophie was such a sweetheart, though tough as nails, and she'd be a great mother figure for Vieno, Lidon realized. The food was perfect, though he hadn't expected anything else, and conversation flowed easily.

"That was delicious," he told Vieno as the omega got up to clear the plates. "Thank you for cooking, sweetheart."

Vieno beamed with pride, and it made Lidon's belly go weak. "Come sit with me for a spell," he said, pulling Vieno onto his lap.

"I need to..." Vieno protested, but Lidon held him close.

"We'll do it," Palani said and got up to clear the plates, Enar following suit.

His uncle's eyebrows raised at the highly unlikely gesture from an alpha, but Aunt Sophie didn't even appear surprised. It wouldn't surprise Lidon if she'd seen something different in Enar for a long time. She'd known him since his childhood, what with Enar spending so much time on the ranch. Hell, he'd barely gone home during the summer breaks, since he loved it too much at the ranch. They'd spent whole days playing outside, riding horses, fishing in the pond, running with the dogs, building tree houses, helping with chores.

"I'd love to see what you're planning with the renovation," Uncle Leland said. "Jawon said you had big plans, but refused to go into details."

It warmed Lidon he had his cousin's loyalty. "We do. It was Vieno's initiative," he said, nuzzling his mate's soft neck, smiling when Vieno let out a little giggle. He was so wonderfully responsive, his body tuned in to Lidon's.

"I wanted to restart the vegetable garden," Vieno said.

"I've always wanted one, but I never had the opportunity. We're also rebuilding the barn, but bigger, so it has room for big equipment and machinery. And my chickens are arriving tomorrow, and I'm super excited about that."

The enthusiasm in his voice rolled through Lidon like a caress. Vieno was helping the ranch become a true home again, and it was something wonderful.

"Can you give us a tour?" Aunt Sophie asked. "I would love to see it."

"I'd love to," Vieno said, sliding off Lidon's lap.

Minutes later, they stepped outside where the sun was still setting, throwing a warm glow over the land. Vieno showed them everything, and they rewarded him with lovely reactions that he deserved every bit of.

"This place is magical," Uncle Leland said, taking up position next to Lidon as Vieno and Aunt Sophie examined the vegetable plot.

Before, Lidon would have categorized a remark like that as a creative expression, but now he wondered. "I'm sorry I let the ranch go so badly," he said.

His uncle's hand clamped down on his shoulder. "It's okay," he said, his voice warm. "It hurt, but I understood. You were dealt a rough hand, losing your parents so young and so unexpectedly."

"Uncle Leland, I've realized that there was a lot my father never had the opportunity to tell me. Things that are important, maybe even crucial to who I am, to who we are."

"I doubted if you were ready to hear them, if you even wanted to learn about them. You seemed to have closed yourself off from your past," Uncle Leland said carefully.

Lidon sighed. From the corner of his eyes, he saw Palani and Enar walking up, and knowing that his men were near settled his heart. "I think I had. It all hurt, you know? Everything reminded me of Dad and Daddy, of what I lost."

The hand on his shoulder squeezed. "I understand. But it seems you found your way back. Your blood has shown up, Lidon. You can't deny who you are."

Lidon frowned. "What do you mean?"

"Your foursome... You're the alpha of our family, Lidon. You're upholding a long and rich family tradition, one that continued unbroken for centuries...until your father."

Lidon turned around to face him. "Uncle Leland, what are you talking about?"

His uncle's eyes widened. "You didn't know. He never told you *that* either."

"Told me what?"

"Lidon, the alpha heirs in our family have always been in poly relationships. Always. Three, four, even five men, sharing one omega...and always a male one. Grandpa, my father, was the alpha, but he mated a beta and an omega, my other two dads."

Palani and Enar came up beside him, steadying him with their presence. "Dad never said a word. I thought it was just Granddad and his omega," Lidon said, shocked to his core.

"Your father was ashamed of it, I think, since by then, poly relationships had become uncommon. So he only mentioned our biological father and Daddy, but Papa was very much there as well, a beta who stabilized the three of them."

"That's why you weren't shocked by our foursome," Enar said.

"No, on the contrary, I'm elated. You're going back to traditions, and I couldn't be more excited. Lidon, your father was the first in his line to break that tradition when he married only your daddy, and your grandfather, my dad, was not amused. They had a huge fight over it, but in the end, your father went ahead with the marriage."

Lidon stood, trying to process his uncle's words. "I...this is new to me. Why did my father break the tradition? Was he that in love with my daddy?"

He'd always remembered them as loving and affectionate, but had his memories been tainted? Had something else happened?

"He loved him for sure. I won't deny that. But he was also stubborn as fuck and refused to take our dad seriously. Dad warned us we were the last of our kind, that we had to stick to our traditions to survive. We were the last shifters. *He* was the last shifter. All around us, families had lost that ability, but Dad still possessed the ability, though it became harder for him as well. He impressed upon us it was because of the traditions, because of the pack. But your father denied it. When he reached fourteen, the age our father shifted for the first time, and he didn't shift, he blamed it on nature, on evolution. It was bound to happen, he claimed, since no one else could shift anymore."

"What happened on the day I was born?" Lidon asked, feeling like cold bands had wrapped around his heart.

His uncle's eyes grew moist, and he seemed to gaze far beyond the present. "When your daddy became pregnant, Dad said it would be an alpha heir. He had no doubt. He wanted to be present at the birth, as had been custom through the ages as well. All living alphas witnessed the birth of the next heir. But your daddy never felt accepted by the family—not entirely without reason—and he didn't want him there, and your father backed that decision. So Dad waited outside until you were born, and I joined him. I remember feeling something rippling in the air."

He fought for composure for a second. "My skin stood on end, and I felt lightheaded. He hadn't shifted in years by then, claiming it had become too hard for him. Rightly so, because we all saw how it drained him to shift back. But then your daddy delivered you, and your first cry sounded... and Dad growled, like full-out alpha wolf growled. Your dad stepped outside minutes later, holding you to show you to us, and Dad took you. He blessed you with the ancient blessing, kissing you, crying with joy. He said a True Alpha had been born, the one who would protect the pack, and then he gave you to me, and he shifted."

A look of wonder transformed his face, and even the birds around them hushed as he continued. "This beautiful gray wolf stood before me, and he took my breath away, so majestic and powerful... He roared, an alpha roar unlike I'd ever heard before, and then he howled. And, Lidon, you were minutes old, but you stopped crying in my arms and howled with him, this tiny baby howl that stabbed my heart because I knew... I knew he was saying good-bye."

He was crying now, tears streaming down his face, Aunt Sophie comforting him while Vieno crawled into Enar's arms. "I...I bent down, and he licked you with his big tongue, and you smiled... I swear, babies that young can't smile, but you did. You were connected for a moment, two souls merging, and then he shifted back, and he passed out...and I knew. He transferred his powers to you, Lidon, because your father didn't want them. That's why you are so powerful."

"How...how am I powerful?" Lidon asked, trying to take it all in.

"You're so much like him, my dad. Looking at you is like looking at him from how I remember him. You have the same voice, the same commanding presence, the same sweetness toward your omega. And the power ripples around you. I feel it every time I enter the gates, every time I see you. You're special. You're the True Alpha."

"The True Alpha?" Palani asked. "What does that mean?"

Uncle Leland smiled through his tears. "Rumors say you have Grayson Whitefield staying here, yes? Ask him about the legend of the True Alpha."

13

When Palani walked into the kitchen after a long day at the paper, he expected Vieno to be there, preparing whatever meal he had planned for that night. Instead, the kitchen and living room stood empty. Where was everyone?

Lidon hadn't returned yet from work, he knew, as he'd texted he was running late. He'd been working long hours after his uncle and aunt had come over for dinner, something about a big drug bust he wasn't sharing much about with Palani, which he completely understood. They'd barely seen each other aside from a quick shower fuck that morning, and Palani missed it. He missed him.

They had so much to talk about, so many things Palani wanted to ask him and Grayson, but he'd have to wait. It proved to be challenging, coordinating schedules when three of them had irregular jobs.

He walked to their bedroom to change into shorts when he heard Vieno's voice. Or rather, his moans.

He smiled as he opened the door. Vieno was riding Enar, his back toward the man, his ass sliding up and down that fat cock. Enar's hands held his hips, and the look of bliss on his face told Palani he needed only seconds to orgasm. Underneath the sexual bliss, Palani spotted the stress on the alpha's face.

Ah. He must have had a rough day, and Vieno, being the sweet little omega that he was, had tried to let him fuck the stress out. Vieno had tried hard, but it looked like Enar needed something else that Vieno couldn't give. And as luck would have it, Palani's day had been shitty as well, and he couldn't imagine anything better than taking it out on Enar's ass. God, he hoped Enar would let him, as so far that privilege had only been granted to Lidon.

They hadn't heard him, too caught up in the lovely way Vieno pleasured himself on that cock. Enar's eyes stayed glued to that perfect view in front of him, and who could blame him? The sight of that bubble butt taking in a big cock again and again was mesmerizing and erotic as fuck. And Palani wasn't interrupting, not until Enar had come. The man deserved his orgasm.

"Ungh!" Enar moaned. His hands tightened on Vieno's hips as he lifted his ass up and rammed inside him with three, four deep thrusts before he groaned low and deep, his body tightening as he came.

Palani waited till Enar had caught his breath again. "Fuck, you're so sexy when you come," he said.

Two heads turned toward him, and he'd already stripped out of his clothes before he crawled onto the bed. He kissed Enar first, a slow, wet kiss, the alpha still panting into his mouth from his release. Then he scooted over to Vieno, who sported that smile, which made him so ridiculously cute.

"Hi, baby," Palani said. He found a spot between Enar's legs, facing Vieno, so he could kiss him. What a joy it brought to no longer have to hold back in his affection for Vieno.

"And you are so damn gorgeous when you're riding a big alpha cock. Show me how you fuck yourself, baby. Show me how beautiful you are when you come."

Vieno lifted his head as he resumed his rhythm. Palani watched, enraptured, as he shifted his hips, finding a position that allowed him to impale himself over and over again until his cheeks flushed with desire, his eyes glazed over, and his cock wept precum. He was so beautiful like this that it took Palani's breath away.

Vieno's hand circled his own dick, and it only took a few tugs before he sprayed his fluids. His eyes fluttered as a long moan fell from his lips. Palani caught it, pressing their mouths together for another long kiss, wanting to drink in every little sound Vieno made in his pleasure. Finally, he dragged his mouth away.

"He needs you," Vieno whispered.

"I know, baby. Thank you for taking care of him."

He gave Vieno a last kiss before allowing him room to climb off Enar, who watched them with guarded eyes. God, Palani hoped he'd be granted the permission to take care of him the way Enar needed him to. He stretched out next to Enar, then held out his arm. It only took a second before Enar rolled over and came to him, burying his head against Palani's shoulder.

"Shitty day?" he asked.

"The worst."

"Will you allow me to take care of you?" he asked. He almost held his breath, waiting for permission, but it came fast.

"Please."

They cuddled for a minute or two till Palani felt Enar

relax in his arms. Only then did he kiss his head and roll both of them over, then positioned himself on top of the bigger man. He loved exploring Enar's body, but now wasn't the time. He was probably nervous, seeing as how this was Palani's first time topping him, so Palani would skip the foreplay and focus on the end goal.

He slid down Enar's body, nudging him to open his legs so he could kneel between them. He quietly signaled Vieno, who had wrapped a sheet around him and sat at the foot end of the bed, to grab lube, which he handed over.

When he pressed his slick index finger against Enar's hole, his eyes pinched shut. "Eyes on me, Doc," Palani said. "You're not hiding from me, not now."

"It's hard," Enar confessed, meeting Palani's eyes.

"I know, but there's nothing to be ashamed of. I got you, but you need to focus on me, okay? Don't hide from me."

He kept talking as he pushed his finger in, his eyes trained on Enar's. Finally, the alpha allowed him in, his tight ring of muscles relaxing. "That's it, Doc. Damn, you're tight. You're gonna clench so fucking snug around my cock, aren't you?" Palani said.

He added a second finger when Enar loosened up, then a third, all the while encouraging him with sexy talk. His own cock was leaking by the time Enar was ready for him.

"Pull your legs up, Doc. Yeah, like that. Vieno, baby, why don't you melt the man with one of your kisses while I take his ass, hmm?"

Vieno crawled past him and dropped himself like a stone on Enar's chest, making Palani grin. Seconds later, their mouths were fused together, and sucking sounds filled the room. Good. That would help the alpha relax. Palani figured Lidon achieved the same effect with sheer intimidation and alpha dominance, but since he didn't possess that, he had to work with what he had.

Enar's body tensed when Palani pushed the head of his cock in, but then relaxed again. He took him slowly, staying shallow until he felt his hole open for him. "You ready for me, Doc? You ready for me to pound your ass? Hang on."

He planted his knees so he'd have a good grip, then surged in. He'd been right. Enar's ass gripped him like a tight fist, hot and slick and perfect.

"Damn, you feel good, Doc. I'm gonna ravish your ass. You feel that? You feel me bottom out inside you?"

His balls slapped against Enar's flesh, a wonderful sound Palani loved almost as much as the sloppy sound his cock made as it thrust balls deep inside the alpha. Then there were the soft moans Enar let out, muffled by Vieno's mouth against his, and Palani's own grunts as he fucked him deep, every thrust precise.

His hands found grip on Enar's legs, spreading them wider, folding them tighter until he had the perfect position to slam in. Enar's grunts sounded harder now, and Palani looked up to find Vieno cradling his head, no longer kissing him. The omega looked at Palani with love in his eyes, and they shared a moment, taking care of Enar.

The opening of the door interrupted their moment, but it was Lidon who stepped in, his face breaking open in a sexy smile when he spotted them. "Now that's how I like to come home," he said.

He kissed Vieno first, as he always did, a deference to his position as omega, which never failed to make Palani's insides go weak. He always took his time too, never satisfied with a short peck but ensuring Vieno's mouth was claimed.

Palani stopped thrusting to receive his own kiss. He loved how Lidon kissed, all possessive and dominant, simply taking what he wanted. What he deserved, somehow. And Palani gave freely, gladly, until he damn near ran out of breath.

He expected Lidon to come for Enar next, but he didn't. Instead he shedded his clothes. His cock was already hard when he stretched out next to them, putting his big hand on Enar's neck and pulling his mouth toward him. "I'm damn proud of you," he said before kissing him too.

Palani watched as the two alphas kissed, his stomach once again doing funny things. The kiss was hot, sure, but it went beyond that. What the four of them shared, what they were starting to build was extraordinary. It was so much more than sex, and watching Enar surrender to Lidon was the proof. He was so close to taking that final step.

Lidon broke off the kiss, then sat up and smacked Palani's ass. "Wreck him."

"I plan to," Palani said, grinning.

He'd been worried for a second Lidon would tell him to pull out, that he would claim the right to fuck Enar, but he'd seemed more than happy to let Palani do the honors this time. Lidon stretched out next to Enar on his back, and seconds later, Vieno all but dove on top of him, eager to get more kissing in, by the looks of it.

Palani had no trouble finding his rhythm back and let out a content moan as he sank his cock back deep inside that tight heat.

ENAR'S BODY was on fire but in the best way possible. The muscles in his legs twitched from being in the same position for a while, his hips burned from moving against Palani's thrusts to get him still deeper inside him, and his ass. Oh god, his ass. It throbbed and stung so deliciously that he didn't even have words to describe it.

Having Palani take him, it was...everything. Why had he waited this long? When Lidon fucked him, he chased the release, the domination, and the not having to think. It was being used and taken and not having a damn say in it. With Palani, it was pure erotic pleasure, Palani focusing on making it exquisite for Enar. He'd taken his time in prepping him, and his thrusts were deep and precise, aimed at bringing them both pleasure.

It was heaven.

And he hadn't been weird about it, hadn't so much as hesitated or given Enar a strange look. Vieno either. The omega had been so super sweet when Enar had come home from work, his eyes red-rimmed from working for almost twenty hours straight. He'd been so fucking tired but too wound up to sleep, and Vieno had taken one good look at him and had led him into the bedroom where he'd stripped and basically lowered himself onto Enar to ride him into an orgasm.

Palani's hand wrapped around Enar's slick cock with a delicious pressure that had him moaning. A few more jacks like that and he'd come again. But Palani kept his movements slow, bringing Enar to the brink without sending him over.

Enar growled, then brought his own hand to his cock, where Palani swatted it away. "Hands off. I got you, Doc."

"You need to..." Enar started, then moaned low and deep as Palani squeezed his crown hard enough to make Enar dance on the edge of his release a few seconds longer. His balls pulled up, but Palani squeezed again, the pain just enough to stave off the orgasm. Oh god. He would fucking kill him with this.

He closed his eyes, no longer able to concentrate.

"Uh-uh, eyes on me, Doc. I don't want you to forget who's fucking you," Palani said.

He opened them again, let out a frustrated grunt. As soon as he did, Palani's body stilled, his cock halfway inside him and his hand still on Enar's cock but without any pressure. What the hell was he doing?

"Nononono," he pleaded. "Don't stop! You have to..."

Palani looked at him, his brown eyes calm. "I have to *what*? Who's in charge here, Doc?"

Dammit. The beta had his number, didn't he? "You are," he admitted.

"So what did you want to tell me about what I have to do?"

"Nothing," he said. He sighed, a strange sense of calm filling him. "Nothing at all."

"Good."

Palani thrust back inside with a force that slammed the air out of Enar's lungs, at the same time putting the pressure back on his cock. Oh fuck, that was amazing.

A sound to his right made him turn his head. Vieno sent Lidon a sexy smile as he lowered himself onto the alpha's big cock, taking it in like it was nothing. His cum still lingered in there, Enar realized, and it was both erotic as fuck and deeply gratifying to know that Vieno would have both him and Lidon inside him. They shared him, like they all shared each other. For the first time, Enar felt like he did belong, like he formed an unmissable part of them.

"Doc, eyes on me," Palani told him, and Enar whipped his head back.

God, the beta was glorious when he acted like this, all sassy and mouthy and bossy as fuck. He played Enar like a finely tuned instrument, and damn if he didn't love it. In the past, it had always been a bit of a struggle to surrender to Lidon, but after this, he'd willingly surrender to Palani every single time. Somehow, he knew exactly what Enar needed.

The pressure in his balls built again, and he moaned as he tried to reach for his orgasm, wanting it so desperately. But as soon as he did, Palani's hand loosened its grip again, and his release danced away from him, always close but just out of reach. When would Palani let him come, dammit?

"You'll come when I think you're ready and not a second earlier," Palani told him, reading his mind, apparently. The beta's cheeky smirk shouldn't be so hella sexy, but it was. It made Enar's heart do a little jumpy thing he'd noticed more when he was around Palani.

"And when am I ready, oh great and all-knowing master?" he shot back at Palani, not willing to give him all the power.

The smirk widened. "You'll know it when I'll let you come."

Palani sped up, his thrusts pummeling Enar's hole, wrecking it in a way he'd never experienced before. He let go of any thought of coming anymore, too busy focusing on staying in the present and not losing himself to the sensation. His eyes drilled into Palani's, which darkened with desire as he let out a deep moan. His hand squeezed Enar's cock, then again and again.

Enar's eyes never left Palani's as the beta spasmed deep inside him, then flooded him with his fluids.

"Now it's your turn," Palani panted.

His hand gave one last jack on Enar's cock, and his orgasm slammed into him, leaving his vision white-spotted and his head reeling. His muscles jerked as a wave of pleasure barreled through him, radiating tingles through his entire body.

Palani dropped like a stone on top of him, and Enar's arms came around him, even as the man's cock still jerked inside him, releasing the last of his juices. Enar had spurted all over himself, and his cum was now being smeared all over his body by Palani, and he didn't care one bit because this sex had been filthy and bossy and absolutely fucking perfect.

His eyes drifted shut as his breathing slowed down, and seconds later, he was asleep.

14

His uncle's words had kept buzzing around in Lidon's head, ever since the visit a week ago. The story of his grandfather passing on his powers to Lidon sounded like science fiction, and yet...deep down, it felt true. Not with his mind but with his soul. He connected with this truth, acknowledging it deep inside his alpha.

He'd looked at family photo albums again, and lo and behold, his uncle had been right. His beta grandfather had been there all along, but his father had never identified him as such to Lidon. Both his beta and his omega granddaddy had died days after his grandfather, which made sense if they had been fated mates. Melloni had explained to Palani and Enar that the lifelines of fated mates were connected, that they usually could not survive without each other, especially not if they'd been together a long time.

But Lidon needed to learn more about that last statement his uncle had made.

"Grayson," he started on a Sunday afternoon as they all lounged in the cool shadows of the porch with a beer. "Have you ever heard of the legend of the True Alpha?"

Grayson looked up from the crossword puzzle he'd been doing on his phone. "I have, but who mentioned it to you?"

Something in the man's tone was sharp, sharper than Lidon had ever heard him speak.

"My uncle."

"Your uncle Leland, the younger brother of your father?" Grayson asked with that same sharpness.

"Yes, but why does that matter?"

"I'll explain in a sec, but just to verify. He's your oldest living male relative from your father's side, correct?"

"Yeah. My dad had younger sisters who got married, but only one brother, Leland."

"And he mentioned this to you? What did he say precisely?"

"He said I was the True Alpha, and when we asked what that meant, he said to ask you."

Grayson gasped. "He called you the True Alpha?"

"You're freaking me out, Grayson, and not in a good way," Palani commented from the swing where Enar lay cuddled up against him on one side and Vieno on the other.

"I'm sorry. I'm sorry." Grayson held up his hands. "It's just... Fuck, this is big. Okay, let me explain 'cause I see you're getting frustrated with me."

"You got that right," Lidon mumbled, taking another swig from his beer.

"The legend of the True Alpha is not common knowledge. It's passed on from storyteller to storyteller...and beyond that, only those who are related to the True Alpha can know about it. Your grandfather was a True Alpha, which is why your uncle knows. But he couldn't have told you unless he knew for certain you were a True Alpha because he would've brought dishonor on himself and his family."

"You'll need to explain what this whole True Alpha thing is, but if what you're saying is true, how do you know about it and why are you telling us?" Palani asked.

Grayson smiled. "Because I'm a storyteller...who heard the legend from my grandfather, another storyteller. And look around. Lucan is not here, and neither is anyone else but us: me, the storyteller, and the four of you, Lidon's family. By telling Lidon and mentioning me by name, his uncle has sanctioned me to tell you."

"What is the True Alpha?"

Grayson leaned forward. "Every generation, there is one alpha who will lead all shifters, one alpha with extraordinary powers who will bring about change for the good of our kind: the True Alpha. It's been like this for centuries, and there are stories of each True Alpha and what he has done for his kind. Your grandfather was the last True Alpha. None have been recorded in the generation after him, though some claimed to be. But a True Alpha can't be faked. The power is felt by everyone and can't be denied. It's confirmed by the alpha's oldest living male relative..."

"And you think that's me?" Lidon asked, too stunned to grasp what Grayson was saying.

"I know it's you. I've known from the moment I set foot inside the gates, from the second I met you. But I couldn't confirm it, couldn't even mention it, because that's not my task. But now that your uncle has, I'm at liberty to talk about it with you."

"I... I don't know what to say," Lidon stammered. He leaned back in his chair, his head a whirlwind of thoughts and emotions.

"What do you mean by powers?" Enar asked.

"Extraordinary senses," Grayson said.

Enar looked at Lidon. "That's true. Both your eyes and your hearing are exceptional, way beyond what's standard."

"A strong intuition, an innate sense of right and wrong."

"Look at the job you chose," Palani commented.

"Physical and mental strength combined with a high level of discipline."

He couldn't deny that one, Lidon thought.

Grayson cleared his throat. "No need to confirm this one but a high sexual libido is also one of the characteristics."

Vieno giggled. "We're not saying anything."

"A stronger alpha compulsion, which we've already seen evidence of."

Lidon swallowed. "If this is true, why didn't it manifest sooner? Why didn't my uncle tell me before?"

"Because it didn't manifest until you chose the old ways. As long as you were single, dedicated to your job, the power was there, but it was untapped, unfulfilled. Like a natural talent that hadn't been honed yet. Once you chose Vieno, Palani, and Enar, when you made the decision to rebuild the ranch and honor the pack traditions of your blood, your powers rose to the surface. Your uncle didn't tell you sooner because you would have rejected it, like your father did."

Lidon frowned. "My father was a True Alpha?"

"No, he wasn't. I meant to say he rejected the traditions of the bloodline he was a part of. He didn't want them, at least most of them, instead only allowing those traditions that he was comfortable with."

"Like the rule about not allowing strangers within the gates," Lidon said.

"Yes. Some pack traditions would have been too ingrained for him to ignore, or they must have seemed harmless to him. But the ones that truly mattered, like having multiple mates, he chose to diverge from."

"You do realize that if my father hadn't married my daddy, I wouldn't be sitting here?" Lidon asked Grayson.

Grayson smiled. "Of course, and I get this must be hard for you to hear, but your father weakened himself and his bloodline by letting go of his strength. A pack's strength is always in numbers, most notably in the numbers of the alpha leading it."

"Yet here we are," Palani remarked. "With, apparently, a True Alpha. What does that say?"

"It means nature finds a way. It means that whatever your grandfather did on the day you were born was strong enough to overcome your upbringing."

"What traditions are you talking about?" Enar asked. "Like, what specific things should Lidon do if he wanted to honor his bloodline or however you called it?"

"That's a question Lidon should ask. No offense. I can't show what he's not willing to see."

"I'm asking," Lidon said, and he hadn't realized how much he meant it until he spoke.

Grayson leaned forward. "Danger is coming, and you need to be ready. Build and grow your pack and name your beta, your second-in-command. Protect your pack above all, at all costs. Trust your instincts, your alpha. Claim what is yours and mark it. Lead, and others will follow you, alpha."

15

Palani was determined to get to the bottom of the mysterious fertility drug they suspected caused the genetic mutation, but due to everything going on in his life, he hadn't found the time yet. His work had kept him too busy.

He'd finished a series of four articles on the Anti Wolf Coalition, whose ideas were equally shocking as those of their counterpart, the Conservative Wolf Party. Palani thought them both fringe-style lunatics, but their popular appeal couldn't be denied. He still wondered how two parties with such extreme ideas amassed such support, and Franken was bewildered as well, so he'd asked Palani to investigate further. So far, he hadn't made much progress, but he'd figure it out.

He hadn't made any headway in his Excellon investigation either. Truth be told, the threat against him and Lucan had him rattled. He felt safe on the ranch with Bray and his men around, but even with a massive bodyguard called Adar shadowing him—he had Lidon to thank for that, as he insisted Palani be protected by one of Bray's men at all times

—he was apprehensive when he set foot outside the gates. Adar was built like a fucking tank, but even that didn't lift the sensation of being watched off Palani's system. It was like Lucan had described, an awareness of being tailed, even though he never saw anyone. He wouldn't let go of his investigation into Ryland, Excellon, and Lukos, but he'd damn well tread more carefully.

He had off today, so he made it his priority to determine if their theory about the fertility treatments was plausible and to find out who'd been behind this. He'd made calculations based on the data on the carriers of the gene. The drugs had to have been available for at least fifteen years, but most likely longer. No trial could ever last that long, so how had they managed it?

Rosalind and Abby McCain, two of the McCain sisters, had been more than willing to talk to him. "Anything to shed more light on what happened to our sons," Abby told Palani. She'd lost her son, Robert, the computer programmer, and her sister Rosalind had buried her son Lance, who'd been safe in the flower shop until that fateful delivery. Their third sister, Gillian, was Colton and Adam's mother, and Abby explained she was unable to speak to Palani as she struggled with her unfathomable loss. They were kind and sweet to Palani, their faces older than their age suggested, marked by the grief that hung around them like a cloak.

"You entered the trial first, correct?" Palani asked Abby. With their permission, he used their first names as the "Mrs. McCain" would get too confusing.

"Yes. We'd been married for five years, and when I still hadn't conceived, I sought treatment. A friend of my husband's was a doctor, and he'd heard of a successful trial, so I applied, and I got in."

"Do you remember the doctor's name?"

"Yes, of course. Dr. Morton Baig. He was young, only mid-thirties back then, but ambitious and smart. Very friendly too."

The name tickled Palani's brain, but he couldn't place him. He filed it away to do more research later. "And he worked in a hospital?"

Abby nodded. "Yes, he was on staff at the Women's Clinic with his own room and everything."

"The one with the wolf poster," Rosalind said, a smile on her face. "Remember that poster with the big gray wolf?"

Abby smiled as well. "Gosh, I'd forgotten, but yes. Every time you hung in that chair with your legs in the stirrups, you felt as if that wolf was watching everything!"

They giggled, and it warmed Palani's heart to see them smile, if only for a little bit.

"What did he tell you about the drugs?"

"It was called X23, and he explained they affected the embryo right after conception. His theory was that I could conceive, but that the embryos didn't survive that initial stage because they were too weak, so I kept having early miscarriages—if you can even call them that at that stage. He said these drugs would produce stronger embryos that would survive. And he turned out to be right."

"How long did it take for you to get pregnant?" Palani asked. "I'm sorry, these are quite personal questions."

"Mr. Hightower," Rosalind said.

"Call me Palani, please."

"You explained the Melloni gene to us and your reasoning that it was the likely cause of the depression that drove our sons to suicide. Your questions make me feel like you think the fertility drugs are the cause. Is that right?"

"Yes, that's what we suspect."

"We?" Rosalind asked.

"I have a friend, a doctor, who's helping me get to the bottom of this. We're also being aided by Dr. Melloni himself, the man who discovered the genetic mutation."

Abby and Rosalind found each other's hands, and Palani was struck by their strength. "I'm so sorry for dredging up emotions," he said. "I can't even imagine the grief you must be coping with."

Abby nodded. "I hope you'll never experience this," she told him. "But if we can do anything to prevent other mothers and fathers from losing their son, we'll do it. We'll answer any question you have, no matter how personal or intrusive."

She shot a quick look at Adar, who stood at a respectful distance. "Is this the reason you needed protection?" she asked. "Because of you investigating the gene?"

"No. It's because of another investigation, which angered some people. It's a precaution from my employer," Palani said.

The employer part was a little lie, though Franken had readily agreed with Palani's request to let Adar shadow him after Palani had explained his investigation into dirty cops had pissed off some people. But he couldn't burden these women with the details of his personal life and his work, not when they didn't need to know.

Abby took a deep breath, then dabbed her eyes with a tissue. "I got pregnant two months after taking the first shot. Dr. Baig said I would feel differently about a month after, and I did. I had...an increased sexual appetite, as he had predicted. Even during the pregnancy, my sex drive was strong."

Rosalind nodded. "When Abby got pregnant, Gillian and I wanted in on the trial as well. I'd been married three years, and I, too, struggled with getting pregnant. Gillian too. Dr. Baig accepted Gillian into the trial first, and she became pregnant within two months. A few months later, he contacted me to inform me a spot had opened for me, and three months later, I was pregnant with Lance."

"Did Dr. Baig guarantee you would get X23? Or did he mention you might get a placebo or another fertility drug?"

Abby and Rosalind shared a look. "No, he made it clear we'd be given X23 from the start," Abby said.

"That's strange because usually drug trials are double-blind, meaning both the doctor and the patient are unaware which drug will be administered, so the results can't be misreported by the patient," Palani explained.

"I didn't realize that," Rosalind said.

"Did you ever feel like something was off about the trial or about Dr. Baig? Or now, looking back and knowing this might be the cause, can you remember anything out of the ordinary? Anything he said or did?"

Abby said, "I always thought it was weird that he didn't track us during the pregnancy. He only did the initial exams and administered the shots, but once I was pregnant, my regular ob-gyn did the rest. And Dr. Baig stressed not to inform my regular doctor about the treatments, as it could influence how he treated me."

Palani nodded. It made sense for Baig to keep his distance once the women were pregnant, as not to arouse any suspicion. His warning not to inform their regular doctor fitted the profile as well of someone who wanted to cover his tracks.

"And you?" he asked Rosalind. "Anything strike you as odd?"

She looked pensive. "I remember contacting him after Fredric, my second, was born, because I was surprised he, too, was a male omega. Dr. Baig said that the drug might affect the embryo's sex and identity, so we had a higher chance of getting an omega."

"You used the drug for all your pregnancies, correct?" Palani asked Abby.

She looked at her hands, her cheeks growing red. "I wasn't supposed to tell anyone. Even my husband doesn't know. Only Rosalind and Gillian. After we had three omegas, my husband wanted me to stop with the drugs. But he wanted an alpha so badly, so I tried once more without him knowing. I contacted Dr. Baig and explained the situation, and he agreed to give me the drugs free of charge and outside the trial. I know it wasn't legal, but I—"

"I completely understand," Palani assured her. "No judgment from me. Did he come to your house?"

She shook her head. "No. He asked me to come to the research facility where the drug had been developed."

Palani leaned forward. This was interesting. "What can you tell me about that?"

"I went there as well," Rosalind said. "My husband wanted me to quit the drugs after our first, since he'd seen Abby only had omegas, but I went behind his back. I wanted more kids, you know?"

"It was small," Abby said. "And it had a super weird name. Do you remember what it was, Rose?"

Rosalind frowned. "Something with Mais...Mait...Wait, that's it. Maiitsoh."

"Maiitsoh?" Palani repeated. "Can you spell that for me?"

"M-a-i-i-t-s-o-h. I looked it up years later because a friend asked me about the drugs and Dr. Baig had left the hospital, but the facility was closed, and I couldn't even find that weird name online anymore. Like they had never existed."

"Baig left the hospital?" Palani asked.

Abby and Rosalind both nodded. "Yes. It was weird," Abby said. "One week he was there, and the next he was gone."

"We got a letter that he'd resigned," Rosalind said. "We suspected he'd been fired for..." Her voice trailed off, and her hand found Abby's arm, gripping it so hard her knuckles turned white.

"What's wrong?" Abby asked. "You turned all white."

"What if it was because of the drugs, the X23? You said the trial ran way too long, that it wasn't double-blind, that something was off about it. What if the hospital found out?"

"That's good thinking, Rosalind," Palani said. "I'll verify that with the hospital."

He asked them a barrage of other questions, and they answered each one. By the time he left, he had a whole stack of notes. He'd gotten answers, but in turn these had resulted in a ton of new questions.

Rosalind's suggestion to check with the hospital had been a good one, so Palani called the Women's Clinic first. It was the oldest hospital in the city, and they had digitalized all their archives two years ago, meaning Palani's request for information was an easy one. It helped that he was on good terms with a clerk in the archive office, a lovely elderly lady by the name of Kaila Kelley, who regularly called in tips for Palani.

"Dr. Baig," she said. "That's over twenty years ago. I even remember him. Handsome lad. Real ladies' man. I always figured he got fired for being a little too personal with a patient, you know?" She chuckled as her fingers clicked away on her keyboard.

"Huh, that's strange," Kaila said. "He's not on any patient records. He should be because I know damn well he treated patients, but he's not. There are no patient records attached to his name."

"Any chance you could get into his personnel file?" Palani asked.

"You know, I really shouldn't, but you and I both know I will. I can't stand it when something doesn't add up. Hold on a sec."

Her fingers rattled on the keyboard again.

"His file is blocked. I've never seen this before, but I can't access it."

"Do me a favor, would you, Kaila? Keep digging to see what you can find out? Something fishy is going on with this guy, and I need to find out what. I'll bring you a box of those expensive chocolates when I drop by next time, promise."

She laughed. "You got yourself a deal, kid. I'll call you when I have news."

So Baig had been wiped from the hospital records. Yeah, everything told Palani he was on the right track. But what about that research facility both Rosalind and Abby had been to, Maiitsoh? He had to check his notes again for the spelling. What kind of weird name was that, and more importantly, where had they gone?

He did a quick online check and found nothing. No company records, no proof a company with that name had ever existed. Had Rosalind gotten the name wrong? He tried a few variations in the spelling, but with the same result. What did that name mean anyway? He typed in "maiitsoh meaning," and a result popped up. It was the Navajo word for wolf.

Wolf.

Why would they name a research facility after the word

for wolf? What was up with people and their fascination for the wolf shifters? He came across it all the time recently. George York and the whole wolf party, Grayson and his wolf shifter stories, the whole pack thing with Lidon, and now this Maiitsoh company. And of course, there was the Anti Wolf Coalition, who was fed up with the whole wolf shifter fascination.

Something tickled his brain. He'd seen another wolf-related name, but where? He tried to dig it up from his brain but got nowhere. Still, it wouldn't let him go.

It wasn't till he drove through the gates of the ranch that it hit him where he'd seen it. He raced inside, opening his laptop while he hurried into the kitchen, where Vieno and Enar were making out, the smell of a roasted chicken in the air.

"Hey, baby," Vieno said, his face beaming and his lips swollen from Enar's kiss.

"Not now. Oh, fuck, what if I'm right?" Palani muttered. He plunked his laptop onto the kitchen table, his fingers flying over the keyboard.

Lukos. The company who made Excellon. Lukos was a different spelling for lycos, the Greek word for wolf. And suddenly he knew why he'd recognized the name of Dr. Baig.

"Palani, what's wrong?" Enar asked, letting go of Vieno and walking over to Palani.

Palani's heart stopped when he saw his suspicions confirmed. The website for Lukos showed the board of directors. Their medical advisor was an ob-gyn by the name of Dr. Morton Baig. That's why the name had sounded familiar when Rosalind and Abby had mentioned it because he *had* seen it before on the website of Lukos when he did research.

Dr. Baig now connected Lukos and Maiitsoh. But there had been another doctor who had worked at two companies, and that company possessed an unusual name as well. What if...?

His fingers flew over the keyboard again, Googling the meaning of Ulfur, the company Dr. Eastwood worked at before being employed by Lukos. What do you know? Úlfur was the Icelandic word for...wolf.

He gasped. It was all connected.

Lukos, Ulfur, and Maiitsoh were the same company, terminated and reborn to continue their work.

Lukos was behind the Melloni gene.

Oh god.

16

Palani carefully put the two cups of coffee in the car first, then walked back to get his messenger bag and placed it on the back seat. He'd already slipped behind the wheel when Enar called out to him, "Who says you're driving?"

Palani merely smiled and closed the door, waiting for Enar to get in on the passenger side. "When you stop looking like you're gonna keel over any minute, that's when you get to drive. Now shut up and drink your coffee."

Enar grumbled, but more out of habit than anything else, Palani thought. Enar still worked too hard, and it worried him. The man was rarely home, and when he was, he was exhausted. Two days ago, he'd fallen asleep during dinner, Palani catching him right before he would've face-planted into his plate. It wasn't healthy. Not for himself, but also not for their relationship. They barely had time to talk, even with everything that was happening. Something had to change, but Lidon seemed reluctant to bring it up.

Palani had hoped Enar moving in would help, that it would provide Enar with the affirmation he needed, but so far, it hadn't changed much. Aside from Enar working too much, everything was good between him and Palani, and he seemed to have grown closer to Vieno as well. It was Lidon he still struggled with. Palani wanted to smack their heads together at times, these two, who had such a hard time talking to each other. How could Enar talk to Palani but struggle with Lidon, who was so trustworthy and honorable? Didn't he realize the alpha wanted nothing more than to solve all his men's problems? Maybe he should play interference again with them, though he wasn't sure how to do it without either one of them blowing up at him for even trying.

"That's something, huh, that whole True Alpha story?" he reverted to a safer subject. "Had you ever heard of it before?" He checked in the mirror to make sure Adar was still behind him. Hmm, he appeared to have brought someone else with him, judging by the second man in the passenger seat. No problem for Palani, who still felt watched often.

"No. Then again, my family was one that lost the ability to shift early on, and my father was never big on the old ways, to use Uncle Leland's term."

"So what are your thoughts on that whole pack thing?" Palani asked, shooting a quick look sideways.

Enar looked pensive. "You can't deny Lidon's influence," he said. "I knew he could influence me, but I reasoned it was because I'm a weak alpha. The fact that he can compel Grayson is almost unbelievable. I wouldn't have believed it if I hadn't seen it with my own eyes."

"Same here. When Grayson first said he'd felt the power ripple through him as soon as he entered the gates of the ranch, I thought he was imagining things. I mean, the man is a writer, and his books are phenomenal, so I chalked it up to an overactive imagination."

Enar chuckled. "Yeah, right? But not when Lucan confirmed it, 'cause it was clear he wanted to deny it so badly but couldn't do anything else but tell the truth. He's not exactly a fan of his dad's theories." He was quiet for a bit, then added, "Do you sense it? The power they referred to when entering the gates?"

"I don't know. I always feel something when coming home, but I associated that with you guys, with being happy and good emotions."

Enar nodded. "Yeah."

"Did Lidon say anything to you about the True Alpha thing?" Palani asked.

"No, but we haven't really spoken since."

Big surprise there, Palani thought. You couldn't talk if you were never home. "What do you think?" he asked instead of voicing that thought.

"It sounds like science fiction, and yet I find myself believing it. I've seen how special Lidon is over the years, you know? His powers, his character... The legend of his grandfather's last shift and death on the day he was born always fascinated me. As a doctor, I'm inclined to say it's impossible that a newborn baby smiles or connects with his grandfather. And yet I want to believe it because it makes sense on a level I can't even explain."

Palani nodded. "I deal in facts, but there's a power in these stories that's so real that I can't reject them out of hand as legends or myths." He hesitated, then decided to add at least a little more. "Uncle Leland's stories about the old ways fascinated me, especially what he said about poly relationships, how inextricably linked the partners were. It helped me accept the reality of the four of us even more."

Enar sighed, a sad sigh that broke Palani's heart a little. "I guess," was the noncommittal answer.

He'd let it go for now and focus on the reason for their trip. After his discovery that Maiitsoh and Lukos were linked, they'd immediately wanted to contact Melloni, but the scientist had called Enar before Palani even had a chance to explain his whole theory to his men to set up an appointment for the next day.

"Melloni said he had news for us?" Palani asked, since he hadn't had the opportunity to ask Enar why Melloni had asked them to come down to his lab.

"Yes. He called me and said he had made a ground-breaking discovery that he didn't want to share over the phone."

"Did he hint at what that discovery was? Are we talking a cure?"

"He wouldn't say, but I doubt that. He wouldn't be able to find a cure until he knows for certain what the gene does and how it originated. My money is on him finding out more about either of those."

"Hmm. That makes sense."

"So what did you find out?" Enar asked.

"Do you mind waiting till we're at Melloni's? I have to tell him as well, so I might as well explain the whole thing once, since it's rather complicated."

"Sure. My brain is still struggling to wake up anyway," Enar said and yawned as if on cue.

"I'm glad you could make the time to take this trip," Palani couldn't resist saying.

Enar sighed. "Passive-aggressive jabs are beneath you, Palani. You have something to say to me, come right out and say so. You never mince your words, so why start now?"

"You're right. I'm sorry. I worry about you, you know."

Enar's head turned sideways. "You worry about me?" he repeated, the incredulity clear.

Palani made sure his voice was soft when he spoke again. "You work too hard, Doc. You're running yourself into the ground."

He shot a quick look to the side. Enar rubbed his temples with his thumbs. "I know. It's just that…"

He was silent for such a long time that Palani was about to say something when Enar finally spoke up again. "One reason is that the clinic I used to rent facilities from has canceled their contract with me, citing legal reasons. I'm now using another facility, but it's not as well maintained, and I'm wasting a lot of time cleaning and preparing for each procedure. And it's on the south side, so the commute is killing me."

Palani let that information sink in. "It seems like an inefficient use of your time if you're cleaning and sterilizing rooms," he said carefully. "Couldn't you hire someone to do that for you?"

"Sure, if I had the money. Most of my patients don't have insurance, and even if they did, I can't bill half the stuff I do because it's illegal."

Palani frowned. "But you sold your townhouse, right? When you moved in?"

"Yes. I used the money to update some of the equipment I need that the clinic doesn't have. I operate at a loss, Palani. I always have."

Palani had to admire the man's ethics and generosity, but at the same time, he recognized this wasn't a tenable strategy in the long term.

"You could ask—"

"I'm not asking Lidon for money," Enar interrupted him, his voice firm. "I never have, and I never will. He can't be anywhere near what I do because of his job, and I would never ask him to compromise himself. Besides, it's complicated enough between us without adding money to it."

"What do you mean, complicated?" Palani asked, shooting another look sideways. He did not like the expression on Enar's face. "You said one reason was that you had to move your practice. What's the other reason you've been working so much, Doc? I thought you guys had talked, that night when you came home late and you took a bath together, and then again on moving day, when you stayed behind?"

Again, it was quiet for a while before Enar answered. "We did, and he assured me he wants me there, but... You don't understand how hard it is for me to find my role under him. I wanted to give you the opportunity to see if you liked it better without me. If you would be happier without me."

A wave of anger rolled through Palani, so sharp and stinging it took his breath away for a second. It left him reeling, his heart hurting, and his head buzzing with fury. He clenched his teeth, grateful when he spotted an exit to a rest stop so he could get off the freeway and park the car. He set the transmission in P and shut off the engine before he spoke.

"I am so fucking angry with you for saying this that I can't even find the words right now. You'll have to give me a minute, okay?"

He unbuckled, then leaned forward to rub his head.

"Palani, I'm... I'm sorry, okay? I know it sounds lame, but I can't help feeling like I don't belong."

Palani opened the door and got out of the car, his body too restless to stay confined to such a small space anymore. Enar got out as well, his eyes tracking Palani's movements.

"I see how well you three connect, how in sync you are, and I can't help but wonder if—"

Palani closed the distance between them with a few long strides, then shoved Enar back with both hands. "Shut up."

Enar's hands came up in a lame-ass attempt to defend himself. "But I..."

Palani shoved him again. "Stop talking. Right fucking now. I have done nothing but listen to you, and now it's time for you to stop talking and listen for a change. You need to get your head out of your ass and fucking hear what I have to say."

Enar's eyes widened. "I just want to..."

Another hard shove. "God, you suck at following orders. I am so angry with you right now that trust me, you don't wanna mess with me. I could fucking knock you on your ass for what you said."

"It's how I feel!"

Palani's fist shot out and connected with Enar's jaw. It wasn't even that hard, but the crack stunned both of them into silence. Enar's hand flew to his jaw, where he rubbed the area where Palani's fist had clocked him, and he was staring at Palani with big eyes.

Palani's anger seeped out of him, leaving him with a sense of remorse he'd rarely experienced before. "I'm sorry," he said, his voice breaking. From the corner of his eye, he saw Adar stepping closer, and he signaled him everything was okay. Dammit, they'd gotten quite the show here.

"You hit me." Enar's voice was full of disbelief.

"I know. I was so angry... Are you okay? Did I break something?"

Enar shook his head, removing his hand from his jaw. "Your hand, maybe, but my jaw is stronger than a beta's fist."

Palani flexed his hand, which started to throb. Fuck, he was such an idiot.

"I have a cooling pack," Enar mumbled before opening the back door to grab something from his medical bag he always carried with him. He broke a cooling pack, starting the chemical process that would cool it down, then handed it to Palani.

"Your jaw," Palani protested.

"I told you, your hand hurts more than my face."

Palani took the pack hesitantly, then wrapped it around his hand. "I'm sorry," he said again.

"So you told me."

"No, please don't, Doc. Don't retreat into that closed-off mode you have. Not now."

"What choice do I have when you won't respect how I feel?"

"Because I don't believe for a second that's how you feel. It's what you think, what your scared self deep inside you is telling you because it's afraid to get hurt again, but it's not what you feel. It's the reaction to what you feel, your brain coming up with something to protect you from what it perceives as a threat."

Enar blinked, a myriad of emotions flashing across his face. "How would you know what I really feel?" he said, his voice constricted with emotion.

Palani stepped in close, his throbbing hand forgotten. "Because I feel the same way. I'm in love with you, Doc, and I'm pretty sure you feel the same way about me."

ENAR'S BREATH caught in his lungs as Palani's words reached deep inside him. Enar would've brushed them off as a joke, as something to make him feel better if he could, but Palani's face told him the beta was speaking the truth. Palani was in love with him. How the hell was that even possible?

"How can you love me?" he asked, his throat clenching so painfully it made him wince. "I'm—"

His words were cut off when Palani placed his index finger on Enar's lips. "Stop. You need to stop talking about yourself as if you're unlovable. You're not. The opposite, in fact. I find it very easy to love you."

He took his finger away and replaced it with his lips, treating Enar to a soft kiss that made him want to crawl into the beta's arms and never leave.

"I'm so confused," Enar said, leaning his forehead against Palani's.

"I know you are, but I'm not. We can figure it all out, but you have to stop running from it. From us."

"I'm scared," he admitted, and something inside him cracked when he spoke those words.

Palani kissed him again, his lips quieting Enar's tornado of emotions. "I get why. You've been deeply hurt in the past, rejected for who you were, and you've never experienced a sense of belonging. Now that you do, it scares the crap out of you."

"What if you—"

"Stop. You're doing it again. You're always expecting the worst, and I understand why, but you've got to stop. We are not happier without you. We are not in sync more with the three of us than with you. You saw what happened with Vieno when he was stressed out. You responded too. He needed you as much as he needed me and Lidon. You sensed him, didn't you?"

"I did... It's just... What if that's only because Vieno chose me but he made a mistake?"

"That's a lie your brain is telling you. You belong with us, Doc. You know you do. You're part of what makes us work, what makes us whole. You're a part of me."

The words grabbed him by his heart, shook him. How he wanted to believe this. Palani's hand wrapped around his neck. "Tell me the truth, Doc. Tell me what you feel. Not what your brain is trying to convince you of, but what you sense deep down in your heart."

With Palani's kind, strong eyes focused on his, Enar allowed himself to open up to his feelings. He'd been shoving them down for so long releasing them was like being swallowed whole by a sinkhole, like being swept away by a flash flood.

But Palani was his foundation, the thing that he could grab hold of, that would prevent him from being sucked under. He'd been there from the beginning, a man who looked deeper than Enar had wanted him to, but without ever making him feel threatened. He'd chipped away at his defenses, enticing Enar to lower them one by one, simply by being himself. And he'd never judged, not even once. Instead, he'd offered quiet acceptance and...love.

Palani loved him. And he loved him right back.

"I love you," he said, his voice filled with the wonder of the discovery. "I didn't realize it, I swear, but I love you."

Palani smiled, his breath teasing Enar's lips. "I knew you did, Doc, but I'm glad you told me. We'll figure it all out, I promise."

Enar let himself be held, putting his head on Palani's shoulder. "You really love me?" he asked.

"I do. Very much, in fact."

Enar tried to let it sink in, but it was hard to wrap his mind around. Had he ever felt this loved? Probably not. Lidon loved him, sure, but it was different. More like friends, still, even though their relationship had changed as well. And Lidon had known him for years, so it was different. Palani loving him, that was...magical. Enar had been himself with the beta, more than with anyone else, and Palani had still fallen in love with him. Maybe that meant... That thought was so big he hesitated to let it in. He'd have to think more about this, though Palani had been right about his thoughts deceiving him.

"How do I change the way I think about myself, about us?" he asked.

"You're the doctor. Tell me how that works."

Enar sighed, still wrapped in Palani's arms. That in itself was a miracle, that he'd feel so safe in the arms of a man who was so much smaller than himself.

"It's a neuro pattern, formed over time, like a deeply rooted cascade of thoughts. Each step triggers the next, like a well-oiled machine. In order to change that, you need to form a new thought habit, create a new pattern."

"And how do you do that when the brain is naturally resistant to a change of that magnitude?" Palani asked.

God, he excelled at asking the right questions, didn't he? He had such a sharp brain, phenomenal analytical skills. Enar kept being impressed by him.

"Rewards. The original pattern formed because it was rewarded in some way, so a new pattern can be formed if you have enough of a reward to do so."

"What would you like to be rewarded with, Doc? Tell me."

Enar stood there in the parking lot next to the freeway, held tightly by a man much smaller than him while his mind found a peace he'd rarely experienced before, his heart growing like it was about to burst out of his chest. All because of Palani. Somehow, he'd found the key to Enar's heart, to his emotions, to his real self.

"You," he said. "You're my reward. And Lidon and Vieno." He lifted his head and leaned back. "I want this. Us. I didn't realize how much until now, but I do. I've just been so scared to lose it again, to lose you...and Lidon and Vieno."

Palani's face broke open in a wide smile that made Enar stagger. His heart tripped, skipping a few beats before settling back in the rhythm.

"You're not gonna lose us, Doc. You're part of us. We'll work through whatever fears you have until you feel what we do, I promise."

He nodded, his eyes welling up. "Can you tell me you love me one more time?" he begged.

Palani grabbed his neck again, a gesture that never failed to make Enar feel safe. "As often as you want or need me to. I love you, Doc."

The last doubts drifted away when Palani kissed him until every corner of his mouth was claimed and loved and his whole body sung with pleasure and contentment.

17

After his little run-in with Enar in the parking lot, Palani had messaged Melloni to inform him they'd be half an hour late. He hated arriving late, but in this case, it had been worth it. Something had changed in Enar; he felt it. The strong hand Enar had put on his thigh as soon as they'd started driving again had been proof. Of course, he'd fallen asleep right after, but Palani didn't mind. The man needed his sleep, and Palani vowed he'd do a better job of taking care of Enar 'cause clearly the man sucked at that himself.

He woke him up when he'd parked the car at Melloni's research lab, Enar instantly awake as soon as Palani touched his shoulder.

"Damn, I fell asleep," Enar said, his voice all guilty.

Palani leaned in for a quick kiss. "It's all good, Doc. You needed it."

Enar grabbed his neck when he wanted to pull back, and Palani smiled against his mouth. "I'm not ready to let you go yet," Enar whispered.

He kissed Palani again, a slow kiss this time. Palani's

neck hurt from the weird angle, but he didn't care. He bit Enar's bottom lip and caught the little gasp that elicited. "Can't get enough of me?" he teased.

Enar rubbed his stubble against Palani's chin. "No. I need more."

"After," Palani promised. "First, we do this, and after, I'll let you do whatever you want."

"Palani... I'm not ready yet."

Palani wasn't sure how he knew what Enar was referring to, but he did. "I know. You set the pace, Doc. You'll tell them when you're ready."

Their foreheads leaning against each other, Enar's eyes expressed his gratitude. "I love you," he said.

What a rush it was to hear these words out of the man's mouth. "I love you too. Now let's go."

They needed a minute outside to cool off before going in, Enar especially since his cock was rock hard, he explained with a slight blush to a grinning Palani. When they walked in—waving at Adar, who took up position at the entrance while his companion, another bulky alpha named Isam, walked around the building—Palani was determined to keep his distance, but Enar reached for his hand, lacing their fingers.

"No secrets," he said. "I never want to feel like I need to hide what we are to each other."

That almost led to another make-out session against the wall, but they broke off their kiss quickly, both realizing this was not the time and place.

"Young love," Melloni greeted them with a smile.

"Excuse me?" Palani asked, certain he'd misheard.

Melloni pointed toward a large screen that showed security footage from around the building. "I've had some vandalism, so I had this system installed. I saw you arrive," he said, his eyes twinkling.

All right, then. No sense in denying, then, was there? Maybe he could use it to ask some questions? "Yes, we are," Palani said, tugging Enar toward him. "With two others, actually, another alpha and an omega."

Melloni's eyes widened. "A foursome? Excellent!"

"Excellent?" Enar repeated. "That's not what I expected you to say."

"Sit, sit," Melloni said, gesturing to a corner of his lab with comfy chairs. "Will you allow me to bring someone in to participate in our conversation?"

Palani and Enar shared a look. "Sure," Enar said. "An associate of yours?"

"In a way," Melloni answered. "Give me a minute."

He walked out of the lab into a dimly lit hallway and disappeared from sight.

"I didn't know he was working with anyone," Enar said.

"He's not. At least, not according to the information I found. He's not even part of an institute or research facility anymore. This building, this lab, it's his. He had a falling out with some leaders in the research community a few years back, and he went rogue," Palani said. He'd done his research into Melloni.

"Does he have a family? He's what, late fifties?"

"Sixty-one, according to his official bio. And I have no idea about his family, because it says nothing about his personal life...which makes sense because I don't think he wants to advertise he's a beta."

He stopped talking when Melloni walked back in, a slender man on his heels. An omega, Palani saw with surprise. What the hell?

"I'd like you to meet my son, Allessandro Melloni, Sando for short. He's my research assistant."

Palani and Enar both introduced themselves to the shy omega, who barely met their eyes. Palani wondered what the story was here. Melloni was sixty-one, but Sando couldn't be over twenty-five. That was a big age gap. Also, an omega in a role like this was highly unusual, especially in a complicated field like this. The love Melloni had for his son was obvious, though, as he looked at him with paternal pride.

"You said you had something to share with us?" Palani said as they'd all gotten seated again. Sando was sitting slightly behind his father, watching them with sharp eyes.

"Yes, yes," Melloni said. "But after that, you must tell me about the foursome."

Palani shot a quick look sideways to Enar. Why was Melloni so interested in their relationship? It was a bit odd. Disturbing, even? Still, he'd play along if it would help them get the info they wanted. "Sure," he said, then added, "We have a theory and some news we want to share with you."

"Oh, interesting. But let me start with what we found. Since the discovery of the gene, I've tried to find out its origins and what it does exactly. We have the symptoms from what carriers describe, but we haven't been able to pinpoint all of them, since some could be environmental or caused by effects of the gene. But last week, Sando and I made a breakthrough discovery."

He pointed toward a large computer monitor. "This is what the genetic sequence looks like compared to a normal omega. Or a noncarrier, I should say, since normal is a meaningless term."

He shared a look with his son that made Palani wonder all over again what the story was there. He refocused on the screen, which showed a schematic, but he had no clue what he was looking at.

"Can you spot the difference, Dr. Magnusson?" Melloni asked.

"Enar, please. And yes, it's right there, correct?" Enar pointed to a small piece in the middle. Even then, Palani didn't see it, but he trusted Enar to explain it if necessary afterward.

"Yes. As you can see the change is almost insignificant, yet it has far-reaching effects. Now, I've zoomed in on just that bit from a carrier and a noncarrier omega."

The screen changed into the same schematic, only on a far bigger scale, and now Palani noticed they were different, though it was more like a "point out the ten differences between these two drawings" game to him than an ability to distill any meaningful interpretation from the schematics.

"Now watch this," Melloni said, and a third schematic popped up on the screen. "What do you see?" he asked Enar.

"It's been a while for me since I had to interpret these, but that third one looks remarkably similar to..." Enar stopped, then squinted and moved in closer. "It's almost like... It looks like a mix between a carrier and a noncarrier. Like, it shares some details with each. What am I looking at?"

Melloni leaned forward in his chair and folded his hands. "Wolf. You're looking at the genetic sequence of a wolf."

A WOLF?

Enar got up to get a closer look at the screen. It had been

a decade since he'd done this in med school, but he'd always liked biology at this level and had excelled at it. There was no denying the similarities, and there could only be one conclusion. He felt like he stood at the edge of a cliff, about to jump in. If this were true... God, this was so big he didn't even know where to start.

"The Melloni carriers have wolf DNA in them?" Palani asked, his voice tight with emotion. Did he know more? Was this somehow linked to what he had discovered?

Melloni nodded. "Yes. Somehow their DNA has been mixed with wolf DNA to create this...this mix. It's been done deliberately, targeted at this specific sequence. It's too obvious to be a coincidence."

"Enar, it fits," Palani said, his voice a mix of excitement and fear. "It all fits together, the whole wolf thing. This is... god, what have we gotten ourselves into?"

"What do you mean?" Enar put his hands on Palani's shoulders to make him face him. "What did you discover?"

"We've discovered a few things of our own about how they gained access to the mothers, and maybe even why, and it ties in with this," Palani said. "I'll try to start at the beginning."

"We haven't been able to find out how they got access," Sando spoke up for the first time. "What did you find out?"

Enar reached for Palani's hand, linking their fingers together and drawing strength from that connection.

"There was a fertility drug called X23," Palani said, then explained what they had discovered about what at least the McCains had in common.

"I can't believe I missed this," Melloni said, his face excited and upset at the same time. "It's so blindingly obvious. I had discovered they all had mothers, but not this. How could I miss this?"

"You've focused on the biological aspect from the start. You discovered this gene, and you wanted to understand it, but you approached it from your own field. It's been about genes for you from the start, about this," Palani said, pointing at the monitor. "You've tried to understand the gene in your terms, your jargon. I came at it from a completely different angle. It's been about the people for me from the start, and that made me look at the whole problem differently."

"One thing doesn't add up, though. How could they run a trial for over a decade?" Melloni asked, his faced puzzled. "I'm doing the math, but we're talking about at least a fifteen-year period."

Palani nodded. "Yeah, we haven't figured that out yet, but we're also not certain how long they continued. Omegas don't get tested until they show symptoms, which means the youngest confirmed carriers are twenty years old. We could look at god knows how many more that are still too young to have been tested."

Melloni nodded. "That's something Sando has been working on, developing a test that's less expensive and faster."

"You said the fertility drug was linked to the wolf DNA," Sando said. "What did you mean by that?"

Palani took a deep breath. "This is where it gets truly shocking because I think the whole goal has been to bring wolf shifters back."

Enar couldn't hold back his gasp, and Palani squeezed his hand. "It sounds crazy, but hear me out. The company that made X23 was called Maiitsoh, which is the Navajo name for wolf. The McCain women remembered visiting the facility and seeing posters of wolves in the room. It's a small detail, but it all adds up. Their doctor was a man named Morton Baig, a young, ambitious doctor, who was later fired from the Women's Clinic for unknown reasons. Then we have Lukos, a young company that has launched three successful drugs targeted at omegas, two birth control meds and a heat suppressant."

Melloni nodded. "I've heard of them. Their success is rather astounding."

"Yes. On the board of directors of Lukos sits a doctor called Morton Baig, the very same doctor who gave the McCain women their infertility treatments. And Lukos's chief of research, Dr. Jerald Eastwood, worked at another company before Lukos, called Ulfur, where he registered more patents, all for drugs aimed at male omegas. Now get this. Lukos is the Greek word for wolf...and úlfur is the Icelandic. Maiitsoh, Ulfur, and Lukos, they're all the same company, reinvented to keep going. They're behind the Melloni gene, and I reckon their aim was to bring back wolf shifters."

Palani stopped, almost out of breath after his explanation.

"Holy fuck," Enar said, his head hurting with the implications of what Palani had said. "I can't even wrap my head around this."

"All their products are targeted at omegas, but not just omegas. They're all countering the effects of the gene: high fertility, excessive heats, antidepressants, you name it. It's as if Ulfur and Lukos are trying to fix the side effects of what X23 had done," Palani said.

Melloni shook his head slowly. "It's...it has to be true. I don't believe in coincidences like this. We'll need more proof, but I agree that your theory fits. My god, what have they done?"

"But if this is true, then who is trying to stop Lukos from

marketing their drugs?" Enar asked. Melloni and Sando looked at him with similar puzzled expressions, so he quickly explained. "One of Lukos's drugs is a birth control called Excellon. Data shows it's much more effective than the most commonly used birth control meds, but Palani discovered doctors have been bribed not to prescribe the drug."

"I still don't know who's behind that, but my latest working theory is that we're looking at high-level government involvement, since all three of Lukos's products seem to be targeted. Insurance companies or their competitors wouldn't be able to go that far. They lack the reach to block approval of a drug by the Drugs Agency," Palani added. "I started out thinking that Lukos was the good guy in this, the little company that got blocked by the big bad drug companies. Now, I don't know. Maybe there are no good guys in this story."

"There's us," Enar said, squeezing his hand. "We're the good guys here."

"Yeah, and we're paying the price," Palani mumbled.

Melloni's face tightened. "What happened?"

"The beta who gave Palani the tip about Excellon was threatened, as was Palani himself," Enar explained. Palani squeezed his hand again. "We don't know by whom yet, but they have to be connected to this. That's why we have security now...just a precaution. They're outside, since there was no need for them to come in."

"It almost sounds like science fiction," Melloni remarked.

Enar's head shot to the side as Palani's hand grabbed his in an iron grip. His eyes were wide open, and his mouth was dropped in a little O.

"What..." Enar started, then thought better of it. Something had clicked in Palani's brain again, which meant he needed a little time to work through it.

He shushed Melloni when the man cleared his throat in preparation to speak, and the scientist leaned back in his chair. It took thirty seconds before Palani spoke.

"It's not science fiction. It's very real. I think there's a dedicated group of people who wants to bring back the shifters: their societal structure, their laws, and even their DNA. It's all connected. Dammit, how big is this thing?"

Enar frowned. What was Palani talking about? Bringing back the shifter society, who would...? It hit him. "George York. The Wolf Party. You think they're connected."

Palani let go of his hand and got up from his chair. "They have to be. Don't you see? They all want the same thing. They want the shifters back. You said it yourself, Dr. Melloni, no one knows why our kind lost the ability to shift. They may have figured that out, or they're guessing, and they're trying to fix it. The Wolf Party is going after the political side, and Maiitsoh/Ulfur/Lukos is going after the omegas. Hell, George York even referenced Excellon when I interviewed him, and he knew about your work with omegas. The man knows, I'm telling you. It's all connected."

Enar's head dazzled with the implication of what Palani was suggesting, but he couldn't deny the connections. Then something struck him, and he frowned. "Dr. Melloni, has there been any follow-up research into the kids of the gene carriers?"

Melloni shook his head. "No. I did a research proposal, hoping to attract a resident, but few people want to be associated with omega research. It's not where the prestige and the money is, as we're all aware? Why are you asking?"

"If the goal of X23 was to somehow bring shifters back, they may not have failed with the gene carriers. They may not be able to shift, but what about their kids? What if the gene causes a genetic mutation in the second generation, allowing them to shift again?"

Melloni's lab was dead quiet as his words hung heavy in the room.

"We won't know until these kids are fourteen. That was the age shifters could first shift," Melloni finally said.

Enar and Palani looked at each other, and Enar knew they were thinking the same thing: Vieno. What would happen to Vieno when he got pregnant? What would happen to his child?

"Is it possible the children of the gene carriers could shift again?" Palani asked.

"I would have to do more research," Melloni said. "I can't possibly conclude this without more data."

Enar put his hand on the man's arm. "I understand that as a scientist, you're inclined to trust facts and scientific methods, but what does your gut say?"

Melloni shared a long look with his son before he answered. "My gut says it's possible. But if we consider how many unintended side effects their fertility treatment had, there's no saying what genetic mutations they have unwillingly triggered that will manifest generations down."

18

Vieno was singing along to the radio while baking cookies. Lidon loved his chocolate chip cookies, and they'd run out, so he would make a new batch. He loved taking care of his men like this, figuring out what made them feel loved and special and providing that.

Every morning, he got up early to make sure his men enjoyed a full breakfast before leaving for work, and they never failed to be appreciative. It was what he loved and what made him feel like he'd finally found his place in life.

After fixing them breakfast, he'd work on their lunches. He'd been preparing a lunch box for Palani to take to work for years, and ever since Palani had pointed out Enar sucked at taking care of himself, Vieno made one for Enar too. He prepared thick sandwiches, fresh fruit, and veggies, and always an extra snack or two. Enar loved nuts, he'd discovered, so he made sure he included a little container with mixed nuts. And the man loved his chocolate, so he got that too. Lidon had eyed the lunch boxes for a while now, Vieno noticed, so he figured he'd ask for one soon as well.

He loved doing things like that for his men, making sure

they were well fed and happy. So he made cookies for Lidon, knowing his alpha would come home tired today—he'd mentioned something about being home late because of a stakeout—and would love this show of care and affection. It wasn't like he minded, since he loved baking, and he'd made chocolate chip cookies so many times he didn't even need a recipe anymore.

Grayson had set up a desk in his bedroom, which sat close to the kitchen, and the click-clack-click of his keyboard was audible when there was a lull in the music. The man got completely immersed in his writing, Vieno had found out. You could call him, but he wouldn't answer, not until you were standing right next to him, and then you had to be careful not to scare the crap out of him. Lucan had scolded his dad to set timers, and ever since, Grayson popped up every two hours. He was unfailingly kind, the alpha, and Vieno hadn't felt unsafe in his presence even once.

Lucan was visiting a friend in town, escorted by his brother, much to his frustration, but Bray had insisted. Palani had much less trouble accepting Adar's presence. He'd had a short argument about it with Lidon, but he'd given in fast enough to make Vieno think he appreciated the safety the bulky alpha's presence brought.

No wonder, after the scary threat against him and Lucan. Even the little info Lidon had been willing to give about it to Vieno had been enough to make him worried sick, so he was happy with the protection Lidon had insisted on. Even more after what Palani had told him about the origins of the gene and his hunch the conspiracy was far bigger than they'd suspected.

Vieno's head had dazzled at the complexity of it all. He knew it was highly stereotypical not to worry his pretty little head over it, as some would say, but it suited him damn fine.

He'd had enough shit to last him a lifetime, and he didn't need to stress himself out by worrying over things he had no influence on. Simple matter of self-protection.

He had put two sheets of cookies in the oven when he felt something. It was like a cold band wrapped around his heart and tightened. He couldn't explain it, but something was happening. Something bad.

He turned off the music, his breath stuck in his lungs. What the hell was happening? Then he heard it, faint but unmistakable. Gunshots.

Oh god.

On instinct, he turned off the oven, then ran into the hallway, where Grayson stormed out, his face displaying the same worry as Vieno's.

"Did you—?"

"Come with me," Grayson interrupted him.

Vieno didn't hesitate but allowed the alpha to grab his hand and pull him with him. They ran through the house to the door that led to the cellar.

"Where are we—?"

"Do you trust me?" Grayson asked Vieno, his eyes burning into Vieno's. Vieno nodded. "Then please, follow me and don't ask questions."

Grayson opened the door and led him downstairs, not turning on the lights. Much to his surprise, Vieno's eyes adjusted to the dark quicker than he had expected. Grayson never stopped but led him toward a corner of the cellar where he reached under a mattress and lifted up a hatch. He let go of Vieno's hand and opened the hatch high enough so they could slip in. The mattress seemed attached to the hatch, as it rose up when Grayson pulled it open.

"Let's go," he said, and Vieno obeyed, instinctively knowing Grayson was protecting him.

They hurried down an old wooden stairway, and Grayson closed the hatch behind them, then locked it from the inside. The mattress would cover the entrance again, Vieno realized. The stairway led deeper underground than he'd thought possible. He hadn't even known it existed, but Lidon must have told Grayson at some point.

It was eerily quiet down here, the only sounds their ragged breaths. Grayson put a calming hand on his shoulder, and Vieno sensed something, like a peace that exuded from the alpha. Was he using his alpha powers to calm Vieno down? It sure felt like it, and fuck, he appreciated it.

Grayson waited till Vieno made eye contact with him, then let go of his shoulder to put his finger on his lips, indicating he wanted Vieno to be silent. Yeah, smart. Vieno wasn't sure what was happening, but Grayson's reaction showed he'd felt threatened as much as Vieno had, so lying low and staying silent seemed like their best option.

Vieno found a wooden bench, and he lowered himself, shivering as the tension of the situation hit him. What was happening? Who had fired a gun? It had to be the men who were after Lucan and Palani, right? Thank fuck they weren't home.

But what if...? His heart stopped at the thought. What if they got to Palani at his work? Or to Lidon and Enar? Vieno had never been so scared in his life, and it wasn't even for himself but for those he loved. His head jerked up to beg Grayson to call them, but he was already furiously texting on his phone. Vieno's own phone was in the kitchen, sadly, as he'd put it next to the stove to use it as a timer. He'd have to rely on Grayson doing the communicating for him. Of course, Lucan was in danger too, his son...and maybe Bray as well. Grayson had to be as worried as Vieno.

A strange sense of calm filled him. He loved them. Not

only Palani but Lidon and Enar too. He loved them with all his heart, his men. And they were meant to be together. Fate would not be so cruel as to bring them together and then rip them apart? No, impossible. He felt it, just like he'd known trouble had arrived, even before he'd heard the shots.

Grayson tapped him on his shoulder, holding out his cell for Vieno to read. He'd group texted Vieno's men, and Lidon had already responded he was okay and on his way. Then another text came in from Palani that he, too, was safe. Thank god. But what about Enar, Bray, and Lucan? He pointed toward Grayson and asked with his eyes. Grayson nodded and showed him another text, from Lucan this time.

"We're OK. Bray got urg call from men. Sit unsafe. stay where u r."

It took harrowing minutes before Enar's text came in that he was fine. Vieno let out his breath. At least everyone was okay, for now, though he didn't know about Jawon and Lidon's other cousins. Had they been at work today? He remembered something about them not coming in because of an urgent job elsewhere, but had that been today? He tried to recall if he'd seen them. No, there had been no trucks in front of the house, which meant they hadn't been there. Maybe that's why whoever had attacked had chosen today because they'd spotted fewer people there?

But Palani and Lucan hadn't been home either, and if they'd watched the house, they would've known that. Which mean they'd come after him. Or Grayson. Or both. With the two of them, they would've been able to pressure both Lidon and Palani into doing anything and Lucan as well. It was a perfect strategy...if they would succeed.

Vieno wasn't sure how long they sat there, quietly waiting in the dark, until Grayson looked up from his phone and spoke for the first time since they'd hidden here. "The situation is under control. We can go back upstairs."

Vieno wanted to get up, but something held him back. "Says who?"

"Bray. He got the all clear from his men."

Vieno shook his head. "No. We're staying here until Lidon gets here. I'm not trusting anyone else but him."

Grayson, who had already gotten up, sat back down. Vieno's eyes had gotten so used to the dark that he could make out the man's baffled expression. "What?" Vieno asked.

"You alpha compelled me," Grayson whispered.

Vieno shook his head. "Don't be ridiculous. I did no such thing."

"But you did. You said 'no, we're staying,' and I had no choice but to sit down."

Vieno gasped. "How is that possible? I'm an omega."

"I don't know, but it was Lidon's power I felt. It was less than when he compelled, but that's probably because he knows how to use it and put his full force behind it, but I'm telling you, Vieno, you used his alpha powers. I've never seen anything like this."

The wonder in his voice was unmistakable. "Have you... have you read about it? In legends?"

"I don't know if..."

Vieno had never heard the older alpha's voice so insecure and hesitant. What did the man know that he was reluctant to share?

"I could make you tell me," he said, teasing him to lighten the mood.

It worked as he was rewarded with a chuckle. "You're something special, Vieno," Grayson said. "I've watched you the last two weeks with growing admiration."

Vieno blushed, glad the alpha couldn't see it. "Why?"

"You're soft and strong at the same time. You bind your men together with love, and you take such good care of them that they would do anything for you, and at the same time you make them listen to you, and you insist that your place is at the center of their attention. It's mesmerizing. It makes me believe the legend could be true."

Vieno swallowed. Did he want to know what Grayson was referring to? "What legend?"

"The legend of the True Omega."

LIDON HAD BEEN HOLED up in a fake construction van for three hours with Sean, watching a house they suspected of being a meeting place for a local gang up to their eyeballs involved in drug traffic. It was slow and tedious work, sitting and not moving, not drawing any attention to themselves. You had to both disengage and stay alert, a skill Lidon had mastered but that Sean still struggled with.

He'd scolded his rookie partner already for drinking too much. Not alcohol, obviously, but coffee. Caffeine made you need to pee, and that was not a good thing when you couldn't leave the van, which Sean was discovering the hard way now. He'd been shifting in his seat for the last fifteen minutes, and Lidon expected a desperate request for permission to relieve himself any minute.

Then his heart stopped, his system flooding with a boost of adrenaline so strong he gasped. He felt him, sensed Vieno's fear thunder through him, almost heard his heart-beat go through the roof. Something was wrong with Vieno, something bad. His omega wasn't upset; he was deadly afraid. Oh god.

"Lidon, what's wrong?" Sean whispered with an urgency that alerted Lidon to the fact that he must've asked before. He hadn't been able to hear it over the roaring in his ears.

Lidon took out his phone, forcing himself to stay calm and use his brain. No, his instincts, he should use his instincts. He called up his alpha, allowed the power to fill him. Its message was clear. *Go home. Vieno needs you.*

"Lidon, you're scaring me..."

He whipped his head toward Sean. "I need to leave. I can't explain. Something is wrong with Vieno. Stay here and call in backup. Do not engage until backup is here, you got me?"

Sean nodded, fear showing on his face. "Your eyes..."

He didn't have time for this, not when Vieno needed him. "We'll talk later," Lidon snapped.

He put the cap low over his eyes and exited the van, dressed in the worker's coveralls and boots he'd donned as part of their cover. He walked until he turned the corner, and then he ran. He'd parked his own car a few blocks away in case he needed to make an escape when shit went wrong. He put his light on top of the roof and turned his siren on, something he rarely did because some criminals noted the license plate of cops' cars so they'd recognize them. But he had no choice. He needed to go home.

He was two minutes en route when his phone dinged. Grayson had sent him a text.

"Read message," he snapped to the voice control.

"Gunfire at ranch. Vieno and I are in hiding. No details yet. Contacting Bray now."

"Call Bray," he ordered.

"Calling Bray Whitefield... The number is engaged. Would you like to leave a message?"

"No. Call again."

"I'm sorry, what would you like me to do?"

Lidon bit back his anger. It wouldn't help him. Vieno was safe right now. That was the most important thing. He felt the omega's emotions settle a bit.

"Text Palani," he commanded.

"What would you like to say to Palani Hightower?"

"Unknown attack at ranch. No details yet. Go in hiding. Don't call. Will call you with details."

"Sending your message," his system cheerfully told him.

"Send message to Enar," he followed up, then sent him the exact same text.

"Call Bray," he tried again.

This time, he picked up and started talking immediately. "Five men, heavily armed, through the front gate. I have two men down, but the others are still engaging. My dad confirmed he has Vieno underground."

Thank fuck the man knew to skip the details. "You and your brother?" he asked.

"We're on our way back. Adar texted he has Palani safe."

Lidon let out a sigh of relief. "I'm on my way, fifteen minutes out. I'm coming in blazing."

"Has Enar checked in?" Bray asked.

Lidon checked his phone, and his stomach sank. "No. I texted him, but message shows unread. He may be in surgery."

"I'll have my man secure him."

"You have a man on him? How...? Never mind. Thank you. Now, go!"

He hung up, knowing Bray needed to focus on other things than explaining why he'd also shadowed Enar without Lidon knowing about it. And without informing Enar because he would've blown a gasket had he found out.

Thank fuck for Bray's initiative because at least now Lidon knew Enar would be safe.

But Vieno...oh god, his sweet omega. He'd calmed down somewhat, but his fear still pulsated through Lidon's veins, a constant call that his mate needed him. Grayson had been right about their connection. Lidon didn't understand it, but after this, he'd no longer doubt it.

The text that Enar was safe came a few minutes later, and Lidon breathed with relief. All his men were safe. For now.

He didn't drive up the main road but shut off his siren and light and took a back road that led to an east entrance on the property where he parked his car under some trees. One advantage of being a cop and a narcotics one at that was that he possessed a license to transport all kinds of guns in his car. A locked box in the trunk that only opened with his fingerprint held various guns, and he took out his .45. He was already armed with the standard issue Glock 17 all cops carried, and he'd tucked a much smaller .22 in an ankle holster because of the stakeout. He took his Colt M4 Carbine out and slung it over his shoulder with the strap. Bray had reported the attackers were heavily armed, so he'd better come well prepared.

He hated the coveralls he was wearing, but at least the work boots were well suited for the terrain, protecting his ankles and his feet from all kinds of branches, stones, and even a rattlesnake or two that jumped up as he flew past. He slowed down as he got closer to the house, then stopped behind a large bush to listen. It was quiet, no sounds other than what could be expected.

He checked his phone, which he'd put on silent. Bray had texted. "Sit rep that sit is under control but use caution. Source may be compromised."

His respect for the man jumped several grades. Thank fuck he'd hired someone who didn't take things at face value but was naturally suspicious.

"Dad still safe with V."

Okay, so Grayson and Vieno had stayed holed up. That was smart thinking. With care, Lidon moved forward till he reached the gate surrounding the house. It was too tall to climb without props, but Lidon knew two spots where a tree provided natural assistance. These were also the two spots he had cameras on at all times as well as motion sensors. That meant that if the attackers were still inside and had access to the security feed, they'd be able to see him coming. He had to risk it. Coming in through the front gate was not an option.

He hoisted himself up the tree, then inched over the large branch that brought him close to the top of the gate. He winced as he calculated the jump. If he shorted his jump, he'd end up with a spike through his... Yeah, he'd better estimate it right.

He took a deep breath, then launched himself from the branch over the gate, his gun strapped to his back. His hands found the pales of the gate on the other side, and he hung on with all his might to break his fall. He still hit the ground hard but bruises-hard, not break-every-bone-hard. As soon as he landed, he moved, not staying long enough to become a target.

Everything was still quiet. He'd go in through the back door, less chance of encountering anyone there. He took out his Glock, the rifle still strapped to his back. Gun drawn, he moved as he had done a million times, the movements as familiar to him as breathing.

He found the first body at the back door. Not one of Bray's men but an alpha completely dressed in black. He checked for pulse in his neck, even though the large pool of blood he carefully stepped around confirmed the man was dead. Still, he made sure. He didn't touch him other than that, not wanting to disturb the scene. Someone would investigate this, and he wasn't gonna walk into a trap that implicated himself.

The back door stood wide open, and Lidon went in. His heart rate was elevated but steady as he systemically swiped each room. The second body lay in the laundry room. This time, he didn't have to confirm as the man's face was blown away. Bray's men weren't joking around with their armor, he noted with satisfaction.

A soft squeak alerted him to someone else's presence. It could be one of Bray's men, since so far, he'd only found dead attackers. But how did he check? He hid behind the big dryer and checked his phone.

"All clear confirmed. Identify yourself to my men," Bray had texted.

Now it came down to how much he trusted the man. If he wanted to fuck Lidon over, this was the perfect way to do it. He could have Vieno, Palani, and Enar for all Lidon knew.

No, he couldn't. Because Lidon would know if Vieno was in that much danger. He checked in with him, not even sure how he could, but he felt Vieno's emotions steady though scared. But not in mortal danger, which meant he was still in hiding.

He remembered something else from that night with Grayson, something he'd been pondering in the back of his mind. He hadn't tried it since, but it was worth a shot, right? Especially in a situation like this. If these were Bray's men, they might be part of his pack, whether or not he'd realized it before.

He took up position behind the dryer, which would

protect him somewhat, then called out, allowing his alpha to roll through him like never before.

"This is Lidon Hayes, alpha of this house. Show yourself with your hands in the air!"

Muttered curses sounded, mixed in with footsteps and gasps of surprise.

"What the fuck?" someone said.

"I can't... How does he do that?"

Seconds later, three men appeared, their faces showing complete surprise. Lidon relaxed when he recognized them as Bray's men.

"What's the situation?" he called out to the leader, still not lowering his weapon.

"We took them out. Three dead, two wounded but secured. We lost one man, and one is wounded, but stable."

"You're sure there aren't more?"

The man who'd answered him nodded. "Yes. We finished a complete swipe of the house. I can't guarantee what's going on outside the gates, but inside is all clear."

Lidon lowered his gun. "Thank you."

"How the hell did you do that?" the man asked.

Lidon gave him a dismissive wave. "Not now. I have to find my mate."

"Bray's ETA is two minutes. Can he use the front gate?"

"Only if you're there to lead him in. And have him call up extras. I'll talk to him as soon as I've seen Vieno."

He hurried to the basement, then to the hatch. He knocked as he called out. "Vieno, it's me. Open up, sweetheart."

He heard the lock disengage from the inside and lifted the hatch. Grayson came out first, and then Vieno came up. Lidon pulled him up as soon as he'd reached him. "Oh my god, sweetheart..."

He held him, unable to find the words. It was like his heart was complete again now that he had him in his arms again.

"Lidon," Vieno cried out, and then he burst into tears, his body shaking with deep sobs.

Lidon lowered them onto the floor and held him, tucking Vieno against his chest and whispering sweet nothings until his omega had calmed down.

"I was so scared," Vieno sobbed.

"I know... Me too. I could sense your fear, and I was so worried about you."

"Palani and Enar?"

"They're on their way, and they're safe."

He carried him upstairs, needing him too much to even let him walk himself. Vieno wrapped his arms and legs around him and held on, his head on Lidon's shoulders.

Lidon had no idea who the men were who had attacked his home, but he would find out, and then he'd come up with a plan to protect what was his. What had happened today could never happen again, because he'd come too damn close to losing Vieno, and he could never go through that again. He was the alpha, dammit, and he would protect his pack at all costs.

19

They sat in stunned silence as they puzzled together what had gone down at the ranch that day. Enar had about gotten a heart attack when a tall alpha had burst into his exam room. "My apologies, sir, but you need to come with me right now."

Under other circumstances, he would've been furious at the interruption when he was with a patient, but since he'd experienced a deep sense of unease minutes before about Vieno, he'd known something was wrong. He should've listened to that feeling, should've known to take it seriously after what Grayson had shown them, but he'd convinced himself he was wrong, that he was imagining things.

They'd gone through all the details of what had happened with Bray's men who'd been at the ranch and had fought off the attackers. No one wanted Vieno there when they talked about the gory details, but he refused to leave Lidon, so Lidon wrapped him in a blanket and held him till he fell asleep. Only then did they start comparing notes.

It was scary shit, what had happened. Five heavily armed men had taken down the security guard at the main gate. They'd counted on that granting them access but hadn't planned on Lidon's system being more advanced than they could break in the short time before Bray's other men had been alerted. It resulted in a furious gunfight with the men gaining access by using gear to climb the gates.

Lidon and Bray both agreed they'd gotten lucky to lose only one of their men, though Enar knew it weighed heavily on Lidon's conscience he'd caused even one death. He'd accompanied Bray when he'd visited the man's mother to inform her because that's the kind of man he was. It had been the only time Vieno had let him go, and Palani and Enar had held him for the entire hour Lidon had been gone.

Lidon called in the cops after they'd all arrived back and he was one hundred percent sure the situation was contained. Two detectives came, then two more, as Lidon explained what happened. It led to a dicey situation where Lidon was forced to omit information about the threats on Palani and Enar, since he couldn't implicate himself. And that was nothing compared to him coming out to his colleagues about being in a foursome. But he'd done it, with a steady voice, unashamed to claim all three of them as his.

Enar watched them react, the judgment and derision on their faces. It was a look he was familiar with after many years. Still, it made him proud that Lidon took a stand for them. And he agreed with him calling in law enforcement, even though Palani had been against it. An attack of this scale wasn't something to keep quiet. That could only become ammunition that could be used against Lidon in the future.

The detectives, of course, had no clues on the identities of the attackers. Bray, bless him, had taken their fingerprints before the cops arrived, and taken pictures of their faces, clothes, and IDs. Enar trusted him, and the guy was street smart, which he appreciated.

"It's too early to say anything about their identities," Bray said, leaning back in his chair, rubbing his temples.

"See what you can find out. Hire an outside expert if necessary," Lidon said.

"Already on it. We need to talk about extra security, though. When you told me the situation, I hadn't expected this."

"Neither did I," Lidon said. "God, Bray, if I'd known, I would've…"

"I know. They caught us by surprise this time. Thank fuck they underestimated the security of the house itself."

"Your men did well," Palani said. "Don't count that out. In the end, it wasn't the gate that kept them out."

"True," Bray said. "And I'm grateful you brought Vieno to safety, Dad."

Grayson nodded. "I'm glad both you and Lidon showed me the hideout on the first day."

"I need to know more about how packs worked back then," Lidon said to Grayson, surprising Enar. "I used my alpha compulsion on Bray's men, and it worked, which meant they were part of my pack, as you call it. I need to understand how this works, what this means."

"We'll talk. I may not have all the answers, but I'm happy to think through it with you. For now, assume that anyone you invite within the gates as a guest is part of your pack."

Lidon looked pensive. "My dad always told me we shouldn't let strangers within the gates, not even delivery guys or whatever."

Grayson's face lit up. "Yes. That confirms my theory."

"Is it a geographical limit, you think?" Enar asked, trying

to figure out how it could work. "Like, it can't be bigger than a certain number of square feet?"

"No. I think it's the boundary the gates represent. As pack alpha, Lidon decides who to let into his pack, consciously or not. The gates represent that choice."

"So Jawon and the others, they're part of his pack as well?" Palani asked.

"I would think so, but, Lidon, you would know," Grayson answered.

"They are," Lidon said. The room was quiet as they all looked at him, his furrowed brows indicating he was working something out. "Bray, I want to widen the perimeter of the gate. I want a gate around the entire property as a first line of defense and then a second, stronger gate like we have now around the house, but also all the outbuildings. Cast a wider net because we may add some buildings. And we'll talk about extra security measures, like trip wires, sensors, and cameras."

Bray nodded. "Yes, alpha."

They spent another hour speculating on who was behind the attack, with Ryland the most likely candidate, according to Lidon, followed by whoever was trying to keep Excellon from becoming a success—Lucan's preferred theory. Then Palani suggested those two might be the same, and things got crazy. Enar had to agree with Palani that the timing of the attack, three days after they'd visited Melloni, was suspicious, and suggested it was a reaction to their investigation into Excellon, Lukos, and the gene. Enar's head was spinning by the time they went to bed, way past midnight.

"You were quiet," Palani remarked as they undressed in their bedroom.

Lidon had already laid Vieno down onto the bed and

crawled in next to him, and Enar watched him, the little one's face all sweet and innocent in his sleep as he lay curled up against his alpha. They'd come so close to losing him today, a thought that made it hard to breathe if he let it in.

He'd been such a fool, fighting the truth for so long. He did belong here with them. If anything, today had proven that because even the thought of losing Vieno made him feel like a part of his heart was being ripped out.

"Doc?" Palani said quietly, and Enar turned around to pull him close.

He inhaled him deeply, this man who had conquered a piece of his heart he knew he'd never get back. "I love you," he whispered. "God, I love you."

"I know you do, Doc. What's troubling you?"

Enar breathed a little easier now that he held Palani. "Today. I've never been so scared in my life."

Palani's arms around him tightened. "Me too. I was frantic."

Enar didn't know how he knew, but he did. He'd come too close to losing it all today, and if he had, he'd only have regrets to look back on, regrets that he hadn't had the balls to go all in, the courage to be himself. It was time to take the jump. He turned around, still holding Palani. "Lidon, could you wake Vieno? I have something I need to tell you."

Lidon nodded, not even questioning Enar's timing. "Wake up, sweetheart," he whispered, and when that didn't work, he rolled on top of Vieno and kissed him until the omega was moaning and rutting against him, clearly awake now.

"I promise you I'll give you what you need after, but Enar wants to say something first."

For a second, Enar hesitated about his timing. Would Vieno feel again like Enar had interrupted him? But Vieno turned around to face him, and there was such love and understanding in his eyes that Enar knew he sensed what this was about.

He climbed onto the bed, his nerves gone. These were his men, parts of his heart. They all looked at him as their hands reached out to touch him. Palani held his hand, Vieno's hand was on his foot, and Lidon's strong hand clamped down on his thigh.

"I've never felt like an alpha," he said, and with those first words, the last of his stress disappeared. "Deep down, I always thought there'd been some kind of mix-up at my birth, like I'd been accidentally assigned the wrong identity. I look like an alpha, but I'm not...and Palani has helped me come to terms with that. I think... No, I *know* I'm a beta inside."

Tears came as he had expected, and the three hands on him tightened, communicating the support he knew he had.

"I know I can't step outside of what society expects of me when I'm outside these gates, but when we're here, when we're home, inside our pack, I would love for you to consider me a beta."

Two seconds after he'd finished, Palani's arms were around him. "I'm so proud of you...*beta*. I love you, Doc. You know I do...just the way you are."

As soon as he let go, Vieno was on his lap, all sweet hugs and kisses. "You can be whoever you are," he whispered and kissed Enar till they ran out of breath.

Then Vieno let go, and Enar faced Lidon, who studied him with kind eyes. "I'm sorry it took you this long to be yourself and that I didn't see it sooner. I'm sorry for missing that, but I'm grateful Palani saw it."

"Is it...is it okay with you?"

"God, yes. All I want is for you to be happy and be with us, and I don't give a flying fuck in what identity that is."

Enar let himself fall over until his nose was pressed against Lidon's stomach. "Thank you, alpha."

Lidon's big hand came down on his head to rest there as Enar breathed him in, the smell of his alpha comforting him. Palani and Vieno reached out to him again, and for a few minutes, he lay there, surrounded by his men, feeling truly himself for the first time.

VIENO WANDERED AROUND THE HOUSE, restless. Palani and Enar were back at work, two days after the attack, much to Vieno's dismay. Bray had doubled the security on them, and the ranch itself was swarming with men as well. Bray had called in reinforcements from a friend's firm, Lidon had told Vieno.

Lucan and Grayson were visiting Lucan's youngest brother, Dane, who lived in a home since he required around-the-clock care. Dane had suffered severe oxygen shortage during birth and was mentally and physically handicapped as a result, Grayson had explained quietly. Vieno's eyes had welled up when Grayson had told him, and he loved that Lucan and his dad visited him at least twice a week.

Lidon had taken a few days off after the attack, and Vieno knew he was shaken by what had happened. He blamed himself for underestimating the danger to his men, Vieno had overheard him confess to Bray. Bray had assured him he'd had the same information as Lidon and that he had underestimated it as well.

Now, Lidon was in the gym room, trying to work some of

his anger and frustration out, Vieno supposed. And Vieno's mental to-do list was a mile long at least, but he didn't feel like doing anything. There was always something to clean, and his vegetable patch needed a little weeding, but he wasn't in the mood. He wanted to do something else to get rid of the pent-up energy in his body. It was a restless itch inside him that demanded to be scratched, to be satisfied and taken away.

He got like this sometimes, even when living with Palani, and he wasn't sure what caused it. Maybe it had something to do with stress? The attack had been damn scary, and he'd been worried sick about the safety of his men. And now, watching Lidon bend under his guilt took a toll on Vieno as well. He hated seeing him like that.

Palani processed through talking, and so did Enar, he'd come to understand. Those two got rid of their stress by talking it through with each other. But he was different, and so was Lidon. Previously, he would've waited till Palani was at work and then fucked himself raw with the biggest dildo in his box of toys, but...

He stopped in the middle of the hallway as a thought struck. He had access to something way, way better than a dildo. And he knew Lidon well enough to be sure that what he came up with would benefit them both. Plus, Lidon was in the gym room, which meant he'd smell all sweaty and masculine and...

Vieno turned around on his heels and hurried down the hall. The gym was a big room that Lidon had converted into a minigym with a weightlifting station, a treadmill, a stair master, and some other benches Vieno had no idea how to use. He smiled. Not for proper exercise anyway, but he bet they could get creative.

When he walked in, Lidon was toweling himself off,

shutting off the treadmill. He was only wearing running shorts, his body slick with perspiration. Vieno smelled him all the way at the door, and his cock grew hard. What was it about the scent of sweat that got to him?

"Hi, sweetheart," Lidon said, his face lighting up as he spotted Vieno, as it almost always did. Still, Vieno noticed the worry lines, the paleness of his face, and the tiredness in his eyes. Vieno locked the door behind him, since Bray and some of the other men used the gym as well, and he didn't intend to provide a show for them.

Lidon lifted his eyebrows, then smiled as Vieno stalked toward him. "You in a mood?" he teased.

Vieno nodded, unashamed. "I am. I have this itch inside me that needs to be scratched with a long, deep, hard fuck. Think you can oblige?"

Lidon's eyes darkened. "Always. I could use one myself."

Vieno whipped his shirt over his head and kicked off his flip-flops, then his shorts and underwear. "I volunteer as tribute."

He jumped into Lidon's arms, which caught him effortlessly, and wrapped his arms and legs around his alpha's body. Lidon's body was slick, and the sensation was perfect. Vieno brought his tongue to his neck and licked, moaned as the salty taste hit him. "Fuck, you smell and taste good. I could lick you all over."

He rubbed himself against Lidon, his own skin getting warm and damp from Lidon's. The alpha breathed in deeply, his chest pressing against Vieno's. "What's stopping you?" he asked, his timbre low. "God, I love it when you smell like me. I wanna get you dirty all over."

Vieno licked again, Lidon's neck, his shoulder, his ear. "What's stopping you?"

Lidon's laugh rumbled through him. "I love you, you little minx."

Vieno stilled as the words hit him. Did Lidon mean it or was it a spur-of-the-moment thing, to be taken in the context of what they were doing?

Lidon's hand grabbed his neck and forced his head back to make eye contact. "I didn't mean to blurt it out like that, but it's how I feel, how I've been feeling for a while."

"You do?" Vieno asked, breathless.

"Sweetheart, I fell for you the moment I met you. I didn't understand what and why, but my alpha knew. And now that I've come to know you with your big heart and your sweet character, the way you take such good care of us, your sense of humor, your drive to make our home into something special, not to mention how compatible we are in bed... God, I love you, Vieno. With all my heart."

Vieno's heart rose up inside him, like a sunflower that felt the warm rays of the sun, giving it life. "I love you, Lidon, my alpha. I feel like I was made for you... Palani and Enar, too, but you're my alpha, my protector. You complete me, somehow."

They stared at each other, two hearts finding peace in their roles in a bigger puzzle, a puzzle that contained four pieces. But he and Lidon, they were the bookends that kept them all together. The alpha and the omega, the beginning and the end.

"Sweetheart, you don't have to say anything right now, 'cause I don't want to pressure you, but would you consider not taking birth control on your next heat? I have this deep longing to have children with you."

"My next heat is less than three weeks away," Vieno reminded him. "That's pretty soon."

"If you want to wait, that's fine," Lidon said. "But I'm ready. I want nothing more than to see you carry my child."

Vieno's eyes, which had been cloudy from the moment Lidon had spoken his declaration of love, welled over. The dream he'd had since he'd been a little omega to one day find his big, strong alpha and have his children was here. Right now, in this moment, his dream had become real, so real he could touch it, feel it, smell it.

"Yes," he said through his tears. "God, yes, Lidon. I'll give you a son, an heir."

Lidon's eyes grew moist as well, Vieno noted with a soft feeling inside. His proud, strong alpha would make an amazing dad.

"I don't care if it's a boy or a girl, an alpha, beta, or omega. It'll be beautiful and perfect and loved. I can't wait to see you carry my child, sweetheart, your belly all swollen and round."

Vieno couldn't explain how he knew, but he did. There was a buzz in his head, a crackle of electricity in his system. A knowledge filled him with a certainty that left no room for doubts.

"It will be a son, Lidon. Your son. An alpha heir. He'll carry your name, and he'll bring change. He'll be the vessel that breaks the chains that hold us back from becoming who we truly are."

LIDON STARED AT VIENO. How...? He couldn't form words. It wasn't possible, what had just happened. Vieno couldn't know, and yet he did...and so did Lidon. His alpha confirmed the truth of Vieno's words. He would have an alpha heir, and that child would bring change. He had no idea how or why, but did it matter? All he cared about was his men, his pack.

"The next heat," he promised Vieno.

"The next heat," Vieno confirmed with the sweetest smile on his face.

Lidon put his hand on Vieno's belly. "You're gonna be so beautiful when you're pregnant. Even more beautiful than you already are."

Vieno melted against him. "I can't wait. It's gonna be a long eighteen days." Then his smile transformed into something slightly less ethereal and a lot more naughty. "Maybe we should practice in the meantime? You know, to make sure we get it right?"

Lidon laughed, a full-belly laugh that shook his body. "Another reason I love you, my little minx. Let's scratch that itch of yours, shall we?"

He walked them over to a bench and gently lowered Vieno onto it. He made short work of his running shorts and underwear, taking off his shoes and socks as well. Vieno lay waiting for him, his eyes trained on Lidon as he licked his lips in a gesture that made Lidon's cock even harder. Would he ever stop wanting him? Probably not, and he was fine with that.

He put up the backrest of the bench, which he always used for weight exercises, then sat down with his back against it and held out his arms to Vieno. "Come here, sweetheart. Sit yourself down onto me. Ride me."

Vieno didn't hesitate for a second, his face all eager as he climbed onto Lidon. Lidon held out his cock until Vieno had positioned himself, and his omega lowered himself. The sounds he made as he took Lidon in were the most intoxicating music Lidon had ever heard. Little whimpers and mewls, soft sighs of pleasure, followed by a deep moan as he was impaled all the way.

"Does that reach your itch?" he asked, his voice hoarse.

"Yes," Vieno whispered. He lifted himself up and lowered, letting out another moan. "Your alpha cock is exactly what I needed."

"Ride me," Lidon ordered. "Ride me until you're satisfied."

Vieno's eyes crossed before he did as Lidon had told him, fucking himself on Lidon's cock. He watched him pleasure himself, his eyes closed and a stream of noises falling from his lips. His hand found Vieno's right nipple, which he loved having pinched, Lidon remembered from his heat. Palani had twisted those little knobs until they had been red and aching, but Vieno had loved it.

Lidon tugged at the little bud, and Vieno's eyes flew open. "Oh!"

"You like that?" Lidon whispered with a satisfied smile. He repeated the move, and Vieno's body shuddered around him.

"Fuck, yes. More..."

The omega's skin was flushed, shiny from his own sweat mixed in with a good dose of Lidon's. He'd never looked more beautiful and healthy, every sign that he was struggling with his health gone.

Lidon teased his nipples, tugging and twisting, as Vieno used Lidon's cock to fill himself again and again till he fell apart before Lidon's eyes. Vieno came all over him without ever touching himself, and it filled Lidon with a deep satisfaction.

He held him as he came down from his high, the slender body trembling in his arms, Lidon's cock still buried deep inside him.

"I'm sorry," Vieno said.

Lidon pushed his head back. "For what?"

"You should come first. It was selfish of me."

"No, it wasn't. I loved watching you pleasure yourself on my cock. God, do you have any idea how sexy it is when you do that? This round was for you. The next is for me. Hang on, sweetheart, 'cause now it's my turn."

He thought about turning them on the bench, then decided he didn't have enough room to maneuver and rose, still buried to the hilt inside Vieno. He lowered them onto a thick floor mat. "Brace yourself," he warned Vieno.

He took his mouth first, wanting to taste him, feel him, breathe him in until all he felt was his omega. Their tongues met, Vieno letting him into his sweet mouth before pushing him out again, their tongues twisting and dancing around each other. Lidon closed his eyes, his senses almost over-loading.

He thrust in hard, catching Vieno's subsequent moan in his mouth. The sounds he made were intoxicating, fueling the desire already storming through his system. He bit Vieno's bottom lip as he thrust again, their slick bodies sliding against each other. They fit so perfectly, his lithe body taking Lidon's cock with ease, his channel slick and ready for Lidon to use.

He stretched out on top of him, buried his face in Vieno's neck, and went to town on his ass. He couldn't be subtle anymore, couldn't be precise. He needed to own him, claim him, mark him all over again so everyone would know he was theirs. Their omega.

Vieno cried out without holding back as he slammed in, his balls slapping against his flesh. "More, alpha, give me more..."

The friction on his cock was insane, Vieno's hole gripping him, squeezing him. God, he wanted to fill him up with his seed, breed him. The thought sent him over the edge, and he gave one final thrust and released balls deep inside him, his body jerking with the joy of his release.

Perfection.

Later that night, all his men were in bed, lazily kissing and making out as usual. Palani was driving Vieno insane with his kisses while Enar was observing with a sweet smile on his face, seemingly content to lie in Lidon's arms after he had fucked him into oblivion. It was something new, the closeness he experienced with his best friend.

"Palani, stop driving him mad," Lidon said with a laugh in his voice. "A few more minutes and he'll spontaneously combust."

Palani lifted his head, causing Vieno to whimper and seek friction for his weeping cock against the beta's body. Palani smiled with that sexy grin, which hit Lidon in his belly. "He's so fucking responsive," he said. "I love driving him crazy with want."

Lidon grinned, knowing all too well how true that statement was.

"He's so mean to me," Vieno complained, but his eyes sparkled this time. "He drives me insane, and then he refuses to fuck me."

"Poor you," Lidon said. "It's a hard life you have, my little horny omega."

Vieno's eyes lit up. "Will you fuck me?" he asked with eagerness.

Lidon reached out with his hand to fist Enar's cock, which was still hard as he'd come only once when Lidon fucked him. "I have a nice big cock for you right here," he said.

Vieno scrambled from under Palani, who protested loudly. "Hey, where do you think you're going?"

"You snooze, you lose," Lidon teased him, rising to his knees to kiss his omega until he trembled in his arms with want. Sure, he could get hard again in no time and fill him, but he loved seeing Enar take him. And Palani could take it, this teasing and rubbing. He'd get his fill somehow, since he was equally happy being fucked as he was doing the fucking.

"Here you go, sweetheart," he said, kissing him one last time before lifting him up and positioning him above Enar's cock.

Vieno reached backward to lower himself, and they all watched in wonder as that gorgeous ass took in the fat cock underneath him.

"Ah..." Vieno sighed. "That feels so good."

"I was robbed," Palani declared, then rolled over to Lidon's arms and sought a spot there. "I guess I'll have to be content watching."

Enar held Vieno's hips as he rose up to surge in deeply, making him moan loudly.

"God, he's so beautiful like this," Lidon sighed, his cock hardening as Vieno lost himself. What a sight it was, that slender body on top of that much bigger one, though the expression of sheer lust on both their faces was identical.

"They both are," Palani said, the love palpable in his voice.

Enar's strong muscles flexed as he sped up, fucking Vieno with deep, hard strokes.

"True," Lidon admitted.

They both watched in silence, enjoying the sight of their mates losing themselves in each other.

"So, a baby, huh?" Palani said.

"Vieno told you?"

"Mmm. He can't wait, you know."

"Should I have asked you? Enar too, maybe?" Lidon wondered.

Palani rolled onto his stomach, seeking Lidon's eyes. "No. This was between you and Vieno, between our alpha and our omega. Besides, you know we want this too."

"You do?"

"Vieno becoming a daddy? God, yes. It's what he was born to do. And you'll make a good father, Lidon."

"I'm sorry that you can't..." He stopped talking when Palani put a finger on his lips.

"No, don't apologize. I don't regret anything. Seeing him like this, knowing he can fulfill his lifelong dream of becoming a daddy, it's all I ever wanted for him. I'm right where I want to be, happier than I ever thought possible."

Lidon studied Palani as behind them, Enar grunted and came, causing Vieno to let go as well. There was not a trace of disappointment or resentment on the beta's face. All Lidon saw was love, and it filled him with a deep desire to do what he could to be worthy of the sacrifices Palani had made.

"About you feeling robbed," he said, smiling when Palani's eyes lit up. "Any chance you'll settle for me instead of Vieno?"

Palani rolled on top of him, already spreading his legs. "Anytime, alpha."

20

Enar felt guilty as shit. He should know because he was quite familiar with that particular emotion. For fuck's sake, his father had excelled at making him feel guilty. Guilty for not being enough of an alpha. Guilty for not being the kind of doctor he should have been. Guilty for not marrying an omega and continuing the family line. The list of things he'd been made to feel guilty about over the years was long.

Today, he could add another one to that list. He should've contacted his brother Sven as soon as he'd found out about the Melloni gene, except he hadn't. Then he should have done it when he and Palani had found out about the likelihood of it being related to fertility drugs, but again, he hadn't.

He knew exactly why. Sven still lived at home, with Lars and their father. Enar's father. Which was the whole reason why he'd avoided this particular confrontation for such a long time. He'd rather have his fingernails pulled than go back to the man who had made his life a living hell. But he had to. For Sven's sake, he had to. And after the attack, after finding the courage to come out to his men, he'd given himself a swift kick in the ass and told himself to man the fuck up.

He'd called Sven the day before to ask him if he could stop by to talk. Sven had been surprised—no wonder, since they rarely talked. Another source of guilt. Enar had left home to go to university when Lars had been four years old and Sven only two. He'd been back as little as possible, and he hadn't returned home in... He did a quick calculation in his head. His mother's funeral had been seven years ago, so that was it. Seven years ago.

At first, he'd attempted to stay in touch with Lars and Sven, but it had gotten harder. Between how busy he'd gotten with work and the bad memories even contact with his brothers stirred up, he'd sort of let them go.

No, not sort of. He *had* let them go. It had been easier than dealing with the pain. And over time, the guilt about it had faded until he barely remembered he had brothers. Now, the guilt was back in full swing, exacerbated by Sven's not-too-friendly attitude on the phone. Enar couldn't blame him, but that didn't make it easier.

At least Sven had assured him their father would be out of the house. He was on a business trip for a few days, so Lars and Sven were by themselves. Much to his shame, Enar didn't even know what they did, if they were in school or worked. Lars was twenty-two, so he could have a college degree by now.

He pulled up in front of the house and parked in the driveway that still looked familiar, even after all these years. The flowers his mother had always planted along the wall were gone, though, replaced by bushes that looked well maintained. The whole garden looked like someone spent a ton of time keeping it up. Definitely not his father because he'd hated getting his hands dirty. No, it had always been his mother who had a green thumb.

As soon as he'd rung the bell, the door was opened. God, Lars had gotten so big. He was a man now. A man who gave him a look that was anything but friendly. He didn't say a word as he opened the door wide and let Enar step inside where Sven stood waiting.

As soon as Lars closed the door behind him, a waft of Sven's scent drifted on the air, and Enar smelled him. He knew, right then and there. Sven was weeks away from his first heat at most, probably less.

But...wait. Why the hell could he smell him? Sven was his brother, and family members weren't supposed to be able to smell each other's heat, and it wasn't supposed to affect him. Was that the gene that had changed that too? And dammit, Enar was still taking suppressants, which meant anyone else would smell him even stronger. He had to have the gene. There was no other explanation. Dammit all to hell and back.

"What the fuck do you want?" Lars said, taking position next to Sven.

"Lars," Sven said, turning away from Enar to shoot his brother a pleading look.

"Can we sit somewhere? I have something I need to discuss with Sven," Enar said after clearing his throat. God, this was hard. Delivering bad news to patients always sucked, but even more if said patient was your brother.

"And, Sven, what I need to tell you is of a rather sensitive nature, so it's up to you if you want Lars to be present or not."

"I'm not leaving him alone with you," Lars snapped at him.

Enar crossed his arms and allowed his alpha to shine through for the first time. "That's not up to you."

Sven put a calming hand on Lars's arm. "It's okay. I want you there. You know I do."

They sat at the kitchen table, the kitchen looking as immaculate and pristine as the rest of the house.

"How have you guys been?" Enar asked.

"Really? After years of no contact, that's what you wanna ask us? Fuck you, asshole."

Lars's eyes spewed fire, his body tight with anger. Sven once again put a hand on his arm, but he didn't say anything.

Enar rubbed his temples. "I deserved that," he admitted. "And the rest of the anger you obviously have stored up for me. I deserve it all and more. But you need to put that anger aside for a few minutes and listen to me because I need to tell you something important."

Lars's eyes lost little of their derision. "I can't imagine there's anything you have to tell that we're interested in hearing."

"Again, I get that, and I deserve it, but this is more important than your anger, okay? This is about Sven and something I need to ask him and tell him that could save his life."

Lars's expression changed at that. "What are you talking about?"

"Lars, can you listen to him, please? I want to hear what he has to say, so can you stop being angry for a little bit? For me?" Sven pleaded with him.

Something transpired between his brothers that Enar wasn't privy to, but Lars turned toward him and said, "I'll listen."

"Thank you. Can I ask you some questions first, Sven? They're rather personal. Medical."

Sven nodded.

"Have you had your first heat yet?" Enar asked.

Sven blushed. "No. I'm a late bloomer, our doctor said. He doesn't know what's causing the delay."

"How is your health otherwise?"

Sven looked to Lars before answering. "Good, I guess. I don't seem to have a lot of energy lately, but other than that, I'm okay."

"And emotionally? Do you ever have bouts of depression?"

Sven seemed to shrink before his very eyes.

"Why do you ask?" Lars asked, still not exactly friendly but not outright hostile anymore.

"Has he been depressed?" Enar asked again. "Are you, Sven?"

Sven nodded. "Yes. The last two years have been hard, and lately it's been even worse."

His answer hung heavy in the air.

"You asked all this as if you knew it already. What do you know that we don't?" Lars said.

"I'm almost certain you have a condition called the Melloni gene, a genetic mutation that's popping up more and more. There's much we don't know about it yet, but we do know it causes the omega to have...excessive heats with stronger sexual cravings than normal."

Enar pushed down his unease at discussing this topic with his brothers.

"It also seems to be correlated to depression, but we're not sure if it's the gene causing that or the consequences of having the gene."

Sven's face had turned white, and Lars wasn't looking

too peachy either. "Can...Can you do anything about it? Are there meds? A cure?" he asked.

"I'm sorry, no."

He let that sink in, allowing both of his brothers to digest the information. "Heat suppressants relieve some of it, but not all. What we know is that knotting helps. Having an alpha help you through it. Are you by any chance seeing anyone?"

His brothers shared another heavy look Enar couldn't place.

"No," Sven said. "And wouldn't using an alpha result in pregnancy?"

"Normally, yes, but I can help you with that." He sighed, knowing the hardest part was still to come. "There's more, though. Part of the effects of this gene is that you're...highly attractive. Alphas and even betas won't be able to resist your smell and will want to have sex with you. Even if they normally would never want to. You'll be literally irresistible during your heat."

Sven's eyes filled with tears. "God, I'm so screwed. What do I do?"

Lars took his hand. "We'll figure it out, okay? Do you need to test him?" he asked Enar.

"I do, but the results won't be in before his first heat starts, so he needs to start making arrangements now to be sequestered."

Lars frowned. "How do you know his first heat is coming?"

"Can't you smell him?" Enar asked, surprised. "I smelled him as soon as I walked in, and I take daily suppressants because of my patients. He's weeks away at most, probably less."

"Of course, I can't smell him," Lars pointed out. "You know family members aren't affected by heats."

"Not normally, but this gene changes everything. I hate to say it, but I can smell him, even with the suppressants I take. I think it's more that you're used to his smell because you live with him, but once his heat starts, it may affect you too, brothers or not."

Enar thought of Palani, who had become somewhat desensitized to Vieno's smell but still got super horny during his heats. There was no predicting what would happen once Sven's heat started, how it would affect Lars. It was weird and somewhat disconcerting to even talk about this, but they had to face the truth.

"Maybe that explains..." Sven said, then suddenly stopped talking.

Lars's eyes widened, and his jaw set. "It's no excuse."

"Explain what? What am I missing?" Enar asked. The words hadn't left his mouth when he realized the answer.

Oh god.

Oh no.

Lars wasn't the only man in the same house as Sven, and he wasn't even an alpha. But someone else was.

"Has...has Dad's behavior toward you changed?" he asked with a sinking sensation in his stomach.

"He tried to kiss him!" Lars exploded. "He fucking groped him, even after he said no."

Enar buried his head in his hands. As much as he hated his father, he couldn't blame him for this, not really. He'd heard Palani's story of how even a straight, mated man had been unable to resist his employee's smell, how he would've raped him had the omega not outsmarted him. What a god-awful mess. The tragedies this damn gene caused were unbelievable.

"You need to leave here immediately," he said, raising his head. "Trust me when I say that once your heat starts, he won't be able to keep his hands off you. You're not safe here."

"But where do we go?" Lars asked. "I've been saving up to move out, but I don't have enough yet."

"Not you. Just Sven. I can take him to my place. Well, my new home." This whole conversation just kept getting better, didn't it? "I've moved in with Lidon, remember him? My alpha cop best friend?"

Sven nodded. "Will he...help me?" he asked, his lip trembling with fear.

"No. God, no. He's...we're...Dammit. Sorry, this is hard to explain. He's mated to an omega, Vieno. And together with a beta, we're a foursome. We're together. With four men."

For the first time, Enar saw something resembling respect on Lars's face. "That sounds cool, but what about Sven? Who will help him through his heat?"

Enar sighed. "I don't know, but I have a few weeks to find a solution. Lidon's ranch is secluded, and we can keep him safe there."

"I'm not going without Lars," Sven said.

Enar's mouth dropped open a little, but Lars spoke before he could say anything. "It's okay. I'll figure out a way for us to find a place together after your heat, but you need to stay safe until then. Enar's a doctor. He can take care of you in ways that I can't."

He reminded Enar so much of Palani in that instant that his heart warmed despite his brother's prickly attitude.

Sven crossed his arms, and a stubborn expression painted his face. "I don't care. I'm not leaving without you. I don't even know you—no offense," he added to Enar.

"None taken." Enar frowned. There was a dynamic here he couldn't quite place, but he lacked the time to figure it out now. "Lars can come. We have enough space at the ranch. Start packing everything you need to bring, and I'll send someone over with a pickup truck to collect you in a few hours, okay?"

LIDON WALKED into the kitchen to find a strange omega sitting at the kitchen table, a mug of steaming tea in front of him and Vieno across from him with a sweet but serious expression on his face as he listened to what the omega was saying.

"I have no idea what I'm even doing here," he said. "Are you sure it's okay with your alpha that I'm here? Enar said so, but he had to work today, and I don't want to be a burden."

"It's fine," Vieno said. "Here he comes."

Vieno got up from the table and gave Lidon one of his hugs that showed how much he needed to be touched after spending a long day apart. He did it with all of them, somehow needing to reconnect when he hadn't been close to them for a while.

"Hi, sweetheart," Lidon said, then kissed him until his taste had invaded his mouth. "Did you miss me?"

He loved how Vieno melted against him, all pliant and soft, seeking his touch. "Always," was the soft answer, and Lidon's heart skipped a step.

He kissed Vieno again, letting his hands roam his body, before reminding himself of the stranger in his house. Not that he didn't know who it was, as Enar had called him. With regret, he let Vieno go and stepped forward to greet Enar's youngest brother.

"You must be Sven," he said, extending his hand.

"Yes, alpha," Sven said, rising from his seat and taking his hand.

"The last time I saw you, you were a toddler, so it's been a while," Lidon said friendly.

"I don't remember you at all," Sven said, then bit his lip.

Lidon sent him a smile. "That doesn't surprise me. As I said, you were still young, and Enar was usually over at my place. He loved it here on the ranch."

As horrific as the attack on the ranch had been, the one good thing that had come out of it was Enar's decision to come out. He could already tell the difference, as the man was much more relaxed. He'd lowered his defenses, and Lidon loved seeing him find his place in their foursome.

Lidon looked up from his musings when a beta walked in. "Lars," Lidon greeted him. "It's good to see you."

He extended his hand, raising an eyebrow when Lars hesitated just a tad too long before taking it. Enar had mentioned his brothers having some animosity toward him, but apparently it extended to him as well. Interesting. Was it because he was an alpha? That wasn't unthinkable, as Enar's father wasn't exactly a role model of how an alpha should behave.

"Thank you for taking us in," Lars said. Lidon held his hand, challenging him with his eyes until he added, "Alpha."

The beta might have grounds to mistrust alphas, but he would have to respect Lidon, he thought. That shit would not fly here, not with everything that was going down. He'd better set Lars straight on that.

"Grab a seat," he told him, and after a slight hesitation and a look he shared with Sven, the beta obeyed.

Lidon didn't need to ask Vieno for a coffee. As soon as he sat down, his omega started the fancy coffee machine for him. He waited till his espresso was done. "Thank you, sweetheart," he said, pulling Vieno in for another kiss.

God, he felt in his system that he'd gotten up early this morning due to a raid they'd planned at five. Vieno had still been asleep, which meant Lidon hadn't gotten his usual morning fuck with any of his men, and his cock let him know it. A high sexual libido, Grayson had mentioned as one of the aspects of the True Alpha. Well, he'd nailed that one. Vieno sent him a cheeky grin, letting him know he'd picked up on Lidon's needs.

"Later," Lidon promised him, his mouth pulling up in a smile.

"Can't wait," was the quick answer.

Lidon sipped his espresso, training his eyes on the two Magnusson brothers. "What do you do in life, Lars?" he asked.

"I just finished up my degree in agronomy."

"Agronomy?" Lidon said, leaning forward. "What do you plan to do with it?"

"I've already sent out a ton of applications, but jobs are hard to find in that area."

The animosity Lars had shown earlier had disappeared, and in its place, a touch of hopelessness had filled his face and voice.

"I can imagine in this economic climate," Lidon said.

"I'm trying to save up enough to get us out of the house," Lars said, then clamped his mouth shut.

Enar had mentioned something about an incident between his father and Sven, and Lidon had no trouble filling in the blanks, not after what he'd heard and experienced himself about the gene. "Well, you're here now, so you got that part covered."

Lars shrugged. "Until after Sven's heat, when you kick us out."

Lidon frowned. "Why would I do that?"

"We can't stay here." Lars's voice was a mix of resignation and the hopelessness he'd shown before.

"Are you willing to work?" Lidon asked, an idea forming in his mind.

"Here?" The surprise was audible.

"Yes. I wouldn't kick you out anyway, as you put it, but you can make yourself useful and earn your keep."

Lars looked around in the kitchen with puzzlement. "Doing what? No offense, but I'm not an omega."

"I wouldn't mind helping with cleaning and cooking," Sven spoke up.

"That's good because Vieno could use the help." His mate's eyes widened with indignation, and Lidon pulled his wrist until his omega gave in and let himself be pulled on his lap. "You work too hard, sweetheart. Sven can help. Ever since Grayson and Lucan moved in, it's been a lot for you. You're doing an amazing job, but I want you to have more time to rest, especially in a few weeks."

The fire disappeared from Vieno's eyes, and he rested his head against Lidon's shoulder. "You're right," he said softly. "And thank you for taking care of me and thinking ahead. I didn't want you to feel that I wasn't doing my job."

"Oh, sweetheart, you're amazing. And no one will ever take your place. You're the omega of this house, of our pack."

Something rolled through Lidon as he said it, a deep affirmation of the truth of his words.

"I love you," Vieno whispered against his lips.

"I love you so much," Lidon whispered back, drawing their foreheads against each other.

He took the time to hold Vieno, waiting till he felt the peace return to his mate's system. Only then did he lift his head, keeping Vieno on his lap but turning him so he could rest his back against Lidon's chest.

"I could use a beta with a strong knowledge of agronomy. Vieno has started a vegetable garden and is looking to expand it. This used to be a working farm, and our intention is to restore it to its former glory. The goal is to be as self-sufficient as possible."

Lars shot up straight, his eyes suddenly alive. "Is this a paid position?" he asked.

"Of course, it is! Did you think I'd make you work for free? Holy hell, what kind of pack do you think I run here?" Lidon shot back, fed up with the hostility the beta was showing him. "I'll pay you a more than decent salary and deduct a fair amount for room and board for you and Sven. You'll find me a more than reasonable employer, but feel free to check with any of the men working for me."

Lars's cheeks colored bright red. "Will you kick me out if I don't take the job?"

Lidon was about to completely lose his patience with him when a booming voice behind him saved him the trouble. "I'll handle this, alpha," Grayson spoke.

He stepped into Lidon's view and pointed a finger at Lars. "You, come with me," he said, his voice heavy with dominance.

Lars rose to his feet, his face set to a thunderstorm, but still obeying. Sven pushed his chair back. "You can stay here," Grayson said, his voice much softer and kinder. "I promise I'll return him in one piece."

Seconds later, Grayson and Lars had walked out of the kitchen, leaving a trembling Sven behind.

"He doesn't mean to be insolent, alpha," Sven said, biting his lip. "He's... It's not been easy for him. For us."

Lidon took a deep breath to make sure he wouldn't take out his irritation on the wrong brother. "I understand, but that doesn't mean he can disrespect me. You'd better make sure he understands."

"Yes, alpha."

Lidon kissed Vieno on his head, then planted him on his feet. "Show Sven around so he can help out, sweetheart."

Vieno nodded, his eyes showing understanding that Lidon needed to cool off. He walked out, Sven's smell reminding him his heat wasn't far off. They'd have to separate him when his heat was close, Lidon realized, as he walked outside. Enar, Palani, and he hopefully wouldn't have an issue resisting him since they were mated, but the other men around would, especially if he had the gene like Enar suspected.

Hmm, how would they pull that off for him and for other omegas that would come to stay? He pulled up a mental picture of the ranch. They could add an omega wing to the main house. There was enough space to do it, but it would still be awfully close to the bedrooms of any alphas staying, too close to keep the scent out. No, that wouldn't work.

He mulled it over in his head as he wandered around the swimming pool, which had been cleaned and was being used daily by Vieno and Enar, who both loved to swim. What if they added an extra building to the compound? They'd have to widen the perimeter of the gates, but it would be safer. They'd need a few bedrooms where omegas could retreat, whether they were riding out their heat alone or with a partner. Each bedroom would need its own bathroom. Maybe four or so? And they'd need a kitchen there as well, so they wouldn't have to come into the main house for replenishments.

He stopped in his tracks as it hit him that he wasn't entertaining the concept of multiple people moving in. He was counting on it. Sven was the first, but more would follow. They'd create a safe haven here for anyone who needed it. He knew Enar encountered many omegas who needed help, for short term or for a longer period. Lidon would love nothing more than to open his ranch to them, but they would need to make adjustments to make it work.

Safety was a number one concern, especially if they were taking in omegas who had the gene. Damn, he recalled how Vieno had smelled that first time—and that was when he'd been weak and exhausted. Palani's stories about those poor McCain kids had been heartbreaking. Lidon would do anything to prevent that from happening on his property, even if it meant investing in self-contained units to keep omegas away from alphas.

Now that he'd made up his mind, he wanted to talk to Jawon to see what the options were. He found him painting the newly built barn, where all the farm equipment could be stored.

"Hey, alpha," Jawon greeted him when he spotted him.

"Why do you keep calling me that?" Lidon wondered. "I have a name, you know."

Jawon shrugged. "It seems appropriate, somehow. I dunno. Do you mind?"

"No, but I don't want you to feel like you're obliged to use it, like I'd insist on it."

"I know. What's on your mind other than that?"

"Checking in," Lidon said. "How are things going?"

He'd spotted Ori and Servas working on extending Vieno's vegetable garden, distributing topsoil and leveling the patch of land. They had gates ready to put around it to keep out deer and other wildlife. He hadn't seen Urien, but maybe he was working on something else.

"Good, we're almost done with the extension of the vegetable yard, so you'll need to tell us what the next priority is."

"Good. It looks great," Lidon said.

Jawon looked around with a satisfied smile. "I love seeing it come to life. Projects like this make my heart sing, you know? We're rebuilding something, and I dunno, but it feels right."

"I know what you mean. Where's Urien?"

Jawon sighed. "He had to leave to pick up his daughter. Her school called that she had a fever."

"Poor kid. Where does he live?"

"Other side of the city, south side. It's quite the commute for him to come here, almost forty-five minutes."

Lidon's eyes widened, and he whistled through his teeth. "I hadn't realized he was that far out. And south side? Ugh, that's a crappy neighborhood to raise a kid."

"True, but it's what's still affordable, you know? Ori, Servas, and me, we've been talking about getting a place together so we can split costs, but with the economy being what it is, we'll probably end up renting on the south side as well."

Something stirred inside Lidon. A deep sense of what was right.

"I may have a solution," he said.

21

L idon ended the call with Detective Helly, who had led the investigation on the attack. The result was as Lidon had feared and expected: nothing. He'd known calling his coworkers in would result in little, but he'd had no choice, given his position. He had to play by the rules, even when those rules weren't gonna get him anywhere. Now that that was confirmed by the detective, it was time to take matters into his own hands.

He still wasn't sure what to make of the True Alpha stuff. It sounded like a legend, like the stuff of movies and made-up stories, and yet he couldn't shake the connection he'd experienced with it deep inside. Grayson's words...they'd sounded like a prophecy almost, and he'd felt them in his very soul. He'd spoken them once, but Lidon could remember every word.

Danger is coming, Grayson had said. He'd been right, hadn't he? Danger had come to the ranch, and they'd almost lost Vieno because of it. Lidon never, ever wanted to experience the terror he'd experienced when he feared he'd lose Vieno. So even if he wasn't fully convinced of the True

Alpha element, he'd follow the man's advice. He'd follow his instincts, and right now, they were telling him to build his pack.

An hour later, the living room was packed to the max with all the men. Every single one of them was there, including all of Bray's men—Lidon had promised he'd keep it short—and his cousins.

When Lidon rose from his chair, Vieno sitting at his feet, a silence fell over them.

"Thank you all for coming. I got a call from Detective Helly that they have no official leads or suspects for the attack on the ranch."

An angry murmur traveled through the room.

"That means it's time we do things our way. Starting today, things will change. We've already started on rebuilding the gate so it protects a bigger part of the surrounding buildings, and we're constructing a second gate around the entire property, but that will take longer. Jawon, Ori, Servas, I want to ask you to move in as long as you are working here on the ranch, which will be a while. We can build a separate cottage for you guys close to the main house, but you're part of my pack, and I want you inside the gates."

Jawon shared a look with the other two, then made eye contact with Lidon, his face serious and his eyes strong. "Yes, alpha. We're in."

Lidon nodded. "Good. Urien, your situation is different, considering your daughter. I'd like to invite you to move in with her into the main house. She needs to be safe."

Urien let out a small gasp. "God, yes, please. Thank you, alpha."

Lidon turned to Bray. "Bray, I need you close to the main house, considering your importance to my security. Choose a few of your men to live here permanently as well. We'll build them a cottage as soon as we can."

Bray nodded. "Yes, alpha."

"Lucan and Grayson, you're free to leave at any time, but we would love for you to stay here, for your safety and for our friendship."

Father and son answered at the same time, their voices strong. "Yes, alpha."

"We're staying," Grayson added. "We love living here and being part of your pack."

Lidon took a deep breath. "About that... I haven't figured it all out, so bear with me as we work out all the details, but starting today, we will function as a pack with me as the alpha. I'm..." He breathed out, trying to find the right words. "I'm not sure of what it all means and how it fits, but after what happened, I need to follow my instincts. This is my pack, and I'm inviting you all in. If you accept, that means you accept my leadership. If you have an issue with that, you'll need to leave. There will be no discussion over who leads. It's gonna be me. This is my home, my pack, and my rules."

Grayson shot him a look of deep pride. "Who is your second-in-command, alpha?"

This was the hard part. It didn't make sense, but it was what his instincts told him was right. Even though he had multiple alphas in his pack, including one in his bed as others would see it, there was only one option for him. "Palani."

Palani gasped, and he wasn't the only one, but Lidon's eyes were fixed on Enar. Would he understand? He never meant to hurt him, and he'd never forgive himself if he had, but he wasn't the right choice, the right fit.

Enar lifted his eyes to look at Lidon. "Excellent choice,

alpha," he said, his voice strong. "He's who I would've picked myself."

A wave of relief rolled through Lidon. "Thank you."

"Are...are you sure?" Palani asked Lidon, who shook his head, amused.

"Did you really think I'd choose you if I wasn't convinced you were the best man for this job?" he asked.

Palani looked sheepish. "True, but it's just... You have alphas here, and yet you chose me."

Lidon reached out for him and pulled him close, putting his hands on the beta's shoulders, not ashamed to show anyone in the room his emotions. "Palani, you have the sharpest mind here in the room. Your analytical skills are second to none. You have a tight rein on your temper... usually," he added, thinking back to the incident Palani had confessed to him where he'd clocked Enar. Wrong as it might've been, it had led to Enar finally opening up.

Palani grinned, then shot a cheeky look in Enar's direction. "I only hit people when they deserve it."

"I need someone I can trust blindly, someone who won't impulsively decide but follow the facts. I want you by my side," Lidon said. "This pack will judge people by their talents and competence when it comes to jobs, not by their status or identity."

Palani's face grew serious again. "Thank you. It's an honor, and I won't let you down, alpha."

Lidon smiled, then kissed him soundly. "I know you won't."

He turned Palani around to face the room. "As my second-in-command, my beta, Palani, will have my authority. His orders are to be treated as if they were mine."

Everyone nodded.

"I haven't figured it all out, what it means to be a pack

and what I want mine to look like, but I do know this. We protect what's ours. Our omegas, our children, our land, our home. We protect our pack. That's our priority. Anyone who has any ideas on how we can do that, please speak up."

"Will you allow new people in the pack?" Ori asked.

"Yes, but after vetting by me or Palani. We may ask Bray to run a background check. And people, remember. No strangers inside the gates."

"What's your policy on relationships within the pack?"

That was Lars. Lidon wasn't sure what Grayson had told the beta, but he'd apologized to Lidon and had told him he'd gladly accept the job offer. He'd worked outside ever since, and Jawon reported he doing excellent work and had made valuable suggestions.

Lidon wondered what had triggered Lars's question. Had the beta spotted someone he was interested in? He frowned. What should be his stand on that? He didn't want drama, but he also couldn't prevent people from hooking up or falling in love. He looked at Palani. Maybe the beta would have an idea on how to handle this?

"If it's consensual, I don't see why we'd have an issue with it," Palani said. "But we'd like a heads-up, just so we're aware. And if it involves an omega, we do need to consent beforehand because we want to make sure the omega enters into the relationship willingly and isn't pressured."

Lidon nodded, happy with that answer. "Yes. That sounds right."

"And what about heats?" Sven asked, surprising Lidon by speaking up. "Do I ask permission before asking an alpha to help me?"

"How was that traditionally done in a pack?" Palani asked Grayson.

"The omegas would ask the beta, the alpha's second-in-command, for permission," Grayson said. "Sex was always discussed openly in a pack, even shown openly. They all lived in the same house or in close proximity anyway, so it made no sense hiding."

"Okay," Lidon agreed. "So that answers your question, Sven. Find Palani, and he will..."

"Pimp you out," Palani said, grinning. It earned him laughter in the room.

"Can I make one suggestion, alpha?" Grayson said, and it struck Lidon again with how much reverence the older alpha used that title for him.

"Yes, please."

"I think you should declare all omegas off-limits as a general rule. Mated ones obviously, but also the unmated ones. State that anyone wanting to sleep with an omega needs your permission, even if it's for a heat or for a onetime thing. That way, you can protect vulnerable omegas in your pack."

"I like that," Lidon said. "So ordered. Also, anyone who has medical questions or who needs medical care can seek out Enar. Anyone else?"

"Will you allow me to make an announcement?" Enar asked, and Lidon's heart all but burst out of his chest because he knew what his best friend was about to do. He was so fucking proud of him and so...in love.

He *loved* him. He'd always loved him as a friend, a fuck buddy, but watching Enar gather his courage here, his body twitching with nerves, Lidon's heart swelled with a new kind of love. A love that made him want to protect him, cuddle him, fuck the shit out of him, and kiss him senseless. He loved him, and the knowledge made his heart sing.

"Yes, but you'll stand right here next to me when you do," he said.

Enar got up, and so did Palani and Vieno, who had to know what was coming. Hand in hand they stood, the four of them, facing a room of curious faces, though Grayson and Lucan looked like they knew what was coming.

"My request to the pack is to please consider me a beta from this moment on. It's how I feel, it's what I am inside, and I no longer want to be treated or referred to as an alpha..." Enar said, his voice thick with emotion.

Lidon saw some confusion, but others nodded immediately. It couldn't have been that much of a surprise to anyone who had spent any time with Enar lately. The man had been confident to show more of his true nature, and it had been heartwarming to see him blossom.

Lidon squeezed his hand. "Acceptance of Enar's status is required to enter the pack. If anyone has an issue with this, don't join. This pack will allow people to be themselves, no matter what society may think."

They wrapped things up quickly after that, and Lidon sent everyone off, back to their jobs. He asked Vieno, Enar, and Palani to stay back. When the room had cleared out except for his men, Lidon pulled them close. He was so sure of this he didn't even hesitate.

"I want to alpha claim you."

ENAR FROZE as Lidon's words registered. He was kidding, right? Or he meant Palani. There was no way he...

"Both of you. I want to claim you as mine because you are," Lidon said.

Enar swallowed. Did he dare to ask? He chastised himself. He'd come out as beta to a room full of people. Why the hell was he afraid to ask this?

"D-do you love me?" he brought out.

Lidon's face softened as he leaned in for a soft kiss. "I do, and I'm sorry for not telling you. I would have if I'd realized sooner, but it didn't hit me till minutes ago. I've never been more proud of you in my life, Enar, but I've also never loved you more."

Much to his own surprise, Enar burst out in tears. Not a soft welling up of his eyes. No, he shattered into a million pieces, but the pain didn't hurt. It soothed and comforted and made his heart sing like it had never sung before.

"I'm sorry..." he cried as Lidon pulled him into his arms. "I can't seem to..."

"Shut up," Lidon said mildly. "Let me hold you, Enar. Let me take care of you, please."

Enar hid his face against his alpha's strong shoulder and allowed himself to fall apart in Lidon's strong arms, crying until he had no more tears to spend.

"I love you," he whispered when the tears dried up, his voice hoarse. "I think I always have."

Lidon kissed his head, then his mouth, apparently not caring about the hot mess that Enar was right now. "Will you accept my claim?" he asked.

Enar nodded eagerly. "God, yes. Please. I want to be yours."

"You're not concerned what it will mean to your status?" Lidon asked, taking the tissue Palani offered him and wiping Enar's face like he would a child's with incredible tenderness. Enar had to fight back his tears, or he'd fall to pieces all over again.

"I don't give a flying fuck about my status," Enar said from the bottom of his heart. "All I want is to be yours, to be together."

Lidon kissed him again, a kiss that showed every ounce

of emotion he wasn't able to express in words because Enar felt it in the way his alpha claimed his mouth. He didn't let go, clung to him, even as the kiss ended, almost scared to break whatever was holding them together now.

"Palani?" Lidon asked, his voice raw with emotion.

Only then did Enar realize he'd made it about himself when Palani had been there as well. Lidon hadn't only asked him. He wanted both of them, and Enar had selfishly claimed his attention for minutes.

But Palani stepped in, grabbing Enar's hand and pressing it, before offering his mouth to Lidon. "I want nothing more, my alpha."

Vieno squeezed in between them, claiming his spot in Lidon's long arms, and for a full minute they stood, hearts and bodies pressed together as one.

"Bedroom, now," Lidon ordered, and they broke apart, almost racing each other to their bedroom, leaving a trail of discarded clothes behind them.

They hurried onto the bed, four naked bodies and four hungry hearts, all desiring to be truly one. Enar saw the hunger he experienced reflected on his mates' faces, and he knew the order in which it would happen. Lidon sought his eyes, the unasked question crystal clear.

"Palani goes first," Enar said the words for him. "He's your beta, your second-in-command."

Lidon cupped his cheek. "It doesn't make you last...or less."

Enar nodded. "It makes me the luckiest man on earth, to have this with you. I belong with you, alpha, with all of you."

Lidon nodded back and let go of Enar, his mouth curving in a satisfied smile. "Palani," he said. "Present yourself to your alpha."

Palani sat on his knees in front of Lidon, and the alpha grabbed his head with both hands. "You haven't asked for the words, but you'll get them nonetheless. I love you, Palani, more than I ever thought possible. Vieno is my heart's mate, and Enar is my childhood's mate, my best friend, but you...you earned my love with your character. It's impossible not to love you, since your heart is so big. Our foursome wouldn't function without you."

God, Enar felt himself get mushy all over again at that declaration of love. It seemed Lidon *could* find the words when it mattered. And Palani, sweet Palani, he lit up like a Christmas tree, his entire face beaming as he radiated the love he felt for Lidon. Enar had known he loved the alpha, but never had it been more clear.

And then he bowed, kissing Lidon's hands in a gesture of sweet submission. "You know I love you," he simply said. "How could I not?"

"You ready?" Lidon asked after kissing him until both their lips were swollen and red.

"Yes, alpha."

Lidon positioned himself on his back, and Vieno scrambled over to lube his cock, then crawled behind Palani to prep him with sweet, soft moves, every caress showing his love. Palani kissed him when he was done and kneeled with his knees on both sides of Lidon.

"Take me in," the alpha ordered.

Palani did as he was told, his face tight with concentration. Enar knew how big that alpha cock was and how it always hurt so good when you took it in. The beta winced, then visibly relaxed, and Lidon's cock disappeared inside him. He did a few careful thrusts until Enar saw him relax.

Lidon sat up, holding Palani and looking at him with love. Vieno found a spot between Enar's legs, and he held him close, feeling privileged he could watch this special moment.

"Do you accept my alpha as your mate for life, sealing our unbreakable bond as long as we both shall live?" Lidon asked, repeating the words he'd once asked Vieno.

"Yes, alpha." Palani's voice rang out confident and steady, not a trace of nerves audible. "Do you accept my beta as your mate for life, sealing our unbreakable bond as long as we both shall live?"

"Yes, beta."

This time, Lidon didn't ask for permission to claim him. His hips flexed, and he thrust deep inside Palani. The beta groaned as the alpha roar filled the room, Lidon claiming every cell of them. He thrust deep inside Palani again with an aggressive move and came at his neck with his teeth.

Enar froze as he noticed Lidon's eyes. They were gleaming, shining unnaturally, much like an animal, like a... Enar gasped. A wolf. He was looking at the eyes of a wolf as Lidon sank his teeth deep inside Palani's neck.

In that moment, Enar realized that everything Grayson had told them was true. Lidon was so much more than a mere man... He not only was their alpha but also the True Alpha, and he'd bring change. A peace settled in Enar's heart at the knowledge that he was a part of this, that he would not only witness history being made but also would help shape it himself.

A little trail of blood trickled down Palani's neck, and Lidon licked it up, moaning low and deep. Without saying a word, he rolled Palani onto his back and slammed inside him, forcing the air out of his lungs with an audible swoosh. He repeated the move as Palani held on to his shoulders for dear life.

"Mine," Lidon snarled. "You're mine."

The possessiveness was unlike anything Enar had seen from him before, and it showed the alpha claim had taken root.

"Yours, alpha," Palani repeated, his voice raw.

Lidon fucked him harder than Enar had ever seen him do before, but Palani took it, encouraging Lidon with grunts and moans. "I'm yours," he kept repeating until Lidon sped up and came inside him, throwing his head back and letting out another alpha roar.

He collapsed on top of Palani, whose arms came around him as he nuzzled his neck, mumbling things too soft for Enar to hear. Enar smiled. Even Lidon couldn't resist Palani's cuddles. The man was too damn inviting not to seek shelter in his arms. He was their safe spot, the place they could be themselves, vulnerable.

He held Vieno as they watched in silence how Lidon returned to earth, finally pulling out of Palani, kissing him before rolling off him.

"It's your turn," Vieno said softly but with excitement in his voice.

"Thank you for sharing him with us, little one," Enar said.

Vieno turned around in his arms. "He was never only mine. He always was ours, just like you're ours."

Enar nodded, finally feeling the truth as much as he believed it and knew it in his head. "Will you prep me?" he asked Palani. The mark on his shoulder was furiously red, but Enar looked at it with longing. A few minutes more and he'd have one of his own.

"Gladly."

Palani took his time, stretching him with slow, sweet gestures, kissing him until he was a writhing mess, dying to be filled. "I love it when you get all needy," the beta whispered against his lips. "My beautiful, strong man. I'm so proud of you."

"I love you," Enar said, his throat constricted. He'd never thought he'd ever be in this position, to be claimed. For so long he'd believed he should do the claiming, even though it had felt ten kinds of wrong. The freedom of this moment, it was indescribable.

"He's ready for you, alpha," Palani said.

Enar expected Lidon to take position on his back again, but the alpha hesitated. "This one is different," he said. "He completes us, so it should be all of us, united."

Enar frowned. What did Lidon mean?

"Enar, on your knees, your ass toward me," Lidon commanded. "Palani, take position in front of him, and, Vieno, you're in front of Palani. All four of us, connected."

Only then did Enar understand. Vieno and Palani took position, Palani sinking deep inside the omega without a problem. No wonder, Vieno had to be horny as fuck after what he'd witnessed. Enar positioned himself behind Palani and entered him, his hole still slick and stretched from Lidon's not-too-gentle claiming.

Lidon's head pressed against him, and he opened up, spreading his legs as wide as they would go and pushing his ass back. Palani and Vieno moved with him, never losing their connection.

"My man," Lidon said, pushing inside with one steady move. "My men."

"Yours, alpha," Palani mumbled, echoed by Vieno.

"How about you, my beta?" Lidon asked, wrapping his strong arms around Enar. "You ready to accept my claim?"

Enar raised his head. "I'm yours, alpha."

"Do you accept my alpha as your mate for life, sealing

our unbreakable bond as long as we both shall live?" Lidon asked again.

"Yes, alpha." Enar's eyes filled, and his voice broke as he spoke the words he never thought he'd utter. "Do you accept my beta as your mate for life, sealing our unbreakable bond as long as we both shall live?"

"Yes, beta."

Lidon was quiet for a second, but then he continued, his voice ringing out.

"We are four, and we are one, alpha, beta, beta, and omega. Four hearts, one soul. Four bodies, one mind. What we bind together, no man will ever break apart. I am the alpha, and I claim these men for life!"

Lidon roared, and Enar's ears rang with the force. He roared again, and the power would have knocked Enar over if Lidon hadn't held him. On the third roar, Lidon snapped his hips back and drove deep inside Enar, making him dizzy with the force. Once more he roared, and then his mouth descended on Enar's shoulder, and his vision went white hot, then black. He was split in two, made whole again, and he cried as he came, as they all came.

A haze settled over him, over them all, and he was hard, so hard, so hungry for sex, for cock, for his men. Was this how Vieno felt during his heat? Like a hot, throbbing ball of need, that wanted to come, then come again, and then again until he was full and empty at the same time?

He took, and he was taken, again and again and again, until he went limp, and he slept in his men's arms.

22

Palani couldn't explain it, but when Franken called him into his office a week after the alpha claiming, he knew it was bad. Franken hadn't said anything, but Palani had sensed it. Maybe it was because he'd seen the big brass who owned his paper come in yesterday and talk to Franken. He wasn't sure, but something was going on, and it had to do with him.

When he walked into Franken's office, his boss's face was tight. "Have a seat," he told Palani, and his friendly tone affirmed something was up.

Franken leaned forward in his chair. "There have been complaints from the cops since you started your investigation into corruption," he began. Palani nodded, since he was well aware. "And we've always supported you, since you could back up your findings with evidence."

Palani nodded again, and Franken sighed as he dragged a hand through his receding hairline. "Your last piece, about the corruption in the White-Collar Division did not go over well."

Palani had debated hard whether he should write the

piece, scared he would trigger Ryland into more violence like the attack on the ranch. In the end, he'd decided not to name him by name but paint a bigger picture of incompetence and corruption in his division. He'd also omitted any mention of Excellon, since he felt it was too soon to go public, since he still didn't have all the facts. If the conspiracy was as massive as he feared, showing how much he knew could prove catastrophic.

"I'm guessing that's an understatement?" Palani asked with feigned indifference, since he knew all too well the absolute chaos and fury his piece had caused at police head-quarters, courtesy of Lidon.

"The chief of police was livid, but..." Franken hesitated. "Look, there's been a ton of pressure from high-ranking offi-cials on me and the paper to make your investigations stop. The reasoning is that people are losing trust in cops, and that's a bad thing for all of us, since it erodes trust in government."

"The truth gets too painful, huh?" Palani said with a sinking feeling in his stomach. He knew where this was headed. Dammit.

"Well, they're claiming it's not the truth, but that the evidence you showed was fabricated by an inside source."

Palani's hands started to sweat. This was worse than he had expected. "An inside source, sir?"

"Yes, a cop. They're saying he helped you fabricate this evidence to further your career."

"What cop, sir?" He knew, but he had to ask.

"Palani, is it true you are involved in a clandestine four-way relationship with three other men, one of whom is a cop?"

His heart dropped out, but he looked Franken straight in the eyes as he answered. "Yes, sir. But there's nothing clandestine about it. Our alpha alpha claimed all three of us, and none of us are hiding it."

"What you do in your home and especially in your bedroom is none of my concern, but—"

"No," Palani interrupted him. "It's not. We are four legal adults in a committed, consensual relationship. That is no one's business but ours."

"It is if the cop you're sleeping with is accused of doctoring evidence for you, so you could write flashy pieces and get famous."

"You don't seriously believe that, sir."

Franken's body language was contradictory. His stern face and tone seemed to say he was upset with Palani, but the hesitance in the rest of his body, the slight twitching of his fingers, told Palani there was more to this.

"I don't know what to believe."

"Sir, my first articles came out before I had even met Lidon. And I showed you how I collected evidence, every step of the way."

Franken's face softened. "You did, and I gave the okay, but now I'm telling you that we can no longer support you in this. You've gone too far, pissed off the wrong people."

Ah, now they were getting to the real issue. "What people would that be, sir?"

Franken leaned back in his chair. "My hands are tied. I hope you realize that. I've stood by you, but I'm not willing to lose my job over you."

"Am I...am I being fired, sir?" Palani asked.

"You're suspended without pay. For now. The board wants a full investigation into your sources and methods."

Palani shook his head. "I won't give up my sources, sir."

"No, I didn't think you would. But it's what they're

demanding, so you need to ask yourself how much you're willing to lose over your ethics."

"If I don't give up my sources, they'll fire me?"

"Count on it," Franken said. "For now, you're suspended, which will give you a little time to figure out your strategy, but if you don't cooperate, they will boot you."

Regret colored the man's voice, and Palani took comfort in that. "I appreciate the heads-up, sir," he said. He rose from his chair.

"Palani," Franken said, using his first name since he'd started working for the paper. "For what it's worth, I'm truly sad to see it play out like this. You deserve better."

He nodded. "Thank you, sir."

He walked over to his desk to grab his bag and discovered two security guards waiting for him. "We're here to escort you out. You can take personal items only," one of the guards said.

Palani nodded. Good thing he always scanned his notes into his own laptop and then destroyed the paper copies. He never stored any privacy sensitive information on his work laptop, knowing it wasn't safe. Journalism 101, always protect your sources.

He slung his messenger bag over his shoulder and walked out, sending Adar a quick text he was already on his way. He waited outside the office till Adar had shown up.

"I thought you were staying in all day," the bulky alpha greeted him.

"So did I. I got suspended."

Adar's eyes widened. "Interesting timing. Isam just called me, said something was going down at the clinic."

"What's happening? Is Enar okay?" Isam was Enar's security guard. Enar had left early that morning because he had a full day of procedures at the clinic he rented an OR from.

"The Health Department is raiding the clinic, from what I understand."

"Oh, shit," Palani said. If they discovered the illegal procedures Enar did, the meds he gave patients without prescriptions, he could not only lose his medical license but also go to jail. That in itself was worrisome enough, but the timing was conspicuous, the fact that it happened on the same day as Palani getting suspended.

"Have you checked in with Bray? Is Vieno okay at the ranch?" He hadn't felt anything from Vieno, but he couldn't rely on that, since they still weren't sure how that connection with the omega worked.

"Yeah, everything is fine, but Bray is on high alert."

"Can we go to Enar? Is he still there?"

"Yes. They told him he couldn't leave until they'd concluded their on-site investigation." Adar looked as worried as Palani felt. "Will they find anything?" he asked Palani. "Does he keep any proof there of what he does?"

Palani's eyes narrowed. "How do you know what he does?"

Adar's strong hand landed on his shoulder. "He helped my youngest sister when she was pregnant at eighteen. I took her, and he took care of it, of her. She'd been foolish and careless, but her life would've been over had she kept it, so he helped her. He's a good man."

Palani's face softened. "Yes, he is. And no, they won't find much. He keeps records of his legal patients only. The rest is in his head. He's as careful as he can be."

"Good," Adar relaxed a bit, though he was always on alert, constantly checking his surroundings. "And you showing up won't complicate things?"

Palani smiled. "I always complicate things, but that's what makes life interesting. No, he needs me, even if he doesn't know it yet."

THE MEN HAD SHOWN up midway through a surgery. Enar had been tying his patient's tubes—a perfectly legal procedure, thank fuck—when he'd heard the commotion outside his OR. Loud voices, lots of footsteps. His stomach sank. He'd feared this day would come.

"What the hell is going on?" Nancy, his OR assistant, asked.

"I don't know, but can you find out, please?" Enar asked. "And make sure they don't step foot inside because we can't contaminate the OR."

Nancy walked out, leaving Enar with Jaser, the anesthesiologist, and Maz, an ob-gyn resident, who volunteered with Enar as much as he could. He was a fourth-year resident and a gifted one who shared Enar's passion to better to health and lives of omegas. He'd done countless procedures with Enar, knowing damn well at least half of them weren't legal.

Jaser knew too, but if that man cared about anything else than money, Enar hadn't discovered it yet. He wouldn't sell Enar out—the man assisted in clinics like this all over the city and wouldn't want to lose that lucrative side business—but he wasn't exactly an ally either.

"Do you know what that's about?" Maz asked.

"I have a suspicion. Don't get sucked into this, Maz," he warned the man.

"Into what?" Maz asked, his tone light.

Enar had met him at a mandated training from the

Health Department, and they'd hit it off instantly. Maz exuded a calmness that Enar appreciated, and so did patients.

"Sir, no!" he heard Nancy say outside. "That's a sterile environment."

The OR sliding door swooshed open, revealing two men in suits.

"Enar Magnusson?" one of them asked.

"That's Dr. Magnusson to you. Who the hell are you?"

"We're inspectors from the Health Department, performing an inspection on your facilities after complaints."

Complaints, his ass. They'd found out about his illegal activities somehow and were trying to find evidence. Good luck with that. "That's all good and well, but you need to get the hell out of my OR because I have a woman exposed on the table here. You're contaminating the OR." Enar pushed as much alpha into his voice as he could.

"What procedure are you performing?" the other man asked.

"A bilateral tubal ligation. Can you leave now? I'd like to focus on my patient here before I accidentally kill her, if you don't mind."

"We'll stay right here until you're done, Doctor."

They stayed in the doorway, at least, while Enar finished the procedure. Luckily, the ligation went flawless, and his patient should be up in no time. And their timing was perfect because an hour later they would've caught him performing an illegal abortion on a male omega.

He waited before speaking till Nancy had wheeled their patient out of the OR into the recovery room. "Now, what the hell is going on?"

It was amazing how much effort it cost him to be so

alpha after having the freedom to be himself at home. It felt forced, unnatural.

The two inspectors stepped into the OR. He could complain about contaminating the room, but that was a lost cause anyway. Besides, he wouldn't be performing any more surgeries today, that much was clear. Behind the two men, Nancy gave him a quick A-okay sign, and he breathed with relief inwardly. It was the signal to confirm she'd managed to send out an emergency text to his illegal patients from today that they shouldn't show up. It ran through an untraceable online service, so Enar wouldn't be caught doing it either.

"As we said, Dr. Magnusson, we're here to inspect your clinic after a complaint."

"It's not my clinic. I rent an OR here to perform procedures like the one you witnessed. And what complaint? This is the first I've been made aware of any complaint against me. Aren't these supposed to go through the medical board?"

"Not when it concerns a public safety concern, like the sterility of your equipment."

"If that's a concern, you shouldn't have barged into my OR," Enar pointed out.

"We needed to make sure you wouldn't have the opportunity to hide any information pertaining to our investigation."

"Hiding information? Where? Inside a patient?"

"No need to get riled up, Dr. Magnusson. Why don't you wait in the waiting room while we do our inspection of your facilities here?"

Technically, it was a suggestion, a question even, but the way the inspector worded it, it was more like a command. Enar did as he was told, signaling to Maz to follow him as they took off the rest of their surgical wear, then washed their hands. Enar didn't have to tell Maz not to say anything. Maz was well aware of the risks and the most likely real reason the inspectors were here. It could cost him his career as well, so he kept as quiet as Enar.

It wasn't till he settled in the waiting room that Enar realized he hadn't seen Isam. The man always stayed outside the OR for obvious reasons, but he usually hung around Enar's office. Had he seen the men arrive and decided to hang back? If so, that was a smart choice because Enar wasn't sure how to explain to the Health Department he had a bodyguard.

Thank fuck he had his phone on him, as he always did. He'd switched it to do not disturb in the OR, but he always had it on him. Should he inform his men?

He smiled at the thought. His men. It had taken him a while to get there, to understand and accept his role, his part, but he no longer had doubts. He belonged with them as much as they belonged with him. If anything, Lidon alpha claiming him had made that clear. And yes, they'd want to know, he was sure. He sent them a group text, keeping it vague, just in case the inspectors somehow took his phone from him. "Health Department raid at clinic bc of complaint. Will keep you posted."

Palani responded first. "On my way."

On his way? Why would he come over for that? It was sweet but also a bit much, maybe? Still, Enar appreciated the thought. Palani always was protective of Enar, which was endearing and sweet and made Enar's heart go all warm and fuzzy.

Five minutes later, Enar's phone buzzed again. "On my way as well."

Enar frowned. Lidon was coming over too? Why wasn't

he at work? What the hell was going on? A raid on his clinic wasn't cause for both of them to show up here. It was sweet that they wanted to show their support, but... He stilled. Unless something else was going on, something that involved all three of them.

LIDON KEPT his temper in check as the chief of police chewed him out for falsifying evidence. He knew what this was about, who was behind this. Ryland. Lidon cursed his own naïveté. He should've known Ryland wouldn't meekly lie down and let it happen. Not after the attack on the ranch, which he still suspected Ryland to be involved in.

Still, it stung that after so many years of service and an exemplary record, he'd be accused of this. He still trusted the system enough that in the end, the truth would come out, but for now, he was livid that his integrity was taken into question, and he told his boss as much.

Right after he'd been escorted out, he saw Enar's text. It was like the bottom dropped from under his feet. Him getting suspended on the same day as Enar was getting raided? No way that was a coincidence. And Palani being on his way? That had to mean something, too, because he didn't have a job where he could just up and leave. He debated calling him but decided it could wait till they saw each other. With everything that was happening, he wanted to be careful.

He caught Palani at the clinic's entrance, Adar standing close and alert. Lidon walked straight up to his man, who had no qualms about burying his head against Lidon's chest. Lidon held him, kissing his head first, then grabbing his neck and taking a real kiss.

"What a shitty day," Palani said against Lidon's lips. "Though I'm feeling better already."

"What happened?"

"I got suspended."

Lidon let go of the embrace, though he still kept his hands on Palani's shoulders. "I feared you were gonna say that. So did I. Let me guess, for falsifying evidence?"

Palani's eyes bulged. "They suspended you?"

"Yes. For falsifying evidence to help one of my boyfriends get a scoop."

"I'm sorry. This is—"

Lidon put a quick hand on his mouth. "Not your fault. We both know it's not. You exposed the truth and nothing else. We know who's behind it. We just don't know why."

"If they have enough reach to get you and me suspended on the same day and get Enar raided, we're not talking about Ryland anymore. This is much, much bigger."

Lidon nodded. "I agree. We'll discuss this at home. First, let's go get our man."

They walked inside, hand in hand, and found Enar in the waiting room. Palani let go of Lidon and watched with warmth in his belly as Lidon hugged Enar and kissed him, right in front of other people. It was funny how easy it came, their dynamic. He'd known Lidon should greet him first, that that was the way it should be. He'd always come second, after their alpha, and he was fine with it. It felt right, in a way he couldn't explain.

Lidon pulled him close when he was done kissing Enar, and Palani hugged him. "How you holding up, Doc?"

He held him tight, knowing Enar needed that sense of security.

"I'm good, but what the hell are the two of you doing here?" Enar asked.

Palani leaned back and subtly shook his head. They couldn't talk here, not with strangers around. He let go of Enar. He'd met Nancy before, Enar's OR assistant, but the young alpha wearing scrubs was a new face. That had to be Maz, Palani deduced, having heard Enar talk about him.

"Nancy, Maz, these are two of my mates, Lidon and Palani."

They shook hands, exchanging pleasantries, when two men dressed in suits walked in. The inspectors, Lidon concluded.

"Dr. Magnusson, we need the password to your personal laptop," the taller of the two said.

Before Enar could answer, Palani spoke up. "Why?"

Lidon bit back a smile. How he loved it when Palani got all protective.

"That's none of your concern," the inspector bit back at the beta.

"It's outside your authority," Palani said calmly. "You don't have legal access to any of his personal property, not unless you have a warrant signed by a judge."

Lidon would've bet money that Palani had researched this on the car ride here, smartass that he was.

"It is in Dr. Magnusson's best interests that he cooperates fully with this investigation," the man snapped at Palani.

"He's given you access to all his professional files and information. He doesn't need to provide access to any of his personal data under the law, and he won't."

The waiting room grew still, the air heavy with the implications of what Palani had said. As a beta, he couldn't speak like that for an alpha, and it would raise all kinds of questions about Enar and his relationship with not only Palani but Lidon as well. And Lidon saw with sudden clarity that this was what Enar had feared, this public loss of respect. He was caught in an impossible situation, forced to either humiliate Palani by rebutting him or humiliating himself by submitting to a beta.

Then Enar looked at Lidon, his eyes steady as he nodded for Lidon to lead. A rush barreled through Lidon at this incredible sign of submission, though his voice was calm as he spoke. "He's right. As his alpha, I'm telling you that Dr. Magnusson will not hand over any personal data, including his laptop."

The inspector's eyes popped out as he stared at Lidon for a few seconds, then shared a look with his coworker. "His alpha, huh?"

And Lidon raised himself to his full height, allowing every drop of authority he had to seep into his voice. "Yes. Do you have a problem with that?"

They did, of course, but they wouldn't come right out and say it, not in front of Lidon. So they took off after a few minutes, informing Enar his medical license was suspended pending the investigation.

Lidon drove Enar and Palani while Adar and Isam took the other two cars back to the ranch. Once they were in the car, they shared stories of what had happened.

"You were right, Palani," Lidon said when they were done swapping their experiences. "This is much bigger than Ryland alone. What the hell did we get ourselves involved in?"

"It proves what I've been saying all along. It's all connected, and it's infiltrating the government as well."

23

The plus side to having his medical license suspended was that Enar could spend a lazy Sunday with his men. All four of them had been happy to be together, uncertain as the future looked for them, and Enar had remarked how he loved to wake up with all four of them in the bed—a rarity. Vieno had rolled himself off Lidon—the little omega loved to sleep sprawled on top of his alpha—and straight onto Enar, kissing him until Enar had throbbed with need. He'd taken care of that too, his sweet Vieno, and had let Enar fuck him until he'd exploded inside him.

In the shower, Palani had complained he felt left out—though the twinkling in his eyes had belied his real motivation—and so Enar had fucked him against the wall, slow and deep, stopping every time he felt the beta on the verge of orgasming until Palani had begged him to let him come. Enar loved to hear his proud man beg, so he'd pegged his prostate until Palani had climaxed, sagging against Enar.

It was the perfect start to a lazy Sunday, and the rest of the day had been equally relaxing. He'd lounged with Vieno on the porch swing, the omega's small body plastered against Enar's as they both read. Later, Palani and Lidon had joined him, then others as well until they'd decided to do a spontaneous barbecue.

His stomach full, Enar walked back inside to find another book to read. He'd finished the first of Grayson's books, a captivating wolf shifter romantic suspense, and wanted to start on the next book in the series right away. A sound from the fitness room startled him. Wasn't everyone still outside? Well, his brothers weren't, but they rarely joined the rest of the group or at least not when Enar was present.

He stopped as he heard another sound, a low groan. Had someone injured himself while working out? He hurried to the room and swung the door open.

His gasp made Lars and Sven look up, their bodies frozen in what could charitably be described as a compromising position. Lars was balls deep in Sven, who lay on his stomach on a bench, his knees on the floor and his hands holding on to the bench's grips.

"What the fuck?" Enar said, too stunned to understand what he was seeing. Then it hit him. The closeness Sven and Lars had demonstrated. Sven's refusal to come to the ranch without Lars. Lars's overprotectiveness of Sven. This was not a onetime thing. They were lovers, and they had been for a while.

Anger boiled up in him. "Are you two out of your fucking mind? What the hell do you think you're doing?"

"This is none of your concern," Lars snapped at him.

"None of my concern? You're my brothers!"

Lars pulled out, and Enar closed his eyes, not needing to see more of his brothers, his *little* brothers, than he already had. When he opened them again, they both stood, their clothes back on, Sven's face red with shame and Lars's equally flushed with fury.

"Adopted brother," Lars said, but it was more of a sneer than a remark.

"You're not adopted," Enar said on reflex, since there was no denying the physical resemblance between them. Then it hit him. "Is Sven...?"

Sven nodded, biting his lip.

Enar swallowed. "How...? How long?"

Lars sighed. "We discovered it last year, when Sven went to the doctor for his delayed heat. They did blood tests on him, and the doctor told him there was no way he was related to our father or to me."

Enar noted the emotionally cold way Lars spoke about their father, but filed it for later. "Did you ask him about it?"

Lars's face darkened. "No. I don't know if he knew or not, and I don't care. It doesn't make a difference."

Enar frowned as he tried to follow Lars's reasoning. "What are you...? Oh. That's why he can smell him, why I can. Because we're not related by blood."

"Doesn't make it okay, what he did," Lars bit back.

"Of course not," Enar said, his head reeling. "But neither is what you guys are doing. You may not be related by blood, but you grew up as brothers. God, it's...it's wrong!"

"Says the alpha who wants to be treated as a beta...and who is in a foursome, with a beta being chosen as second-in-command over him," Lars sneered.

The pain in his heart was so sharp it took Enar's breath away. His vision grew misty, and he wondered why until he realized it was because of the tears in his eyes. He turned around, blindly staggered out the room, away from his brother, who hated him so much he'd aimed for where he knew he'd hurt Enar the most.

He slammed into a body in the hallway and would have fallen if two strong hands hadn't held him up. "Enar, are you okay?"

He couldn't answer Grayson, couldn't get past the stabbing shards in his heart.

"Palani!" Grayson called out, and seconds later, Enar was wrapped in a strong embrace, Palani's much smaller body holding him.

"What's wrong, Doc?"

Grayson's voice was tight when he spoke. "I have a pretty good idea what happened."

Enar couldn't see what he referred to, didn't want to see. The thought of Lars witnessing his pain was bad enough. He didn't have to see his brother gloat. He'd much rather bury his head against Palani's neck, breathing his scent in deeply, since it soothed his pain more than anything else. Palani's hands found the bare skin under his shirt, rubbing soft circles on his back.

"Motherfucker," Palani muttered with uncharacteristic venom.

"Will you allow me to handle this?" Grayson asked.

Enar stayed in Palani's arms, since the question wasn't directed at him. It should bother him, but it really didn't. All he felt was a massive relief that someone else took responsibility, that he didn't have to take charge for once.

"You'd better make crystal clear that this will not happen again. He hurts Enar again like that, and he's out," Palani snapped, his voice ringing with more authority than Enar had ever managed.

"Yes, beta," Grayson said, not a trace of mockery on his voice.

"Come on, Doc," Palani said, his voice much softer and sweeter. "Let's head to the bedroom and cuddle."

Enar smiled despite his pain. His mate always knew what to say to make him feel better.

PALANI HAD ASKED for all of them to sit together, determined to use the power of their collective minds to find theories and hopefully solutions for the predicament they were in. So four days after they'd been suspended, they grouped in the living room together: Lidon, Enar, Vieno—Palani had insisted he'd be there as they'd kept him out of the loop too much for his own safety—Grayson, Lucan, and Bray. Lidon's Uncle Leland was present as well, per Lidon's request. He'd filled him in on most of the stuff already, but Lidon wanted him there because of his knowledge of the old ways that could shed light perhaps.

He looked at Lidon when they'd all settled, but the alpha smiled at him. "This is your show," he said.

Palani nodded. He was still getting used to the trust Lidon had in him, but it felt damn good.

"Let me start by summarizing what we know for sure," he said. "You may know most of this, but I think it's important to see the whole picture again."

He explained what he'd discovered about the gene, the fertility treatments, Maiitsoh, Ulfur, and Lukos. It took him over ten minutes to connect all the dots they'd found.

"Our working theory is that the whole goal of Maiitsoh was to bring the wolf shifters back," Enar said. "Melloni discovered that the gene modification was done using wolf DNA."

"But they failed," Lucan said. "Because there have been no reported shifts."

"True," Palani said. "But maybe the goal wasn't to create

first-generation shifters but to create male omegas who would bear children able to shift."

Uncle Leland nodded. "My dad believed that one of the causes of the loss of shifting abilities was that male omegas had been discarded due to fertility issues. Many alphas who wanted children chose a female omega because male omegas had such issues getting pregnant and a high rate of complications during pregnancy and delivery."

"We won't know what happens with the second generation until they're old enough to shift," Enar said. "Most of the gene carriers are in their twenties now, so they're only starting to have kids of their own."

Palani's eyes trailed to Vieno, who clutched to Lidon's hand. Enar must have noticed it too because he added, "There's no reason to assume there will be anything wrong with their offspring, just the fact that they may be able to shift again."

"There's been a lot of talk about the wolf shifters lately," Grayson remarked. "The CWP, who is all for returning to the old ways. The AWC, who is dead set against it. Do we suspect this is connected?"

Bray cleared his throat. "Actually, let me share some enlightening news there. I already told Lidon and Palani, but they asked me to wait till now to share it. Ever since the attack, I've tried to find out who was behind it. The cops got nowhere, as we expected, but I had a hard time finding solid leads as well. The men who were killed were all hired thugs. With a little digging, I uncovered their identities. They were all skilled and experienced but motivated by money by the looks of their rap sheets. That meant there had to be someone who hired them, but that's where the trail ran cold."

"Three weeks ago, Enar and I visited Dr. Melloni, and we

discovered some things that made me believe the gene and Lukos were part of a bigger picture, including George York, but also those who oppose him. When I shared that with Bray, it gave him some new leads to follow," Palani said.

Bray nodded in agreement. "I did a little digging, and Palani helped by using his extensive sources and contacts. Karl Ryland, the cop who is involved in covering up the fraud surrounding Excellon, is a member of the AWC, the Anti Wolf Coalition. And the AWC is the political face of this movement, the polite and public face, so to speak, but they have a much lesser-known radical arm—army would be a more fitting term. There's a group of radical AWC members who have started taking action beyond politics. They're organized in cells that are acquiring arms at an alarming rate, and they're radicalizing."

"That's troubling," Grayson said, his voiced betraying his shock. "Where are they getting the money?"

"That's what we're still trying to figure out," Palani said. "But our theory right now is that the men who attacked the ranch were hired by a cell like that, probably in reaction to our investigation into the gene and Excellon."

Vieno bit his lip, then spoke up. "But why would they want to keep what Lukos did, or Maiitsoh or whatever they were called, a secret? Wouldn't they want to expose it? I mean, it was wrong, wasn't it?"

It was the same question Palani had asked himself. "Yes, it was wrong, but considering the wide support the CWP has, my guess is they feared people would condemn the methods but readily embrace the goal. Exposing Maiitsoh would mean affirming that a return to wolf shifters is possible, and that's not news the AWC would want to leak."

"We suspect they're keeping tabs on Palani and Lidon. The warning to Lidon came after he'd accessed that file in the system, and the attack on the ranch came days after you visited Melloni. When that failed, they came after your jobs, though I suspect they've been laying groundwork there for a while," Bray explained.

"For them to pull that off, they'd have to have a far reach on high government levels," Lucan remarked.

"Yeah, that's got us worried, which is why Palani and I have decided to lie low for a while. We're fighting our suspensions, but low-key. We don't wanna rock the boat more than we already have," Lidon said.

"And Enar?" Uncle Leland asked. "What about the suspension of his license?"

Enar sighed. "The problem is that they have reason to suspend me, and they know it. Sure, the charge they got me on now is bull, but if I fight it, they're just gonna dig deeper, and they will find shit to nail me on. So it looks like my medicine-practicing days are over, at least for now."

Palani's hands itched to comfort him, hearing the sadness in his voice, but he wasn't sure if Enar would accept it in this setting. Vieno had no such reservations, and he crawled onto Enar's lap to hug him.

"It wouldn't have to be," Lucan spoke up. He blushed as every head in the room turned toward him. "You can't practice medicine in any clinic or hospital, but you can on private property. It's a loophole in the law some doctors used in the past to help omegas. As long as you're on privately owned property and patients sign a release that they're aware you're not licensed, you're in the clear."

"I'd forgotten about that," Enar said slowly.

Palani shared a look with Lidon and was pretty damn sure they were thinking along the same lines. But they'd work it out together and then present it to Enar. He had enough on his mind right now, so they would keep this stress away from him.

"What does this mean for the future?" Uncle Leland asked. "This threat won't disappear on its own, especially not if you guys keep digging into this whole mess."

"No, it won't." Lidon's answer was firm. "But that doesn't mean we stop digging. It just means we must be vigilant about it. We have a better idea of what we're facing and the lengths to which these people will go to protect themselves and their belief system. We'll adjust security accordingly."

Grayson's eyes narrowed, Palani noticed. "Lidon, have you considered they're targeting you specifically?" the older alpha asked.

Palani frowned. What was he referring to?

"Your bloodline, your heritage, and the fact that you married an omega who carries the gene. You're their worst fears come true."

Grayson's words hung in the room, punctuated by a gasp from Vieno before Enar's arms tightened around him.

"Are you considering children?" Uncle Leland asked after a heavy silence. "I think Vieno's heat will come soon, no?"

"Yes, five more days," Lidon said, his voice calm despite the turbulence Palani spotted on his face. "And yes, we had decided we wanted him to conceive, but..." His voice trailed off. "I'm not sure if we should now, because what you're saying makes sense."

Vieno sat up straight, pushing Enar's arms away. "No," he said, then again and louder, "No."

He got up, stood ramrod straight as he faced Lidon. "We will have this baby. We are not bowing because of threats like this."

"Sweetheart, what if they—"

Vieno planted his feet, his chin raised. "They can't. This is our pack, our home. Men will die to protect this, and we will not cower. I'll give you your alpha heir, and he'll grow up to change our world. I know it, and I believe it with all my heart."

When Grayson had told Palani he felt Vieno using alpha compulsion on him in that cellar, he'd thought him crazy. How could an omega, even an alpha-claimed one, use his alpha's powers? But here was the proof because Vieno spoke with an authority and power that Palani felt roll through him, unable to resist.

Lidon felt it too because his mouth dropped slightly open before he recovered. "You..." He shook his head as if to clear his mind. "You're amazing, sweetheart." He reached for his hand, and Vieno stood between his legs, a look of sheer determination on his face. Lidon kissed him, then pulled him on his knee and faced the room.

"You heard our omega. We're having a baby."

24

L idon raised his head to let the sun beam down on his face and bare torso. It was still early, but the air was already humming around him with the promise of a hot day. He didn't mind. He liked the heat, always had. As a kid, he'd spent hours in the pool, often with Enar, playing tag and lounging on floating devices. It had been heaven, just like he remembered much of his childhood.

The ranch had been a safe haven for him even then, and after hearing Uncle Leland's tale of what had transpired between his dad and his granddad, he understood why. His dad had kept much of the negative influences out, wanting to protect Lidon. But in doing so, he'd also prevented him from learning about who he was, about his heritage. That was a hard pill to swallow. He had so much to learn, and even with Grayson and his uncle helping him, he felt lost. He was supposed to lead his pack, but how could he do a good job when he lacked the knowledge and experience?

He sensed him before he heard him, and then two small

arms wrapped around him from behind. Vieno's head rubbed against his back.

"Hi, sweetheart," Lidon said, breathing him in deeply. Yes, his heat was coming soon, Lidon confirmed, Vieno's scent already hardening his cock.

Vieno walked around him, now hugging him from the front. "Mmm," he said. "I love it when you're not wearing a shirt. All those big, sexy muscles on display."

Lidon flexed, just to tease him, laughing when Vieno did a pretend faint. "What are you doing outside so early?" he asked him. "I thought you were cooking in preparation for your heat."

"I was, but I needed to be close to you."

Lidon's heart melted. He loved it when Vieno got all needy on him. He loved it from any of his men when they leaned on him, needed him. Maybe it was some alpha thing? It made him feel strong and wanted. "I was about to do an inspection with Jawon. Wanna join us?"

Vieno nodded. "Yes. I'd love to see how far we've come."

Hand in hand they walked over to the vegetable plot, which boasted full-grown plants by now, including rows of tomato plants, held up by tall, green stalks. Lars was working there, checking each tomato plant, though Lidon wasn't sure for what.

"He's pinching out suckers," Vieno explained. He pulled Lidon toward one of the plants and showed him a tiny green leaf between the stem and a branch. "If you let those grow, you'll end up with a plant that has a lot of branches and leaves but few tomatoes. The plant needs to focus its energy on a few stems and developing fruit."

Lidon smiled. "You've learned a lot about this."

"I worked my way through a ton of books on gardening,"

Vieno said. "But Lars knows way more than I do, and he's developed a plan for the extension of the plot."

"That's fast work," Lidon commented when Lars stood up and made eye contact.

"I did a quick soil test and made some suggestions on what would work well, considering our climate and the amount of sun this spot gets."

Jawon had made his way over as well and listened as Vieno gestured to the barn, the sound of the chickens in the coop clucking in the distance. "Lars suggested building a trellis system against the barn to grow snap beans. It's the perfect spot, actually. He also had some ideas to improve our zucchini and pumpkin patch, and we've started growing melons there too, which are doing well."

Lidon nodded. "Good. You've made great progress, sweetheart. I'm impressed."

Vieno beamed, and it warmed Lidon's heart. He was in his element here, tending to the garden and taking care of the house. What a perfect fit he was for this place.

"We've made good progress on widening the existing gate as you requested, alpha, working closely with Bray to establish a safe perimeter around the main house," Jawon said as they moved on from the vegetable garden. "I've had a plan drawn up for you for an omega building, per your specification."

They walked over to a folding table placed in the shade, where several drawings were taped to the table. Lidon bent over to study what his cousin had come up with.

"The omega wing is inside the main perimeter, since I figured it would need protection. My idea was to connect it to the house but with a double lock-system featuring a walkway to keep the smell out of the main house. Entry would be based on hand scans, so Bray could program it to only give access to those who'd need it."

Lidon studied the drawings. It was a two-level building, which was smart, since it made optimal use of the downward slope the back of the ranch was on. It provided four bedrooms, each with a private bathroom, and a communal living room and kitchen. There was even a small room for a washing machine and dryer, which was smart thinking because it meant the heavily scented bed sheets and clothes wouldn't have to be carried through the main house.

"I like this concept," he said. "It's private and safe yet connected to the main house and within the gates."

Jawon's face broke open in a smile. "You're gonna love this, then."

He pulled another drawing on top of the omega plans, and Lidon had to study it for a bit before he understood what he was looking at. "You want to build more wings?"

"As needed, yes. Each wing would be connected to the main house but with its own kitchen and laundry facilities. Those would be placed on the outside, with the bedrooms closest to the main house, so the protection is optimal. That was Bray's suggestion, by the way. Four bedrooms per wing, so you could separate alphas and betas, if you wanted, or put my crew together and Bray's men in a separate wing. You could use one for Urien and his daughter, maybe. We could keep adding them around the house as needed, since we have so much open space on every side, and it would further increase security for the core of the house, for you and your men."

Vieno squeezed his hand. "And for our kids," he added softly.

"I didn't want to be presumptuous, but yes. If you'd have kids, they'd be best protected this way," Jawon said.

Lidon pulled Vieno close. "Jawon, this is brilliant. I want to talk to Palani before giving you the green light, but I expect him to be as happy about this as I am. Great thinking, cousin."

"Thank you, alpha. It was a team effort between me and Bray."

As Lidon had expected, Palani loved the concept as much as Lidon did when he showed him the plans in his study later that day. "That's brilliant," he commented. "Both in terms of the use of space as the added layer of security for the main house."

"Yes, and it will give us more privacy in the main house, which is good. I'm fine with Grayson and Lucan staying there for now, but any more, and it will be too much for Vieno, especially once he's pregnant."

Palani smiled. "Did he manage to drag himself away from you?"

"He's with Enar, who promised him a hard fuck if he took a nap. He needs to rest before his heat."

"I know. It's sweet how he clings to you. It does something to you inside, doesn't it, when he gets all needy as fuck?"

"It does. I never feel more like an alpha than when he needs me like that," Lidon admitted.

"I sense the pull toward you as well," Palani said, surprising Lidon.

"You do? How?"

"Not as much as Vieno, but if we haven't seen each other all day, I need to be close to you. It's like you're my compass, my true north. Ever since Vieno's last heat, since you accepted me as mate, I'm a little lost without you, and it's gotten deeper since you alpha claimed me."

Lidon let that sink in. "Does it bother you?"

Palani grinned. "It's not exactly a hardship to be in your presence, you know?"

Lidon's lips pulled up. "Thank fuck for that, then."

"You don't experience the same?"

"A pull toward you?" Lidon considered it. "No. Toward Vieno, I felt it right before his heat last time, so maybe that'll start tomorrow. But not to you or Enar, not like you described, sorry."

Palani cocked his head, his eyes narrowing in a way that told Lidon he was onto something. "Not like I described," Palani repeated. "So, you do feel something…"

There was no way he was confessing to Palani what had flashed through his mind. It was embarrassing as fuck, and he'd rejected the thought every time it had popped up. Lidon's cheeks heated up, and Palani laughed in response. "Oh, this is gonna be good. You're blushing, alpha. Come on, spill."

He should've known he wouldn't stand a chance against this stubborn, bossy beta. Still, he wouldn't give in that easily. "I don't know what you're talking about," he insisted.

Palani jumped into his arms, and he caught him on reflex, pulling him against him so he wouldn't drop him. The beta wrapped his legs around Lidon's waist, holding on to his neck with his hands. "Don't tell me a big, strong alpha like you is scared to admit something…"

"I'm not scared," Lidon defended himself, then laughed as he realized Palani was playing him like a fiddle. Two could play that game, though.

He walked him forward until he'd backed him against a wall. He pulled Palani's hands loose from his neck and pinned them against the wall, grinding against him. The beta let out a soft little moan, and he licked his lips. "I'm pretty sure Enar is balls deep inside Vieno right now," Lidon whispered, bringing his mouth within a breath's distance of Palani's. "How about we have a little...interlude of our own?"

Palani's brown eyes darkened. "If you're trying to distract me..."

Lidon groaned in frustration. He really was too smart for his own good, the sassy beta.

"It's working," Palani finished, then crushed his mouth to Lidon's.

Vieno kissed as if he wanted to swallow you whole, Enar wanted to be conquered by your mouth, but Palani? Palani seduced you with his kisses, Lidon thought. His tongue was liquid heat, teasing and torturing Lidon until his cock was rock hard and leaking inside his shorts and all he wanted was to be buried inside Palani.

"Baby," Palani whispered against his lips, both panting. How Lidon loved to hear that sweet term for him. "You can fuck me anytime, but will you please tell me what was on your mind? You don't have to, but I don't like you being ashamed of anything."

He rested his forehead against Palani's, closing his eyes for a few seconds. Should he tell him?

"Ever since the alpha claiming..." he started, then stopped again. He couldn't do this while he was holding him so close. It would put pressure on Palani in a way Lidon wasn't comfortable with. "I'm gonna put you down, okay?"

He gently lowered Palani to the ground, waited till he'd found his footing, then took a step back. Palani leaned back against the wall, studying him with kind eyes.

"Remember what Grayson said about that True Alpha thing?"

Palani frowned. "He said a lot of things."

Lidon jammed his hands into his pockets, carefully avoiding touching his cock, which was like steel. "The sexual libido." He looked at the ground as he spoke. He'd never been one to blush, but his cheeks heated up a second time.

"Ah," Palani said. "That."

"Yeah, *that*. It's much worse since the alpha claiming."

"I noticed you seek Vieno out more, even at night, in bed."

"Do you think he minds?"

Palani smiled. "He'd sleep with your cock deep inside him all night if he could."

"I don't want him to feel pressured. Or any of you."

Palani's eyes flashed with understanding. "What happened?"

Lidon sighed, lowering himself onto his desk chair. "Remember my second boyfriend, the one I wanted to marry? Or at least I thought I did until he cheated on me. Rodrick complained I put too much pressure on him to have sex, that he felt like he couldn't say no, what with me being an alpha and all."

It had been his biggest failure as a man, to hear those words, basically be accused of taking him against his will. Had he? He rubbed his forehead, trying to remember how it had gone down.

He jumped when Palani's hand clamped his neck. "I have a hard time believing that," he said softly.

Lidon raised his head, looking at him with tired eyes. "You've experienced my alpha powers. You don't think I could've used those on him?"

Palani cupped his cheeks, planting a soft kiss on his lips. "You're far too honorable. You even asked Vieno for permission, in the throes of his heat while his smell must have driven you crazy...and you still stopped to make sure he wanted it."

"But that was after...because Rodrick had told me that," Lidon protested.

"No, you did that because it's who you are. It sounds like your asshole cheating ex tried to put some of the blame with you, but the truth was that he fucked around on you."

"But why? Why did he cheat on me?"

"Oh, baby, are you seriously concerned about that? Do you think it had anything to do with you?"

Palani pushed Lidon's arms aside and straddled him. The beta's easy affection warmed Lidon's heart. There was no denying Palani loved him, not when that love shone out of his eyes, radiated from every cell in his body right now.

"I don't know," he said, then sighed. "Yeah, I do blame myself."

"And you think it was because you asked too much of him in bed," Palani understood. "That's why you didn't do casual sex anymore after him, because you were afraid to make that mistake again."

He was so damn perceptive. "That's why he cheated on me because I pressured him. Don't you agree?"

"No, I don't. People cheat because they get something out of that they don't get at home. I don't know what Rodrick was looking for with you, but he wasn't getting it. Maybe it was because you were slow to marry him, maybe because he wanted you to move to the city...maybe it was because he wanted you to love him and you didn't."

Lidon frowned. "I did love him."

"No, you didn't. You may have thought you did, but you didn't. Baby, you're not someone who falls in love easily, and you're not that easy to love 'cause even though you're honorable and kind and sexy as fuck, you're so damn serious and tough and aloof. It took Vieno to break through your defenses with his sweet and sexy nature.

Once you loved him, you opened your heart for me and Enar."

The words hit him deep. They were sharp as shards of glass, and yet they healed. How was that even possible?

"I thought I loved him."

"I know you did. You wouldn't have agreed to marry him if you didn't. But you can't tell me you felt the same way for him as you feel about Vieno or Enar."

"And you," Lidon added.

Palani smiled the sweetest smile. "And me," he echoed.

"No," Lidon agreed. "It's not the same. How could it be when I've never felt like this? So complete and whole, like I've found my place in the universe."

"Damn, alpha, you say the sweetest things..."

Palani hugged him, and Lidon buried his nose in Palani's neck, breathing him in deeply. It felt good holding him, even if his cock still hadn't calmed down.

"So, high libido, huh?" Palani said after a while, his breath tickling Lidon's skin.

"You have no idea."

"You hard?"

"All the fucking time ever since the alpha claiming."

Lidon felt him grin. "Dude, you have three men to take care of you..."

"*Dude?*"

Palani's body shook with laughter. "Alpha dude?" he tried.

Lidon growled in laughter. "I'll show you who's the alpha here."

It took only a minute or two to get naked, slick himself up, and stretch Palani with rough moves that made the beta moan up a storm. God, he needed to be inside him. It thundered through his veins, this need to take, to possess, to claim. His alpha demanded, and he surrendered, snapping his hips and sliding inside that tight heat in one deep stroke, making Palani clench around his cock. He didn't wait but slammed in again, then again, his hands holding him in place on his lap. He fucked him deeper than he ever had, but Palani took it, opening wide for him.

Lidon nuzzled his neck as he surged in again, his balls slapping against Palani's flesh. God, he loved fucking him like this. It was hard, dirty, and he should feel bad about being selfish about his needs, but he really didn't, not after how Palani had responded to his confession. He needed this, needed him...and Palani was here for him.

He held him for a long time after, content to stay inside him and gently thrust while Palani melted against him, fucked into complete submission.

25

Enar waited till it was just the four of them. They had retreated into the bedroom, and Enar's stress abated for a moment when he saw Lidon and Palani share a kiss. They were so much closer since the alpha claiming. It has resulted in an easy intimacy between all four of them that hadn't been present before.

He sighed. "We have a challenge," he said.

Lidon turned around to face him, still holding Palani, who seemed content to snuggle up to the alpha. "Talk to me. What's up?"

"Sven's heat is coming soon, and Vieno's heat tomorrow may trigger it sooner with all the pheromones we'll be throwing off. He's gonna need an alpha. Who do we ask? God, it feels like I'm pimping out my brother, but he needs one. Not that I want anything to do with it, since they both hate me, but I can't let it go."

Lidon frowned. "Right. Okay, what are the options?" He kissed Palani on his head and sent him to Vieno, who had already crawled into bed.

"Adar," Enar said. "Ori. Isam. Bray and most of his men."

"Does he have a connection with any of them?" Lidon asked.

"No, not as far as I can tell, but we're not exactly close... or even on speaking terms right now." Enar wasn't sure what Grayson had told Lars and Sven after the incident in the gym, but Lars was doing his best to avoid Enar, and it worked for him.

"You freaking out over him and Lars may have something to do with that," Vieno pointed out helpfully, and Enar shot him a dark look.

"They're my brothers. Can you blame me for being shocked?"

"Adopted brother, in Sven's case, which makes a big difference, Doc," Palani said. "That in no way makes it okay what Lars said to you, but you didn't react with much understanding. They're not related by blood."

Enar gave a dismissive gesture. "Semantics. Point is that they're family."

"We'll have to agree to disagree on this one, Doc. I know you're shocked, but it's not helping. They're not gonna break up because you said so, especially not after you ignored them for years."

"Jeez, rub it in, would ya?" Enar snapped.

Palani got up from the bed and sauntered over to Enar, all brassy and confident in his tight red boxers. He met him eye to eye, not backing down despite their difference in size. "I understand it hurts, Doc, but pretending it doesn't gets you nowhere. I've never lied to you, and I won't start now."

"You don't get it, okay? It's easy for you to judge me when you have no idea what it was like with my father..."

His breath hurt in his lungs, even thinking about it. The constant scowl of condemnation and disappointment on his father's face. The below-the-belt snide remarks.

Palani stepped closer and put his hands on Enar's shoulders. "No, I don't understand...because you don't talk about it. But I'm not judging you. I'm not. I wish you would talk to me, to us."

He surrendered, stepping in the embrace he knew was there for him. He put his head on Palani's shoulders, and the beta's arms hugged him tight. "I know. I can't...I just can't."

"Okay, Doc. Talk when you're ready, okay? We'll be here."

He nodded, then pulled him tighter, needing to feel the safety of his arms. Palani held him, and Enar's stress eased, his heart rate and breathing coming down.

"One more thing, Doc, and I want you to think about this, okay?"

Enar hmmed in consent.

"You've asked all of us and the whole pack to treat you like a beta, and I've seen everyone try their best. There have been some slipups but not intentional. We all see the difference in you. But, Doc, when you're with Sven and Lars, you're acting all alpha again. Maybe the first step is to allow them to see the real you as well."

He closed his eyes, forcing himself to stay where he was. It hurt, but Palani was right. "They're my brothers," he whispered. "They're my responsibility."

"No, they're not," Lidon spoke from the bed, where he'd apparently moved to without Enar noticing.

Enar let go of Palani a little so he could look at him. The alpha was propped up against the headboard, Vieno between his legs...maybe even on his cock? They did that lately, Vieno and Lidon, needing that connection more than Enar and Palani. Enar would wake up in the middle of the night, and Lidon would be inside Vieno, half-asleep, the two of them in perfect harmony and bliss and rocking slowly. Enar wasn't even sure if they realized it or if they came. Hell, it didn't always feel *sexual*, weird as that might sound.

"What do you mean, they're not?" he asked Lidon.

"They're my responsibility, not yours. And I agree with Palani that I have no issue with their relationship. They're not blood-related, they're of age, and it's consenting. That means Lars has a say in this, aside from Sven himself, and Palani will talk to them about this, as we agreed in the meeting. This is not your problem, Enar. It's mine."

It shouldn't feel this good to have the weight of the responsibility lifted off him, but it did. He hadn't realized how stressed he was about it until he let go. "Yes, alpha," he said, feeling the words resonate deep inside him.

"Okay," Palani said. "Does anyone else have a suggestion about who to ask? I'll let Sven have the final say but any ideas?"

It was quiet for a bit until Vieno spoke up. "You're forgetting one alpha."

Enar frowned, mentally checking off his list. "Who?" he asked. "I thought I had them all."

"Grayson," Vieno said.

"Grayson?" Enar let go of Palani. "But he's...old."

Vieno grinned. "Old? Dude, he's eleven years older than you. That's not old. That's mature. Plus, he's fucking hot."

"He is," Palani confirmed. "God, his voice alone gives me..." He shot a quick look at Enar, whose mouth had dropped open. "Yeah. Anyway. Vieno's right. And he's stepped in twice already to set Lars straight, so there's definitely a connection there."

"But he's way too old for Sven. God, Sven is younger than Lucan! That's not normal," Enar protested.

"You know, for someone who falls outside of what

society defines as normal, you sure have an opinion on what falls inside the lines," Palani said, his eyebrows raised.

Enar blushed. Dammit, he was right. It was just that... Sven was his brother. Adopted or not, he was a kid, and Grayson was...not.

"Why did you mention him specifically?" Lidon asked Vieno, curiosity lacing his voice. "Has he mentioned anything?"

Vieno shook his head. "No. He wouldn't do that. Not as a guest in this house. But there's tension there, between him and Lars and Sven. I think the other alphas are too young, too inexperienced. I think those two could use someone more mature. And as Palani said, Grayson has volunteered twice already to correct Lars, so there's something going on."

"Hmm," Lidon said. "Let's take that into consideration, Palani. Thank you, sweetheart."

He kissed Vieno, a quick kiss that developed into a deeper one. Then his strong hands lifted Vieno up. He *had* been sitting on Lidon's cock that whole time, Enar realized, and was now settling down on it again, only with his face toward the alpha.

Enar's semi grew hard, and Palani chuckled. "You appreciating the view?"

Enar sighed. "I will never get bored with watching that luscious ass swallow that big alpha cock... Most beautiful sight in the world."

Palani reached for his hand, then jerked hard so Enar stumbled against him. "Oh, I dunno, Doc, I'm kinda partial to the sight of my cock disappearing in your ass."

Enar laughed, then allowed Palani to kiss him till they ran out of breath. A few minutes later, he had to agree that sight was pretty damn good too. And so was the feeling as Palani ravished his ass until Enar had come twice.

VIENO HAD BEEN SLIGHTLY nervous the whole week, but on the day his heat started a strange peace descended on him. When he woke up, his head was buzzing, the warning that he had a few hours at most before the feverish, frantic haze would overtake him. Despite that buzz, his heart was calm, secure in the knowledge he was safe with his men.

Safe, wanted, and loved. So very loved.

He opened his eyes and met Lidon's brown eyes, which were studying him with such love it made Vieno's stomach dance.

"Good morning, sweetheart," Lidon whispered.

Vieno smiled. How could he not when this wonderful man loved him? "Hi."

He let that smile warm his heart a bit longer before he moved in for a kiss, a sweet, lingering kiss that left him tingling.

"How are you feeling?" Lidon asked.

Vieno felt movement behind him, two bodies moving in to surround him. He grinned. "Good. I hope you guys are well rested 'cause it's gonna be quite the ride this time."

Palani circled his waist from behind, then caressed his flat belly. "Are you excited, baby?" he asked.

Vieno didn't need to ask what Palani referred to. They all knew. "I can't wait," he answered honestly.

Despite the discomfort pregnancy would bring and the risks it would entail, he wanted nothing more than to carry Lidon's son. Because it would be a son, an alpha heir. He couldn't explain how he knew, but he did with a quiet certainty that left no room for doubt.

"If we wanna make sure it's Lidon's, should Enar and I not be here for the first twenty-four hours, maybe?" Palani asked. "I know betas can't father a child with omegas now, but they used to, and we've seen so many things change because of the gene that maybe we shouldn't take the risk?"

Vieno sat up against the headboard, his brows furrowed. It made sense, Palani's concern and proposal, and yet. The idea of not being with all his men during his heat was disconcerting, to say the least, if not downright alarming. He needed all of them, not just Lidon. But Palani did raise a valid point. How could he be sure it would be Lidon who impregnated him and not Enar?

Lidon raised himself up, his face showing his thinking frown, as Vieno called it. "I hadn't thought of that," he said slowly.

"What, you thought that your alpha sperm would be automatically dominant compared to mine or Palani's?" Enar joked.

Palani grinned. "He's gonna alpha compel his sperm."

At first Vieno wanted to laugh or maybe stick his tongue out, but then the deep truth behind that statement hit him. Enar was right. If Lidon was the alpha of the pack—and after everything that had happened, Vieno had not even a sliver of doubt that he was—he would come first, even in this. Nature would make sure Lidon would father his child, his heir, before it would allow Enar or maybe even Palani to sire offspring with Vieno.

Vieno looked at Lidon, who met his eyes, his mouth pulling up in a soft smile. "He's right, isn't he?" Lidon said softly.

Vieno nodded. "Yeah. My body won't accept anyone else right now but you. Nature will take care of itself."

"You're gonna trust in something as intangible as that?" Enar asked.

Vieno turned his head. "Yes. They didn't have our level

of medical care a hundred years ago, did they? And yet alpha heirs were produced first consistently, even in poly relationships. Don't you remember all of Grayson's stories? They couldn't manipulate it, and neither should we. Nature will find a way. It always has."

Lidon kissed the top of his head, then pulled Vieno onto his lap. "I agree. And if by chance it will by Enar's child or by some miracle Palani's, then that's what nature intended. The child will be just as loved. It will always be ours, with four dads, not just Vieno and whoever donated sperm."

Lidon held out a hand to Enar and Vieno to Palani, and both scrambled over so they sat on the bed together, legs entwined, touching each other everywhere.

Enar's hand found Vieno's belly. "You're gonna be so beautiful," he said, the awe ringing clear in his voice. "Your belly all swollen and round..."

"We'll take such good care of you," Palani promised. "Everything you need."

Vieno smiled. "I'm gonna hold you to that when I want pickles at three in the morning," he teased, knowing how much Palani hated pickles.

Palani shivered, then looked sideways at Enar. "If you want pickles, you'll get them. I may have to bribe Enar with a blow job to bring them to you, but I promise you'll get them."

Enar shot him a big grin. "I have a feeling Vieno is not gonna be the only one whose needs will be taken care of. Now that I know how to extort you for blow jobs..."

The good-natured teasing warmed Vieno's heart. "I love you guys so much," he said with a happy sigh.

The "I love you too" statements echoed through the room.

"We have one more thing to do," Enar said.

"Yes, a hearty breakfast," Lidon said, and Vieno smiled. The alpha never had enough to eat lately, it seemed. He craved protein especially, finishing off big plates of eggs, fish, steaks, or whatever meat Vieno prepared for him.

"That too, but we need to let an alpha smell Vieno. Not Grayson, since he's been around him a lot and may be somewhat used to his smell by now. One of Bray's men would be best, I think. We need to make sure his alluring smell isn't detectable before his heat starts."

Lidon nodded. "Good point." He looked at Palani.

"I'll ask Bray to send someone," Palani said in answer to the unspoken question.

Vieno marveled again at how automatic the communication between Lidon and Palani was. The decision to make Palani his beta had surprised some people, but a few weeks in, no one had expressed any doubt it had been the right one. Palani could read Lidon's mind, it seemed, anticipating his needs and always ready with the answers Lidon sought.

Ten minutes later, Vieno was in the kitchen, preparing hearty omelets when Palani walked in with Adar. Lidon and Enar got up to flank Vieno, a gesture that helped calm his nerves.

Adar nodded toward Lidon, bowing his head in a manner that had become custom as a greeting to Lidon. "Alpha, do I have your permission to smell your omega?"

Lidon nodded. "Yes, please. Thank you."

Adar's kind eyes sought Vieno's, and he released his breath. It would be okay. Nothing would happen to him with his mates right here with him. Adar stepped close and took a deep sniff, then another one.

He stepped back and turned toward Lidon. "I can detect all your scents on him, and I can smell he's about to start his heat. It has the usual effect on me of making me horny, but other than that, there's nothing extraordinary. He smells like a claimed omega."

Vieno blushed at his candor, then gasped as it hit him. "You can't smell anything special on me? I smell just like other omegas?"

Adar raised his eyebrows. "Should I?" He looked from Lidon to Palani. "Did I miss something?"

Vieno couldn't help it, he had to ask. "You don't want to fuck me?" he blurted out.

Adar took a step back. "No! God, no. You're with... You're the alpha's. You're claimed. I would never... Did I say or do something wrong?"

Palani slapped him on his shoulder. "No, man. You did everything right. Vieno meant no offense, and I'll explain later, okay? It's good news, trust me."

Adar left the kitchen with a last glance at Vieno, then Lidon, his befuddled expression showing he trusted Palani but still wasn't sure what had happened.

Vieno found a safe spot in Palani's arms. "He can't smell me," he whispered. "He really can't smell me..."

"I know, baby. I'm so happy for you. You're free."

The tears came fast, but they didn't hurt this time. They brought release, a sense of freedom and relief unlike anything he'd ever experienced before. He no longer had to fear strangers sexually assaulting him, raping him, because of how he smelled. It was *freedom*. How was this even possible? What had changed that his smell had disappeared?

He tilted his head back to kiss Palani, a frantic kiss that had to express all the swirling emotions inside him he couldn't put into words. And it had to be Palani, the man who'd stood by him all that time, who had slain dragons for Vieno and had come out a victor. Palani kissed him back, all tongue and heat and wetness, pushing Vieno until his back was against the kitchen counter.

"I love you," Palani gasped into his mouth. "God, I love you."

Vieno couldn't find words, his brain turning foggy at the same time his body went into overdrive. "I need..." was all he could bring out. "Please, I need..."

"I know, baby. We've got you."

He was lifted onto the counter, his mouth never leaving Palani's, though it had to have at some point because he was naked, his nipples stiff and demanding touch, his skin feverish and sensitive. Strong hands lifted him, carried him, as his mouth was fucked expertly by...Enar's tongue? When had he...?

They were in bed, the sheets cool against his overheated body, his hole so empty and twitching until he was lifted again, then lowered onto that glorious cock, that alpha cock he needed more than he needed air. He whimpered as it filled him, leaned back against Lidon's warm body behind him.

Enar's strong hands held him as he nibbled Vieno's neck, his stubble rasping his sensitive skin. Palani kissed him, rubbing Vieno's nipples as only he could, playing with the swollen buds until Vieno's face was wet with tears.

Hands and mouths touched him everywhere, stroking, caressing, pinching, licking, biting. He was the center of their universe, the one who united them. Lidon fucked him hard and fast until he came, his alpha roar rattling the windows.

"More," Vieno managed, and he was turned around so he faced his alpha.

His alpha mark burned as Lidon licked it, still hard and deep inside him, and when he opened his eyes, Lidon's eyes glowed. He'd never witnessed anything like it. They were... feral, demanding yet kind at the same time.

"Knot me," Vieno demanded, his voice crystal clear. "Fill me with your seed, my alpha. Breed me."

Lidon's eyes shone so bright Vieno couldn't look away, and he knew. This wasn't a mere man breeding him. This was the True Alpha, the alpha who would bring change, the alpha who would return to the old ways like they couldn't even dream of right now. This was the father of his child, the next alpha heir. And as Lidon's knot swelled, filling him with that torturous mix of pain and pleasure, he grabbed Enar's hand with his left hand and Palani's with his right, bringing them to his belly.

"It's happening," he whispered. "And you're a part of this. I'm his but yours as well. We're four, and we're one, and we're unbreakable together."

It took an hour for Lidon's knot to come down, and all that time they stayed interlinked, whispering sweet words to each other in between lingering kisses, time passing without them noticing.

They were four, and they were one...and they were unbreakable together.

And inside Vieno, new life began to form.

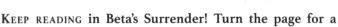

KEEP READING in Beta's Surrender! Turn the page for a sneak peek.

SNEAK PEEK BETA'S SURRENDER

Grayson Whitefield let his eyes wander over the beta in front of him, who had his chin raised defiantly. Lars's usually disheveled hair was an utter mess, and his cheeks were flushed, as were his brother Sven's. Sven wouldn't meet Grayson's eyes, the omega's shoulders hunched as he stared at the floor of the gym room in the ranch. Shame was dripping off him tangibly.

Grayson had no trouble concluding what had happened. These two had been messing around, maybe even fucking, and Enar had caught them. Grayson had picked up on sexual tension between the two brothers before. First, it had been long looks and little touches that had felt out of place, considering they were brothers. Then he'd heard some noises from their room, and he'd wondered about them, his fertile imagination having no issue providing alluring scenarios and projecting them in his mind, those limber, sweaty bodies. They'd look so pretty on their knees, and...

Nope, he wasn't going there. He had to focus on Lars, whose whole expression taunted Grayson to say something. He would—and Lars wasn't going to like it.

Enar's face, as he'd blindly stumbled out of the gym room, had told Grayson everything he needed to know. The man had been wounded deeply—by his own brother, who undoubtedly had lashed out in anger. *Again.*

Grayson had scolded Lars before about his disrespectful attitude—in that case toward Lidon, which was even worse, considering he was pack alpha—but apparently, he hadn't made enough of an impression. He'd have to do better, then.

"We have a problem," he said, keeping his voice level.

"What, you object to me fucking my adopted brother?" Lars snapped.

Ah. He'd been right, then, though the *adopted* part was new. "I do, actually, but that's not your biggest problem."

Lars crossed his arms, lifting his chin even higher. His body language was the complete opposite of Sven's, who now lowered himself on a sweaty bench—undoubtedly the one they'd just been fucking on. Stress and shame radiated from the omega in big waves, and combined with the pheromones he was throwing off, it put Grayson's body on full alert.

You'd think that at forty-three he'd be past that hormonal shit, but apparently, his alpha didn't feel that way. Oh no, it wanted Sven something fierce. Fucking traitor.

"Ask me what your biggest problem is, Lars," Grayson said, his voice not betraying the anger that simmered inside.

Lars shrugged. "Like I care."

Grayson's eyes narrowed. "You *should* care because it's what's gonna get you booted from the ranch."

For the first time, Grayson spotted something on the boy's face other than anger and defiance. Fear. "Lidon promised we could stay. I took the fucking job he offered me, like you told me to."

Oh yes, that encounter had been unpleasant as well,

Grayson impressing upon Lars in crystal clear terms that Lidon's job offer was the best opportunity he would ever get. In the end, the beta had seen reason, or maybe Grayson had scared him into falling in line. It seemed they were back at square one, however.

"That promise was contingent on you obeying his commands as pack alpha, if you recall. One of the pack laws is that you can't have a sexual relationship with an omega without the alpha's permission."

Lars's eyes widened. "You suggested that rule! You fucking set me up," he accused Grayson.

"No, though I did suspect something was going on between you. The walls inside the main house aren't that thick. You should know because I overheard you complain to Sven about hearing the alpha fuck his men. If you can hear them, we can hear you too, you know."

"Why did you propose that rule?" Sven asked timidly. "If it wasn't to spite Lars and me, I mean."

"Because you're vulnerable, Sven, as are many omegas. Ask your brother sometime what heartbreaking stories he's encountered with omegas who were taken advantage of."

"Enar is not his brother," Lars snapped.

Grayson took a step closer to him, raising himself to his full height, which meant he had a good three inches on the beta. "No, but he is yours. Moreover, he's the alpha's claimed mate, which makes him someone you should respect the hell out of, if only out of self-preservation."

"S-self-preservation?" Sven asked.

"What did you say to him?" Grayson asked.

Lars shrunk a little, his eyes dropping to the floor, but he didn't answer.

"What did you say to Enar, Lars? I won't ask again." He

bit back on his alpha, who was getting impatient with the boy's insolence.

"Lars, you need to tell him," Sven said. "He'll compel it out of you, and it will be twice as bad."

At least one of them was using his brain.

Lars shuffled his feet, still avoiding Grayson's gaze. "I...I said he was an alpha who wanted to be treated like a beta... and that Lidon didn't even choose him as his second-in-command."

Grayson closed his eyes for a second. No wonder Enar had looked like he'd been stabbed in his heart. He had been, figuratively speaking...by his own brother.

"Even after witnessing how you've treated him ever since you arrived here, I still find myself disappointed you would sink that low. You deliberately hit him where you knew it'd hurt the most. You should be deeply ashamed of that, Lars."

His words hung heavy in the air, and Lars's shoulders dropped even lower.

"He didn't mean it like that," Sven offered.

Grayson forced himself to stay calm. "That's not something you should decide for him, Sven. If he feels that way, he should have the guts to say so."

Lars raised his head, a spark of fire back in his eyes. "He left us with *him*," he said, his voice thick. "He knew what a massive asshole he was, and he left us with him."

Grayson didn't need to guess who the "he" was in both cases. The little he'd surmised about Enar's father had made it clear the man lacked redeeming qualities.

"Let's assume for a second what you're saying is true and that Enar did that willfully. Does that justify your remarks to him?"

Lars clenched his fists. "You don't understand! I've had to watch my own father try and seduce Sven, and when that didn't work, he tried to force himself on him. And you're saying that I should be all brotherly warm toward the one guy who could've prevented it? Fuck you!"

Grayson's alpha had reached his limit. "On your knees!" he commanded, his voice booming through the gym.

Both boys dropped to their knees immediately...and fuck if that wasn't a satisfying sight. Grayson bit back the mix of anger and lust that thundered through his veins.

"You two need to get through your thick skulls how things work around here. This is a pack, and that means you will damn well respect how things work around here. You do not tell someone to go fuck himself. Do you hear me? Not me, not anyone. You show your fellow pack members some fucking respect. Do I make myself clear?"

"Yes, alpha."

Their responses were instantaneous, and sweet contentment at their submission filled Grayson. He'd never been one to insist on much etiquette as an alpha, but making Lars yield to him pleased him. Very much so, in fact.

"Get up," he told them. "Sit down on that bench and listen."

He waited till they were both seated, Lars sporting a look of begrudging respect.

"We'll continue this conversation at a later time because don't think for a minute that we're done."

"Who made you our boss?" Lars said, and Grayson smiled.

The boy still wouldn't back down, would he? His stubbornness was as infuriating as it was arousing, Grayson's cock still invested in what was happening.

"I did, and I'm gonna love every second of it. You'd better pay attention, boy, because things will not end well if you don't. All I have to do is tell Palani what you said to

Enar. He'll kick you out faster than you can pack up your shit."

Lars paled, shooting a nervous look sideways at Sven, who was on the verge of tears. "Sven's heat is coming."

"I know, which is why we'll allow him to stay. Besides, he's not the one who verbally attacked the alpha's mate... you were. This is your second warning, Lars, and it will be the last one. You may be pissed at your brother, and you may even have reason to be, I don't know, but you will treat him with the respect he deserves as the alpha's mate. If you can't bring yourself to do that, you have no place in this pack."

He waited till Lars met his eyes, satisfied when he saw his message had landed.

"You'll go out of your way to avoid Enar for now until you're convinced you can treat him with respect. Understood?"

"Yes, alpha."

LARS WOULD NEVER ADMIT IT, but Grayson's little speech had scared the shit out of him. The idea of being kicked out of the ranch was frightening, but the thought of being separated from Sven was terrifying. Sven needed him, and if Lars was honest with himself, he needed him right back. He might be the stronger of the two of them, or so he'd always thought, but he'd be lost without his lover, his best friend. It had been the two of them against the world for a long time now, and he couldn't fight that battle alone.

So he'd done as Grayson had told him the last two days, and he'd stayed out of the way of not just Enar but his three mates as well. There was no way he was risking his position here at the ranch. Sven needed to ride out his heat here, though Lars still wasn't sure how much of what Enar had told them was true. Would Sven's heat really be that much different from that of other omegas, or had Enar merely tried to scare them?

But Enar didn't have a reason to scare them, though, did he? Lars had to be honest that he couldn't think of a motive for his brother to fuck them over. He'd never cared about them, so why would he care either way now?

Lars pondered it as he tilled the plot he was working on with a rototiller, preparing it so they could start sowing zucchini, melons, and pumpkins. It was heavy work, especially this time of day, when the sun was burning on his back. He had to wipe the sweat off his face with a bandana after every row of tilling. The music he was listening to with his earbuds did improve his mood somewhat, but he knew it would take him at least two hours to finish this—if he didn't die from a heat stroke first.

Still, it was the perfect time since the soil was dry and easier to move around than when it was saturated with rain. They were expecting rain in two days, so he would make sure the plot was ready by then and distribute fertilizer before the rain hit. That way, it could soak into the soil, priming it for these vegetables, which needed fertile soil to grow.

By the time he was done, he was drenched with sweat, his throat parched. He'd brought a large bottle of water, but clearly, he should have brought more. He emptied it, taking out his earbuds.

"I brought you some more water," Grayson said behind him, making him spin around.

A strong hand steadied Lars as he almost tripped over his own feet. "I didn't see you," he said. "Or hear you."

Grayson studied him with an amused look, holding out the jug of water. "Clearly."

Lars took it after a slight hesitation, then proceeded to gulp down almost half of it. "Thank you," he said after finishing.

Grayson surveyed the plot Lars had been working on. "What were you doing?"

Why was he asking this? Was he checking up on him again, making sure he was staying busy or something? The man had popped up constantly the last two days. "Prepping this plot for planting," he said. "It's what Jawon and Vieno asked me to do," he added.

"I wasn't attacking you," Grayson said. "Merely curious. I don't know much about gardening in general, let alone agriculture."

"Oh." Lars debated with himself for a second, then said, "You can't just sow veggies, especially the ones we want to plant here. They need fertile, loose soil if you want them to grow, so you need to prep beforehand. Like, loosening the soil, removing all big lumps and rocks, and then spreading and mixing in fertilizer."

"Huh," Grayson said, studying the plot again. "That sounds like a lot of work. What made you choose this area to study?"

Damn, what was up with the twenty questions today? Didn't this guy have something better to do than play Spanish Inquisition with him? Still, he'd better answer and not show his feelings.

"I like being outside, and I like working with my hands. This was something that seemed to fit my requirements and that was suitable for a beta career."

Grayson smiled at him unexpectedly. "You don't like me asking all these questions, do you?"

Apparently, he hadn't been able to conceal his frustration. As usual. "Not really, no. Why the sudden interest in me?"

Grayson took a step closer, and even though there was still a yard or so between them, Lars felt his presence. "I told you. I've made myself the boss of you. I volunteered to Palani to make sure you stay out of trouble. And in case you were wondering, I always take my promises seriously."

Just his luck, an alpha with time on his hands who got a kick out of riding his ass. "I'm sure Palani is grateful, but don't you have something more useful to do? I told you. I'll keep my head down, okay? No need to babysit me."

His tone was a tad snappier than he'd intended it, and Grayson's smile grew predatory. "And with that remark, you proved how much you need a babysitter, boy."

That last word got Lars's back up, and at the same time, it tickled him inside. "I'm not a boy. I'm twenty-two, an adult. Old enough to take care of myself and make my own decisions."

Grayson's smile vanished, replaced by a much cooler expression. "Are you, now? You're doing a piss-poor job of both. No, don't bother responding, because we both know whatever you say will only get you deeper into trouble."

Lars's shoulders dropped at the realization that his mouth had once again gotten the better of him. He forced himself to stay quiet, ashamed Grayson was right. He had zero self-preservation skills and had been about to piss off the man who had the power to get him kicked out. Again. He was such an idiot.

A finger lifted his chin up, and Grayson forced him to make eye contact. Lars bit back a gasp at how close Grayson stood, crowding his personal space. The alpha's eyes drilled into his.

"I will keep babysitting you until I am assured you know how to behave. If you keep perpetuating this childish behavior you've demonstrated so far, you leave me no choice but to treat you like a child until you start acting with maturity. The sooner you get that, the sooner I'll get off your ass."

Grayson didn't release him until Lars nodded faintly, and then he abruptly turned around and left. Lars watched him walk away, his insides churning with emotions that were hard to pinpoint. Anger, for sure, mostly at himself for being stupid all over again. But there was also something that wasn't so easy to label, something that felt a lot like regret for disappointing Grayson. Why the hell would he care what Grayson thought of him?

He turned his back toward him and went back to work, his head trying to make sense of it all. Why the fuck had they ever agreed to stay at the ranch in the first place? He should never have believed Enar. He'd always taken care of Sven, so why would he need anyone else now?

KEEP READING in Beta's Surrender!

SIGNED PAPERBACKS AND SWAG

Did you know I have a web store where you can order signed paperbacks of all my books, as well as swag? Head on over to www.noraphoenix.com and check it out!

BOOKS BY NORA PHOENIX

If you loved this book, I have great news for you because I have a LOT of books for you to discover! Most of my books are also available in audio. You can find them all on my website at www.noraphoenix.com/my-books.

Forestville Silver Foxes Series

A brand-new contemporary MM romance series set in the small town of Forestville, Washington, featuring characters in their late forties. These silver foxes think they missed their chance at happiness...until they meet the love of their life, right there in Forestville. A feel good small-town romance series!

The Foster Brothers Series

Growing up in foster care, four boys made a choice to become brothers. Now adults, nothing can come between them...not even when they find love. The Foster Brothers is a contemporary MM romance series with found family, sweet romance, high heat, and a dash of kink.

Irresistible Dragons Series

A spin off series from the Irresistible Omegas that can be read on its own. With dragons, mpreg, stubborn alphas, and a whole new suspense plot, this is one series you don't want to miss.

Forty-Seven Duology

An emotional daddy kink duology with a younger Daddy and an older boy. Also includes first time gay, loads of hurt/comfort, and best friend's father. The third book is a bonus novella featuring secondary characters from the duology.

White House Men Series

An exciting romantic suspense series set in the White House. The perfect combination of sweet and sexy romance, a dash of kink, and a suspense plot that will have you on the edge of your seat. Make sure to read in order.

No Regrets Series

Sexy, kinky, emotional, with a touch of suspense, the No Regrets series is a spin off from the No Shame series that can be read on its own.

Perfect Hands Series

Raw, emotional, both sweet and sexy, with a solid dash of kink, that's the Perfect Hands series. All books can be read as stand-alones.

No Shame Series

If you love steamy MM romance with a little twist, you'll love the No Shame series. Sexy, emotional, with a bit of suspense and all the feels. Make sure to read in order, as this is a series with a continuing storyline.

Irresistible Omegas Series

An mpreg series with all the heat, epic world building, poly romances (the first two books are MMMM and the rest of the series is MMM), a bit of suspense, and characters that will stay with you for a long time. This is a continuing series, so read in order.

Ignite Series

An epic dystopian sci-fi trilogy where three men have to not only escape a government that wants to jail them for being gay but aliens as well. Slow burn MMM romance.

Stand-Alone Novels

I also have a few stand-alone novels. Some feature kink (like My Professor Daddy or Coming Out on Top), but others are non-kink contemporary romances (like Captain Silver Fox). You'll find something that appeals to you for sure!

Ballsy Boys Series: *Cowritten with K.M. Neuhold*

Sexy porn stars looking for real love! Expect plenty of steam, but all the feels as well. They can be read as stand-alones, but are more fun when read in order.

Kinky Boys Series: *Cowritten with K.M. Neuhold*

More sexy porn stars! This is a spin off series from the Ballsy Boys, set in Las Vegas...and with some kink!

MORE ABOUT NORA PHOENIX

Would you like the long or the short version of my bio?

The short? You got it.

I write steamy gay romance books and I love it. I also love reading books. Books are everything.

How was that?

A little more detail? Gotcha.

I started writing my first stories when I was a teen...on a freaking typewriter. I still have these, and they're adorably romantic. And bad, haha. Fear of failing kept me from following my dream to become a romance author, so you can imagine how proud and ecstatic I am that I finally overcame my fears and self doubt and did it. I adore my genre because I love writing and reading about flawed, strong men who are just a tad broken..but find their happy ever after anyway.

My favorite books to read are pretty much all MM/gay romances as long as it has a happy end. Kink is a plus... Aside from that, I also read a lot of nonfiction and not just books on writing. Popular psychology is a favorite topic of mine and so are self help and sociology.

Hobbies? Ain't nobody got time for that. Just kidding. I love traveling, spending time near the ocean, and hiking. But I love books more.

Come hang out with me in my Facebook Group Nora's Nook where I share previews, sneak peeks, freebies, fun stuff, and much more: https://www.facebook.com/groups/norasnook/

My weekly newsletter gives you updates, exclusive content, and all the inside news on what I'm working on. Sign up here: www.noraphoenix.com/newsletter/

You can also stalk me on
Twitter:
twitter.com/NoraPhoenixMM
Instagram:
www.instagram.com/nora.phoenix/
BookBub:
www.bookbub.com/profile/nora-phoenix

ACKNOWLEDGMENTS

This is the part of a book that most people skip, but in case you actually read this, I have some people I need to thank, LOL.

Being an author is often a lonely business, as most of my work is done from the solitude of my home. That's how I prefer it, so no worries, but I love my online tribe who brighten my day every single day.

Vicki: your running commentary, ideas, and suggestions throughout the day keep me sharp, make me a better writer, help me sell more books, and entertain the fuck out of me. You're also a phenomenal PA, and I love the hell out of this cover. Thank you. #SnarkyBitchesForever

The Nookies in my reader group: you guys are amazing, and I couldn't do this without your support.

My fellow writers and sprint partners: thanks for cheering me on and keeping me accountable.

A huge thanks to my beta readers: Britt, Karina, Kyleen, Michele, Racheal, Tania, and Vicki. This one was last minute, so thanks for your efforts into giving me feedback to make the book even better.

Thank you, dear readers, for reading my books and supporting an independent author like me. If you loved this book, please leave a review, as it's one of the most helpful things you can do for an indie author!

Made in the USA
Middletown, DE
28 September 2024